Pr...
The Wedding Beat

"Devan Sipher and romantic comedy? A match made in heaven. *The Wedding Beat*, Sipher's cheeky and charming debut, features a reporter who decides that sharing happy-ever-afters isn't enough—he wants one of his own. . . . Fabulous and funny, a quick, quirky read that marries self-deprecating humor with the bittersweet romantic challenges of a lonely man."
—USA Today

"Sipher, who writes the 'Vows' column for the *New York Times*, delivers in his debut novel a poignant and funny appeal to all singles to let go and give love a try. The clever and snappy prose will appeal to readers who look forward to each new title from Jonathan Tropper. . . . Smart and thoroughly enjoyable, *The Wedding Beat* is recommended for everyone who still sees marriage as a goal, not a penalty."
—Library Journal

"By turns blushingly embarrassing, heartbreakingly true and fabulously funny. . . . Sipher demonstrates he is a true romantic, who has learned much about the inner workings of the human heart."
—Interview Magazine

"Sipher applies the same wit, insight and deft humor to his fiction as he does to his real-world *New York Times* wedding articles."
—Southern California Public Radio

"For any woman who devours the wedding section every Sunday, wondering when her own Mr. Right will come along, *The Wedding Beat* is a romantic, hilarious and inspiring story of the angst behind the announcements."
—Nicola Kraus and Emma McLaughlin,
New York Times bestselling authors of The Nanny Diaries

continued . . .

ALSO BY DEVAN SIPHER

The Wedding Beat

THE SCENIC ROUTE

Devan Sipher

NEW AMERICAN LIBRARY

New American Library
Published by the Penguin Group
Penguin Group (USA) LLC, 375 Hudson Street,
New York, New York 10014

USA | Canada | UK | Ireland | Australia | New Zealand | India | South Africa | China
penguin.com
A Penguin Random House Company

First published by New American Library,
a division of Penguin Group (USA) LLC

First Printing, June 2014

 REGISTERED TRADEMARK—MARCA REGISTRADA

LIBRARY OF CONGRESS CATALOGING-IN-PUBLICATION DATA:

Sipher, Devan.
The scenic route/Devan Sipher.
pages   cm
ISBN 978-0-451-23966-2 (pbk.)
1. Physicians—Fiction.   I. Title.
PS3619.I5763S35 2014
813'.6—dc23   2013050253

Printed in the United States of America
1   3   5   7   9   10   8   6   4   2

Set in Adobe Caslon Pro
Designed by Elke Sigal

For my parents

THE SCENIC ROUTE

CHAPTER ONE

t was the first day of July, which meant that Austin Gittleman had 183 days to find a New Year's date.

Austin Gittleman was the kind of guy who thought about such things. Not in an obsessive way. But when it came to emotional crises, he liked to shop early and avoid the rush.

Austin prided himself on being rational and methodical, and if you were to ask the staff of his ophthalmology practice, they would say that described him to a fault (with a possible emphasis on the "fault" part). So it was out of character for him to be racing ten miles over the posted speed limit on the south 405 freeway. He glanced at the dashboard clock of his rented Ford Focus as if he didn't already know he was ludicrously late. Thanks to Hurricane Bethany, he had arrived in California one day and three hours behind schedule, which was more than he could say for his luggage.

His conversation with a self-important baggage claims "team member" at LAX had been less than encouraging.

"Your bag's not classified as missing in our computer system," the twentysomething underachiever had informed Austin without looking up from his screen.

"But it definitely *is* missing," Austin had pointed out.

"Not according to our system."

The interaction had deteriorated from there. It was possible Austin had suggested the airline employee was a gene short of a full genome. But Austin was fairly certain he hadn't said it in a hostile way.

If his luggage didn't show up, Austin had no idea what he was going to wear to the wedding, or the "weddapalooza," as Stu had come to call it when his fiancée was out of earshot. Austin looked down at his plaid shirt and torn jeans. Definitely not wedding attire. Even if he hadn't spent the last thirty hours wearing them. He took a quick sniff under his right arm. Code red.

"One apocalypse at a time" was the advice he often gave his sister when she fretted about multiple problems simultaneously. He repeated the words to himself as he turned his Focus onto the Pacific Coast Highway, keeping steady pressure on the gas pedal.

He was heading home. Although it had been a very long time since California was home. Since 1985. And it was 2007, so twenty-two years. He had known Stu for twenty-six, since their first day of kindergarten. He found it hard to believe he was old enough to have known anyone for twenty-six years.

He gazed over at the shimmering expanse of sandy shoreline. So many possibilities seemed to hover on the aqua blue horizon. Unlike his sister, he still loved the ocean, or at least he still loved looking at it. He was glad he hadn't lost that.

His thoughts drifted to what he *had* lost, and he turned his head away. He noticed a cute brunette driving a convertible silver Miata in the next lane. She was wearing oversized sunglasses and a playful smile. He wondered if people in real life ever met while driving.

One hundred and eighty-three days . . . really one hundred and eighty-two and a half.

His phone rang. He hoped it was the airline, but it was his office.

This was one of the few days he wasn't held captive there for twelve hours—or on call to come in. Yet they were still calling. Worse, he was considering answering, which went a long way toward explaining why he was still single. This weekend was an opportunity to change that. Spying a Pavilions supermarket up ahead, he decided to make a quick pit stop. What he needed most was fresh clothes, but he'd settle for deodorant.

As he slid out of the car, he caught a reflection of his stubbled and sleep-deprived face: the hodgepodge of Semitic and Slavic features with unruly dark hair, prominent cheekbones, and pale blue eyes that suggested an unkosher dalliance somewhere in his genealogical past. He'd been told several times he looked like the actor Andy Samberg, though he'd also been told he resembled A. J. Jacobs, the humor writer. Austin suspected people were just automatically comparing him to any well-known Jewish male whose name started with an "A." Fortunately, no one ever said he looked like Alan Dershowitz. And, for the record, he didn't.

He briskly traversed the megastore's aisles until he found what he was looking for. Or rather more than he was looking for. There were thirty different brands and formulations of deodorant, yet none of them was the one he usually bought. There was just about everything else, including Old Spice High Endurance, Axe Dark Temptation, and something called Happy Junk Fresh Balls (The Solution for Men).

He grabbed the most innocuous-looking container and momentarily contemplated creating a line of grooming products called "Nothing Fancy" that would each come in only one style and one scent. He imagined men around the world thanking him for simplifying their lives.

He quickly added other essentials to his basket: toothbrush, toothpaste, razor and shaving cream. He deliberated whether buying condoms would jinx his chances of meeting someone over the weekend. It wasn't that he was superstitious so much as he feared being punished for overconfidence.

Not that he was looking for just a hookup. He didn't have a problem getting dates. He actually had pretty good game, if he said so himself (though he was the only person who did). His problem was he didn't like the women he'd been dating. But that sounded pejorative. What he didn't like about the women he'd been dating was that he didn't like them *more*. He wanted to feel, well, more.

For Austin, dating was like a science experiment: first he made a hypothesis about the potential chemistry, and then he tested the hypothesis in a series of one-on-one interactions before analyzing the results. But the testing phase was often cut short when test subjects, well, dates, came to premature conclusions about the depth of their feelings for him, which was inevitably followed by their asking, or more often demanding, that he express similar feelings for them.

But how could he know what he felt until he'd done a proper amount of research? He knew there were people who claimed to instantly fall in love, but it mystified him. He couldn't comprehend how they could figure it out so quickly. Frankly, he didn't understand how Stu was marrying someone he'd known less than a year.

Of course, Stu insisted he'd known Steffi since grade school (and she used the word "destiny" a lot). But going to the same school assemblies seemed more of a nice coincidence on their online profiles than a significant cornerstone of their relationship. Especially since Stu had admitted he had no memory of Steffi at Huntington Seacliff Elementary. Austin was the one who vaguely remembered her, because she was friends with his sister. Yet Stu was about to walk down the aisle, leaving Austin the last of his friends to do so—*if* he ever managed to do so.

He was thinking again about the 183 days. Or, more accurately, he was thinking that 183 was an overly optimistic number, since it included his very long workdays, and Austin had a strict rule against going out with office staff or patients.

Perhaps if he were thinking less, he might have noticed Naomi Bloom standing behind him in the checkout line. With sun-streaked hair, expressive aquamarine eyes and six dozen eggs gingerly balanced in her arms, she was hard to miss.

But Austin was busy admiring the view outside the store's windows and wishing there was someone with him to enjoy the verdant mountains and cloudless sky. That's when he remembered he needed sunscreen.

He abruptly turned around, smashing into Naomi, or, more precisely, smashing into her egg cartons, which bent and burst against her formerly white camisole. Like a juggler who'd missed her cue, Naomi made a frantic attempt to grab hold of the corrugated containers as they toppled from her arms.

It was only then that Austin noted Naomi's delicate curves and her vivid blue-green eyes. He felt like he could have gotten lost in her thick hair—along with the fragments of eggshell.

For a moment, time seemed to stand still, except for the yolks slithering down Naomi's chest. Austin was mortified. He wanted to apologize. He wanted to pay her laundry bill. But first, he attempted to wipe away the gooey mess from the front of her shirt.

And she smacked him.

There was egg on his face, but more than the sting to his pride, it was the lost opportunity that pained him.

CHAPTER TWO

Mandy measured the chimpanzee's swollen vulva.

The freeze-frame of the streaming video from the wildlife preserve flickered on her computer monitor as she aligned a ruler across the screen and recorded the measurement in the lab's database. Then she toggled between program windows and tweeted, "Looks like Anastasia's going to get a lot more action tonight than I will."

Her dissertation adviser frowned on giving the primates names because it could diminish objectivity. But Mandy's adviser frowned on many things. In fact, she frowned in general. Something Mandy was beginning to think was a by-product of getting tenure.

When Mandy was a freshman at the University of Michigan, she'd declared that she never wanted to leave. And she pretty much hadn't. Something her brother reminded her of on occasion (the occasion being whenever he wanted to annoy her). But now she was doubting that she was cut out for a life in academia, which was unfortunate, given there was very little else she could do with a PhD in primatology.

"You don't look like an anthropologist," Tad Emerson told her on their first date. Well, their only "date," if she didn't include sexting and booty calls.

"What does an anthropologist look like?" she remembered asking Tad with a seductive lilt that still made her blush. She had promised herself she wasn't going to think about Tad. But, of course, she was thinking about him. Because she was almost thirty and spending her Saturday night watching chimps have sex.

Tad had called it "monkey porn," which wasn't altogether inaccurate. Bundled up in multiple layers in the frigid basement lab, Mandy felt a bit like a Peeping Tom watching Anastasia parade her engorged derriere before three potential suitors. It wasn't particularly subtle behavior on Anastasia's part, but it was effective. All three males started sniffing and fondling her. Dimitri was the most enthusiastic of the three, but he didn't seem to be her preferred mate. She rebuffed his advances and ran off. Mandy sighed. "Don't be showing your goodies to guys you're not interested in," Mandy wanted to advise Anastasia. "It never ends well."

Tad had said he was going to call on Thursday. The problem wasn't that it was two days later and he had yet to do so. The problem was that if he had called even an hour before, Mandy would have eagerly agreed to meet up with him when she got off work. It was humiliating for her to acknowledge. And it was infuriating. It was one thing to be blown off by a visiting professor of astrophysics, but a trumpet player with ironic facial hair? And what kind of a name was Tad? It was like Chad but without the political significance.

She logged on to her blog and typed in a headline for a new blog post: "Mandy's Manstrosity #37."

Then she hesitated. Was Tad really a "manstrosity"? There was no doubt about #36 (the astrophysicist with the fidelity of a neutron), but Tad was more clueless than cavalier. She had known from the start that she had no business dating a musician. Especially one who was younger than she. He was only twenty-five, which in musician years was like thirteen.

She'd been surprised when Tad contacted her on OkCupid. She hadn't responded to his first two e-mail messages, despite the allure of the pale-skinned boy with overgrown sideburns. (He appealed to the Team Edward girl inside her, not that she'd ever admit to having seen a *Twilight* movie.) He told her he was attracted to older women, which had made her feel like a cougar, and she was too young to be a cougar. At least she hoped she was. She had canceled on him the first two times they were supposed to meet. Yet he had persevered, sending her virtual flowers to celebrate Latvia's Independence Day. He was goofy, and he was sweet. Disarmingly so.

Now she was mooning over him like some hormonal undergrad. Even though he had been the one pursuing her. It was so unfair. Maybe she had played too hard to get. Or maybe he only wanted her when she wasn't interested. Or maybe she shouldn't have had sex with him on the first date.

Anastasia sashayed back over to the male posse, and Dimitri moved in on her again. She hissed and screamed, which must have confused him, given that she had chosen to come back and proffer her ripe parts in his face. Mandy wondered, How was a male chimp supposed to know when "no" really meant no? She was typing the query into her notes file when her cell phone rang. It was Tad. It was insulting that he had waited until after ten. And it was stupid, because there was no way she was answering. Well, not until the fourth ring.

"What's up?" she asked, trying to sound nonchalant.

"Not much," he said, doing nonchalant much better than she could ever aspire to. "I was going to call you earlier," he said, "but I fell asleep while studying."

She tried not to be offended. She tried to focus on the positive: he was studying. Tad was pursuing a master's in trumpet performance, which seemed a rather impractical degree. But people in monkey houses shouldn't throw stones.

"How's work?" he asked.

"Just watching monkey porn," she quipped. She wanted to shoot herself.

"Me too," he snickered. Now she wanted to shoot him. No, she wanted to kiss him. She wanted to do several things to him that required opposable thumbs.

Who was she kidding? It didn't matter what time he called. She couldn't get his lopsided smile out of her mind. Or his unfairly long eyelashes. She was pining for him. Pining in places she rarely pined. She watched Anastasia and Dimitri bump and grind, noting that Anastasia wasn't asking Dimitri to make a long-term commitment. She didn't even seem to like him.

Mandy decided that there was no point in holding out for more than Tad was willing to offer. If her choice was between a booty call and going home alone to watch an *SNL* rerun, she was going with the booty call. At least for tonight. And if she felt differently tomorrow, well, that's what therapy was for.

"Are you making progress on your dissertation?" Tad asked.

No, they weren't going to chitchat. And they definitely weren't going to chitchat about a subject that was stressing her out. They were going to pick a time and location, and she was going to type it into her phone calendar, same as a gynecologist appointment. Mandy could handle having sex without a relationship, but she couldn't handle pretending it was something more if it wasn't.

"Can't really talk right now, Tad," she said. "I've got a chimp in heat."

"Oh," Tad said, sounding like he was hurt. He couldn't have it both ways. Mandy vowed to never again date a musician. Or a twenty-five-year-old.

"I don't mean to be rude," she apologized, twisting a strand of her long auburn hair, as she often did, and lamenting what she considered its dull color, as she equally often did.

"It's okay," he said. "I gotta get going anyway."

Going where? she wondered. To the kitchen of his studio apartment? And he hadn't said what time he wanted to meet up. God help her if she had to be the one to bring up the subject. There had to be some small amount of chivalrous behavior that applied even to the most debased of relationships. But he wasn't saying anything, and she had been the one who wanted to cut the conversation short. "So, what time do you want to get together?" she asked, trying to sound breezy and sophisticated, like Scarlett Johansson, if Scarlett Johansson had to ask a guy for sex.

"Oh," he said again. "I kind of have plans tonight."

"You have plans?" She hated that her voice rose an octave.

"Yeah. But I wanted to say hi and see how you were doing." He said this with complete sincerity. She wanted to smack him.

"You called me at ten thirty on a Saturday night to see how I was doing?"

"Well, I was going to call earlier, but—"

"I'm doing fine, Tad," she said, and she would be, just as soon as she hung up.

"You don't sound fine. You sound unhappy."

Why were men always telling her she sounded unhappy? And why was it always the same men who made her unhappy? She didn't know when Tad had become one of them. More precisely, she didn't remember when she'd let him have that kind of power over her emotions. Maybe it was when he kissed her earlobe and said she tasted like home. He shouldn't have said something like that unless he meant it. She could feel her eyes welling up. She needed to get off the phone before she gave herself away.

"I'm happy, Tad. And I have to get back to work. Really. That's what happy people do." The truth was that she had no idea what happy people did, but she had no intention of telling him that. She wasn't going to explain that her father had died when she was seven. She wasn't going to share that she still had nightmares of drowning in the ocean. "One apocalypse at a time," her brother always said.

"Are you upset with me?" Tad asked.

Don't answer that, she told herself. She wanted to exit gracefully. And swiftly. "Why would I be upset with you?" she heard herself say. "You said you'd call Thursday, and you called Saturday. You said we'd get together this weekend, and we're not. But you checked in to see how I'm doing, so everything's hunky-dory."

"Do you have PMS?"

Mandy would have slammed down her phone if she had an extended warranty on it. Instead, she clicked off and started hammering away at her computer keyboard: "The first thing you need to know about Mandy's Manstrosity #37 is that he's a trumpeter, which means he blows a lot of hot air."

She shivered as she remembered the feel of his warm breath on her neck. Then she zipped up the blue hoodie she was wearing and continued typing.

CHAPTER THREE

Standing under the Frisbee-sized rain showerhead, Austin wanted nothing more than to spend the next hour, or lifetime, letting the Kohler-branded jets of hot water pummel his head and tired muscles.

The truth was he didn't want to go to the wedding. It was something he should have admitted before spending the night on the floor of the Detroit Metropolitan Airport. Or even better, before he purchased the airline ticket.

He had been trying to spin the event as a social opportunity, and in theory, a wedding was a great place to meet someone. But only in theory. In reality, after turning thirty, attending a wedding without a spouse had become a form of public flogging.

Gone were the days of receptions teeming with unattached young professionals boisterously engaged in high-octane flirting. Instead, the solitary "singles" table was often populated by teenage relatives of the bridal couple and stray socially challenged misfits.

Desirable and age-appropriate single women were scarce, and Austin had grown accustomed to married women treating him with a mixture of curiosity and pity. They would interrogate him about his dating history. Then they would offer to fix him up with an obese cousin with a lazy eye. Or worse, they wouldn't.

Austin slapped some of the complimentary Crystal Cove Resort mango-lime shower gel over his torso and under his arms. He poured some more onto his cotton shirt, which he had carried with him into the travertine shower stall, churning the fabric through the flowing water the way he imagined people had done for millennia—in rain showers that weren't trademarked.

He let the water continue to cascade over his shoulders for a precious additional minute as he wrung out the garment. Then he reluctantly turned off the tap and wrapped himself in an oversized, plush white towel before exiting the shower.

As he grabbed hold of the hotel's wall-mounted hair dryer, he felt like he was forgetting something. It was a feeling he'd been having a lot recently. Maybe "forgetting" was the wrong word. It was more like he'd misplaced something. Something other than his luggage. Something was missing. Or there was something he had missed. He thought it might have to do with work and worried he had missed signs of diabetic reti nopathy when he'd diagnosed Myrna Resnick with glaucoma. Or maybe her husband's floaters were a symptom of a missed ocular melanoma.

But maybe it had nothing to do with work. Maybe it was something more intangible. Something he had missed out on. He was too young to feel that way. But then again he had felt like a middle-aged man since he was ten years old. "The little man of the house," his mother used to call him, and "my little soldier." She used to compliment him on how well he took care of her and his sister. As if it were something he chose to do. As if he wouldn't have preferred playing Super Mario to packing his sister's lunch box or organizing his mother's meds.

Austin was gripping the dryer like a gunslinger as he alternated between aiming it at his head and at his shirt. With ten minutes until the ceremony started, the shirt was still drenched. He double-checked to make sure the dryer was on its highest setting, swinging it back and forth over the stubbornly damp material. So much for his attempted ingenuity. If he hadn't already been dreading the evening, the prospect of spending it in wet clothing would have definitely done the trick.

He was starting to resent everything about this forced vacation. Okay, "forced" also wasn't the right word, but the transcontinental trip definitely felt less than voluntary. It wasn't that he didn't want to see Stu get married. He just wished there was a way to do so without being physically present at a wedding. But there wasn't, which was why he had never seriously considered any other option. Going to the wedding was the right thing to do, and Austin always did the right thing. Even if it often turned out wrong.

"Excuse me, sir," the bartender said, "this is a private event."

Austin was loitering in the back corner of the open-air ballroom. No, not loitering. Unobtrusively observing. But it was hard to be unobtrusive in a red plaid shirt. Let alone a soggy one.

"Sir?" the bartender repeated.

The other advantage to Austin's location was that it was next to the bar, and he had just downed his third flute of champagne.

"I'm an invited guest," Austin said. The bartender looked skeptical.

Austin was fairly certain that coming to a wedding in casual clothing did not rank as a major crime against humanity. However, based on the looks he was getting, he might have been mistaken.

He had purposely sat in the back row during the mercifully short outdoor ceremony. Steffi had decided against a bridal party after wearing one too many bridesmaid dresses, so there was no lengthy processional. And since the officiant was a judge, there were no time-consuming religious rituals. It was all very efficient, which was appropriate for a budding software wizard like Stu, and convenient for Austin, who slipped into his white wooden seat moments before the bride walked down the grassy aisle.

But ever since the couple had been pronounced husband and wife, Austin had found himself the object of quizzical and increasingly hostile scrutiny. He didn't consider himself a shy person, but he didn't particularly like being the center of attention, unless he was performing a keratoplasty. And he wasn't doing any corneal implants at the moment, so he wished people would stop staring at him.

He took another glass of champagne, and the bartender whispered something to a passing waiter. What were they going to do? Contact Homeland Security?

Austin had been taking abuse about attending this wedding from the moment he requested the days off of work, which his eagle-eyed senior partner was quick to notice when it was posted on the office schedule.

"Did we institute summer Fridays and no one told me?" asked Len, with more than a hint of sarcasm, since the office staff barely dared to pass gas without telling him.

Austin knew the only reason Len was busting his balls was that Len had wanted to go away for the July Fourth holiday weekend, and one of them needed to be on call. But Len had gone away for Memorial Day weekend. And Martin Luther King Day weekend. And virtually every other holiday for the past four years since Austin had joined the practice. There came a point when Austin needed to stand up for himself.

"I've got three weeks of vacation time I haven't taken, and I put in the request sixty days in advance." Austin hated the way his voice rose in pitch when he was indignant about something. Bad family trait. "It's the wedding of my oldest friend, and I'm going to be there."

"So go," Len said. "Who's stopping you?"

At times Len was Austin's partner. Other times he was his boss.

And sometimes he was a substitute father figure. He managed to be equally irritating in all three roles.

Austin took a swallow of his fizzy drink as he scoped out the crowd, keeping an eye peeled for any unescorted females. To his amazement there seemed to be one approaching him. Someone also dressed informally. Or at least less formally than the other guests, in a skirt and heels. She wasn't clad in wet cotton, but perhaps she felt simpatico. As she got closer, she smiled. She had a warm smile, a toned body—and a ring on the fourth finger of her left hand.

"I'm the manager of Crystal Cove," she said, extending her other hand. "May I help you?"

"I'm the Unabomber," Austin thought of saying but didn't. Instead he flashed his electronic room key with the Crystal Cove logo. If he could afford to pay the four hundred dollars a night, he couldn't be a total derelict. Or at least shouldn't be treated like one.

"I don't know if you realize, but this is a wedding," the manager said as if she were speaking to a mentally unstable person—well, a mentally unstable person with a good credit rating. "Perhaps you'd be more comfortable by the pool."

"I'm not lost or confused." But he was uncomfortably clammy beneath his damp shirt. "In case you didn't notice, I'm more in need of a solarium than a pool." What he really needed was a Star Trek teleporter. But he'd settle for another drink.

"You couldn't find a red plaid suit?" a voice boomed in his ear. Austin pivoted apprehensively toward his next interrogator, but it was Stu, who enveloped Austin in a bear hug as the manager slinked away. "So glad you made it, bro. Was worried you weren't going to."

"There was no way I was going to miss you taking the plunge," Austin said, feeling guilty for having entertained any other thoughts.

"Looks like you're the one who took a plunge. What did you do? Swim here?"

"It might have been quicker," Austin said. Something looked different about Stu. His hair was shorter than Austin remembered. And he was tan. But that wasn't it. He was happy. He was beaming. It wasn't like Stu had ever been a particularly melancholy guy. But he looked euphoric. Or very wasted, which with Stu was always a possibility.

"Did you get Stuffi's message?" Stu asked.

Stuffi was Steffi's nickname, and Austin pulled out his Black-Berry, wondering if he had missed an e-mail.

"No," Stu said. "In your room. She left you a note." Austin hadn't noticed any notes, but he had zipped through the room to the shower and back out again. "She has a surprise for you."

"What kind of surprise?" Austin was leery of surprises, and with good reason.

"Turns out Stuffi has a friend at the wedding who had a crush on you back at Huntington Seacliff. *Big* crush. Still single. And may I add very enthused about seeing you."

Austin felt a flicker of excitement. It was silly that such a small piece of hearsay would make a difference. But there it was: it did.

"Can you point her out?" he asked.

Stu swiveled his head from side to side. "I don't see her. But she's sitting at your table. So you can't miss her."

Stu was already moving on as Austin scanned the room for a familiar face. But it was a futile exercise. Stu was the only person from California Austin had kept in touch with over the years. He tried imagining what each female guest would have looked like as a child, as if he were running some reverse aging software in his brain. But that was even more futile. And his inquisitive looks were inviting more gawking.

He hustled through the French doors to the sunlit garden where the ceremony had taken place, getting unexpectedly dizzy in the process. The champagne and the heat were a potent combination. He leaned against a cypress tree. Or maybe it was a pine tree. His knowledge of trees was pretty much limited to them being tall and green. And he had thought this particular one provided a good place to escape the sting of social censure—and check his e-mail.

Once his eyes came into focus, he could see he had three e-mail from work, none of them urgent, and one new message from his sister with a characteristic subject line: "Mandy's Manstrosity #37." He smiled. Then he dialed.

"I'm working," Mandy answered.

"No, you're not. You're sending out defamatory e-mail." And he was pretty sure he heard music in the background.

"That's a link to my blog that you never read," she accused him with only partial inaccuracy. "And it's not defamatory. It's satirical. And educational. It's *Sex and the City* for women who can't afford to live in a major city and have never paid more than two hundred dollars for shoes."

"You pay two hundred dollars for shoes?" He knew he was busting her chops, but old habits die hard. And he was feeling a little buzzed.

"Is there a reason why you're calling?" She sounded irritated. He sometimes had that effect on women.

"Do you remember a friend of Steffi who liked me?"

"I barely remember Steffi."

"Well, can you try?"

"To remember Steffi?"

"Her friend, who supposedly had a *really big* crush on me," he said, emphasizing "really big" like he was *really* sloshed, though he was sure he wasn't.

"How could I possibly keep track of all of the prepubescent girls who found you a geek god?"

Austin tried again, hoping for a morsel of inside information. "She would have been in your grade at Huntington Seacliff, and Stu said she had a 'thing' for me."

"Austin, she was seven or eight at the time. I'm sure she's gotten over you."

They hung up, and Austin regretted calling. He wouldn't go so far as to say Mandy had burst his bubble, but she'd certainly let a lot of the air out of it. And there was still a roomful of judgmental wedding guests to face, most of whom had taken their seats by the time he returned inside. He took a deep breath as he scooted across the dance floor, or rather lurched across, a little unsteady on his feet. He could palpably feel disapproving looks, but he tried not to care. What did Mandy used to say? "Let your freak flag fly." He hated when she said that.

He kept his focus on finding his table and the mystery woman potentially waiting for him there. The evening had possibilities, and that was no small thing. He approached Table Twelve with an eager bounce in his wobbly step. Until he saw who was sitting there.

Two teenage girls were texting away on their phones. Sitting to their right was a guy who was easily in his fifties, with unnaturally jet-black hair slicked back against his head and his white shirt open halfway to his navel. Next to him was an empty seat. No big surprise.

Continuing clockwise was a woman with purple cat-eye-shaped glasses. Or maybe they only seemed cat-eye shaped, because she was wearing a high-necked blouse with cats embroidered on it and had small silver cats dangling from her ears.

Next to her was a spectacled Asian fellow in a tuxedo and an awkward woman beside him in a fuchsia gown. They seemed to scream out obligatory work invitation. But that wasn't why Austin didn't sit next to them. It was because the juxtaposition of their outfits with his own suggested a support group for the sartorially challenged.

He instead took the seat between the aging Lothario, Jack, and the cat lady, Kitty. (Really.) Jack kept talking about Fergie's new debut album. Austin wasn't sure if Jack was trying to impress the teenagers or if he believed every time he said Fergie's name it subtracted a year from his age.

The only person at the table who could have gone to school with Austin was Kitty. Austin told himself she couldn't possibly be the woman Stu was talking about, but all Stu had said was that she was single. He didn't say anything about that being particularly surprising.

Austin looked more closely at Kitty as she showed him pictures of her "family" (Mittens, Patches and Garfield). She definitely seemed eager to talk to him and was doing so with a sense of overfamiliarity. But there was nothing about her appearance or manner that rang a bell. There was still one empty chair—which he eyed optimistically.

The bandleader asked everyone to stand for the official entrance of the bride and groom. Stu and Steffi strode into the room like they had been waiting for this moment their entire lives. They made a somewhat incongruous pair. Her strapless ball gown made her look particularly short and curvy, while Stu was tall and lean. But they wore matching expressions of irrepressible joy as they danced exuberantly to Natasha Bedingfield's "Unwritten."

Austin couldn't help swaying to the infectious beat of the music, though he didn't recall previously even liking the song. As he watched Stu embrace his new wife and new life, the bubblegum lyrics about releasing one's inhibitions took on new meaning. Austin felt like the song was speaking directly to him:

Reaching for something in the distance,
So close you can almost taste it . . .

There was much applause and clinking of glasses as Stu and Steffi repeatedly kissed. Austin's skin was tingling. He felt like the world was a canvas of new possibilities, and he was about to come face-to-face with one of them. He looked expectantly at the remaining unclaimed seat at his table.

When had an empty chair held so much promise? He knew he was getting carried away. But he didn't care. He was hopeful. He couldn't remember the last time he had been this hopeful. And as ridiculous and irrational as it seemed, he remained blissfully hopeful.

Until Naomi Bloom sat down across from him.

There was no way for Austin to know what emotion he revealed on his face, but internally he was experiencing Edvard Munch's *The Scream*. His first impulse was to run. As for Naomi, she physically shuddered.

Steffi appeared behind her, wrapping her arms around Naomi and squealing with delight: "Thank you! Thank you! Thank you for your wonderful gift!"

"You haven't received it yet," Naomi responded.

"But I've heard all about it!"

"Well, the proof is in the pudding, so to speak," Naomi said. Steffi laughed uproariously, as if Naomi had said something inordinately funny. Austin was wondering if he could still make a run for it. Preferably all the way back to Michigan.

"So, Austin," Steffi said, with the kind of chirpiness that worked best in chipmunk movies, "have you and Naomi been officially introduced? Or should I say reintroduced?"

"I think it was more unofficial," Naomi said stiffly.

"I almost didn't recognize you without the egg yolk," Austin said with a forced laugh that sounded like he was choking.

Steffi looked confused, but she torpedoed on. "Naomi is probably going to hate me for saying this, but she used to have a picture of you taped up in her Barbie Dreamhouse."

"Oh, Stuffi," Naomi said, stiff smile still in place, "I really do hate you for saying that."

Steffi seemed to be waiting for a laugh that didn't come. Fortunately for her, she got pulled away, leaving Austin and Naomi to stew in their mutual discomfort.

It was Kitty who broke the tension by asking, "Why is the bride called 'Stuffi'?"

For some reason, Austin felt compelled to answer a question that hadn't been directed at him. "Because she used to stuff her bra in middle school."

"She did not!" Naomi's eyes flashed with disapproval. "Steffi had bad allergies as a kid and when she got congested her dad would call her Stuffi."

That wasn't what Stu had told Austin, and to Austin's credit he refrained from saying so. But the damage had been done. Through the first two courses of the meal, Naomi interacted almost exclusively with the Asian couple, engrossed in their conversation or doing a good job of pretending to be. Every time Austin glanced in her direction, she seemed to reflexively look away.

However, there were only so many times Austin could nod at something Jack said about Fergie or Justin Timberlake. And Kitty was very focused on slurping her cucumber-lychee gazpacho (while the teenagers remained immersed in their texting). Austin could feel his eyelids growing heavy. It was after midnight in Detroit, and he had been up for most of the last forty hours. He tried to catch what Naomi was saying across the table, concentrating on her voice to stay alert. He couldn't make out the words so much as the timbre. He felt like he was tuning in a low-power broadcast on an analog radio, except his ears were the antennae. He pictured his ears growing in size until they looked like rabbit ears. Then he imagined Naomi also having giant rabbit ears, which looked surprisingly fetching. He thought he overheard her say something about spending a year in Rome.

"That sounds nice," he said.

She looked at him with an odd expression. "Have you also lived there?"

Was it required for him to have lived in Italy to compliment her on doing so? "No. Haven't actually even been there."

"You've never been to Rome?" She asked with more shock in her voice than he felt was necessary.

"I love Rome," Jack said. "Fergie's very popular in Europe."

"Haven't really done much traveling abroad," Austin said, feeling defensive. "But I intend to. It's not like Rome is going anywhere." She seemed puzzled by his statement, as if she didn't understand—or he was speaking in an alien tongue. "I mean, Rome's been around a couple millennia. It's not going to disappear anytime soon."

"Rome disappears every day," Naomi responded, her eyes flashing again, but this time with something more ardent. "Rome as it was just yesterday's already vanished. The bread will never rise exactly the same way. The scent of citrus blossoms will never have precisely the same density. Every day the Colosseum crumbles a tiny bit more. And the Tiber retreats a little lower along its embankment. It's a city of ruins. A city that celebrates things that have disappeared. And it reminds us that everything disappears."

"You're making me want to get on the next plane," Kitty said.

As for Austin, he was a little infatuated by her passion. And a little insulted. Naomi had waxed poetic at his expense while making a specious argument. "Do you really believe," he asked, "if you were to travel to Rome this week and then again the week after that, the city would be in any way noticeably different?"

"I do believe it," she said, "because it's true."

For some reason, her conviction irritated him. "You can claim anything is true if you don't have to prove it. What if doctors went around spouting esoteric philosophies for prescribed treatments without any evidence of scientific benefit?"

"Personally, I'd say science is high on the list of esoteric philosophies."

She was teasing him. Or she was testing him. "Science is based solely on facts," he said.

"But the facts are always changing."

"Facts don't change." He was resolute. "We just discover new facts."

"What we discover," she said with equal resolve, "is how much we got the facts wrong in the past."

Entrées were served, which provided a temporary détente as they focused on their black cod crusted with walnut-edamame hummus. Jack took advantage of the lull in conversation to ask Austin for advice about a recurring sty problem, but Austin disliked talking shop at social events. He recommended Jack make an appointment with an ophthalmologist, to no avail.

"I just want to know how serious it is if I have green ooze coming out of my eye," Jack said.

"People are dining," Austin said, gesturing to their tablemates, who were in fact eating their meals (other than the teenagers—one of whom looked up momentarily when Jack mentioned green ooze).

"I'm not saying I have green shit coming out of my eye *now*," Jack protested, and, indeed, his eyes bore no visible emissions, green or otherwise.

"Without knowing the details," Austin said in his best physician voice, "any green substance would not be associated with optimal optical health."

"Where did you go to medical school?" asked Kitty. It was unclear if she was unimpressed by his diagnostic skills or simply wanted to change the subject.

"I actually went to a combined premedical and medical program at the University of Michigan. So I graduated in seven years with both a bachelor's and a medical degree."

"No wonder you had no time for traveling," Naomi said.

"I chose to focus on my studies." He left out the fact that he couldn't afford to travel because he was putting himself through school.

"I think the problem with those kind of concentrated programs is they force high school students to decide what they want to do for the rest of their lives."

"I wasn't forced." He happened to love Inteflex, his seven-year program, which offered not only an accelerated curriculum, but also an innovative one. Inteflex was devoted to creating more compassionate physicians by training them to treat patients rather than illnesses. And it succeeded precisely because it started with students too young to be thinking like doctors. "I chose to do what I wanted. No one's forced to do anything."

"I was forced to come here today," one of the teenagers volunteered. The other one poked her.

"I didn't mean to insult you," Naomi said. "It's just something I feel strongly about."

"You feel strongly about my medical education?" She was judging him and Inteflex without knowing anything about either.

"I feel strongly about people having to know where they're going in life before they know what their choices are," Naomi said.

"People like me?"

"Not you in particular."

"But you're talking to me." He was being overly defensive and he knew it, but she had gotten him riled up.

"We're taught that the shortest distance between two points is a straight line," Naomi said, "but it's not. It's the fastest distance. It's only the shortest distance if it's your final destination. And no one knows their final destination."

She was mixing science and pseudophilosophy in a disorienting and disconcerting way. "You can't change mathematical reality," Austin objected.

"And you can't know you're on the right path until you get to the end of it," she responded, unchastened. "So why not try an alternative route? Why not turn at the stoplight rather than following directions to go straight?"

"Because you'd be making a wrong turn," Austin said, pointing out what he considered to be an implicit defect in her logic, while the others at the table looked on like spectators at a tennis match.

"I don't believe in wrong turns," Naomi stated.

"What do you mean you don't believe in them?" Austin was bewildered. "They're not like fairies. It's not a question of whether or not they exist."

"What you might call taking a wrong turn, I call taking the scenic route. And you never know what you'll find."

"But you know what you won't find," Austin shot back. "Wherever it was you were driving."

"We have a difference of opinion."

"Do you believe in differences of opinion or are they just mental scenic routes?" He was seething. And he wasn't even sure why.

"So did you decide to be a doctor when you were, like, twelve?" Naomi asked with a noticeable edge to her voice.

"Actually I was ten," he said, once again stopping short of expressing a crucial detail. But if Naomi had gone to his elementary school, she should have been well aware of what had happened to him when he was ten. "Do you also have something against doctors?"

"No," she replied, "I have something against people making life-and-death decisions who never experienced life."

"And have you experienced life?"

She shuddered again. But this time there was something vulnerable about it.

"No," she said softly, before adding, "I'm sorry," as she excused herself from the table.

It occurred to Austin that he was the one who owed *her* an apology, for the spilled eggs and inadvertent groping, and now his possibly excessive combativeness. He vowed to say something when she returned to the table. But she didn't return. And she didn't speak to him for the remainder of the reception.

Going to the after-party was a mistake. Maybe not on the scale of the Bay of Pigs. But Kennedy at least got Castro's attention. Austin couldn't get Naomi to look at him. Not that it mattered. Not that *she* mattered.

She didn't even stick around very long. She slipped out fairly quickly after the dozen or so diehards had followed Stu and Steffi to a small bar at the Crystal Cove Resort, where a rockabilly band was playing classic covers like "That'll Be the Day" and "Wake Up Little Susie." Austin was the only person there who hadn't changed clothes. He was the only person who didn't need to.

He had hoped hanging out in the bar might be an opportunity to meet other single hotel guests, but there were a grand total of five other customers in the beachcomber-themed pub. And the sole female was sitting with two men, all three of whom seemed to be fading into their beers, which didn't stop Jack from introducing himself.

Austin was ready to call it a night. The high-thread-count sheets in his overpriced room were calling to him. Having imbibed numerous Scotch and sodas over the course of the evening, in addition to the initial glasses of champagne, he was ready to veg out and enjoy the sixty-inch plasma television and free HBO.

"Where you going?" Stu called out as Austin lumbered to his feet.

"Dude," Austin said, "it's almost two in the morning, which means it's almost five in Detroit."

"I'm only getting married once," Stu said. Next thing Austin knew he was in a familiar headlock. Stu's specialty.

"Stu!" Steffi shrieked. "Don't strangle our guests." There was some laughing, but Stu didn't loosen his grip. If they were back in Austin's old college apartment, he would have slammed Stu over a couch or a table to get free, but it didn't seem the best approach in the current location.

"Come on, Stu," Austin said, feeling too old and wasted for wrestling in public. "Let me go."

"Only if you promise to stay," Stu said. "You're like my best man. If I could have had a best man, it would have been you."

"Stu," Steffi said, sounding forlorn, "you said you didn't want a best man. You said you didn't want a bridal party."

"I said I wanted whatever you wanted."

"So you wanted a bridal party?"

"No, honey," he said, turning toward her, Austin still caught in his clutch.

"Well, it sounds like you did." Steffi was slurring her words, but there was no mistaking the crestfallen tone of her voice.

"I swear I didn't want a bridal party," Stu said. "I didn't even want a wedding."

Jack laughed.

"Stu!" Steffi bleated.

"I'm joking." He released Austin and embraced her. "What I wanted was to marry you. And I would have a dozen weddings, if that's what it took."

"Aw, that's sweet," she said, adding saucily, "but you couldn't afford a dozen weddings."

"After the IPO," he said, nuzzling against her while Austin rubbed his chafed neck. Austin was deciding whether he should give in and sit back down or sneak out, when the band shifted to a bluesy rendition of "House of the Rising Sun."

"What do you think of the keyboard player?" Stu asked him.

The keyboard player was the one other potentially single female in the room. She had Bettie Page bangs and granny sunglasses that she didn't seem to ever take off. She looked a bit like Katy Perry, if Katy Perry were about ten years older and had about twenty years of hard living showing on her face. But this woman could sing. "House of the Rising Sun" was the first time she had soloed since they arrived, and it might have been the Scotch, but Austin thought she sounded like Janis Joplin mixed with Cyndi Lauper. And that was a good thing.

"She's kind of talented," Austin said, thinking she was also kind of sexy.

"You should ask her out," Stu replied.

But somehow the fact that she had talent depressed Austin. He watched her shake her long, dark tresses while belting a high, plaintive note. He looked around the room at the smattering of inebriated guests. "It's kind of sad," he said, "to be that good and be singing night after night in some half-empty hotel bar. Probably getting paid peanuts."

"Maybe it makes her happy." It was Naomi speaking. She had re-appeared, wearing a clean white camisole and carrying a large tray of white ceramic ramekins. "Maybe singing anywhere makes her happy."

He had stuck his foot in it again. Before he could even think about qualifying his statement, Steffi started clapping her hands together. "Ooh! Ooh! There it is!" She was ogling Naomi's tray with an ecstatic look on her face.

"I present my official, much-delayed wedding soufflés," Naomi said. "Or as Steffi prefers to call them: volcano cakes." Steffi started clapping again and jumping up and down, as Naomi put the tray down on a driftwood table, revealing that each ramekin did indeed seem to contain a miniature chocolate volcano. "It's chocolate ha-zelnut with double chocolate blood orange lava. But, Stu, live and learn: all that matters to Steffi is that it's chocolate."

Steffi nodded in enthusiastic agreement as she grabbed a soufflé and a spoon. Everyone else followed suit, and aside from the sound of scraping spoons, there were several minutes of reverential silence.

It was hard for Austin to describe what he tasted. It was like eating a cloud. A chocolate cloud. But a cloud with varying textures and densities. Just when the delicate sweetness seemed too ethereal, there would come a wallop of citrus, coating his taste buds with an earthy tanginess before sliding down his throat in a slow-moving river of molten cocoa.

"Out of this world!" Steffi declared, and several people concurred with murmurs of "amazing" and "extraordinary."

For some reason, Austin was the only one who didn't know that Naomi was a bigwig Miami pastry chef. Well, actually for a very specific reason. It was because he'd missed the rehearsal dinner, where it turned out she had whipped up a chocolate-blackberry rum cake that people were still swooning over.

"You should open your own shop," Steffi insisted, scooping out one last spoonful. "And forget Miami; you should come back to the West Coast and open a hip little place on Melrose."

"Why not Rodeo Drive while I'm at it?" Naomi said with a laugh.

"Why not?" Steffi replied.

Austin wanted to second Steffi's suggestion. But he was thinking slowly. Responding slowly. He wanted to tell Naomi the soufflé was fantastic. But he didn't want to echo the same flattering words everyone else was using. He wanted to find a way to convey the quasi-religious experience he was having, and he wanted to show he wasn't the cultural Neanderthal she seemed to think he was. He wanted her to know he appreciated artistic endeavors and could be passionate about them.

"Last song of the night!" the keyboardist announced. There was scattered booing, mostly from Stu. Austin caught Naomi's eye for a moment as she collected empty ramekins, but he couldn't read the expression on her face before she quickly turned away.

As the band launched into an intensely rocked-out "Hotel California," Stu pulled Steffi to her feet to dance, but she made him wait while she finished licking her spoon. Others guests accompanied them, shimmying to the raucous music and creating a sort of small mosh pit in front of the band. Though Austin was rarely one of the first people on a dance floor, the combination of the sugar high and the hypnotic beat compelled him to his feet as he joined the dance free-for-all. One moment he was dancing with Steffi. The next with Stu. And somehow he found himself dancing with Naomi.

Well, not so much *with* her as next to her. They bounced up and down, swinging their heads from side to side, not really looking at each other. But he couldn't help sneaking glances at her half-closed eyes, her tangled hair, her nearly bare shoulders. And, yes, her breasts. Which made him feel guilty and uncomfortable after what had happened earlier. He still wanted to apologize. He leaned in to say something to her just as the band kicked things up a notch, cranking the volume and the tempo. As the guitar wailed and the bass line churned, Austin somehow found his arms around her waist, and with the crash of a cymbal their eyes locked and his lips found hers.

Welcome to the Hotel California.

Such a lovely place, such a lovely face . . .

The music kept playing in his head as they stumbled along a garden pathway, fumbling with their clothes. They were drinking each other in, their mouths mingling, their hands exploring. There were so many things he wanted to learn about her. So many places he wanted to touch.

One moment they were nearly horizontal in the hotel hallway; the next he was holding her in his arms with her legs wrapped around him. Somehow he managed to get his key in the electronic lock without dropping her. The light turned green. The door slid open.

And then she was his.

CHAPTER FOUR

Mandy was disoriented. From the darkness of the seedy bar. From the weight of a man's hands resting on her thighs. And from the bourbon. Mostly from the bourbon.

"Who was that on the phone?" the man asked, shifting forward on his barstool. She thought his name was Al. Or Hal. But it probably wasn't his real name.

"My brother," she answered.

"Your mother calls you this late?"

She leaned in closer to his ear, so he could hear her above the Fray. But she misjudged the distance and her lips brushed against his ear unintentionally. Mostly unintentionally.

"My brother," she repeated. He looked at her, doubtful. But she nodded. "Really."

She gave him what she hoped was a playful smile. Or maybe a sultry smile. Like an actress in an old movie. A black-and-white movie. She couldn't think of which particular movie. But women were always saying provocative things in old movies. It was instead of having sex. Back in the days of the Hollywood Production Code, women didn't have sex. Well, no one had sex. But women weren't supposed to even want it.

His hands moved up her thighs. A warning light went off in the back of her head. But it was muted and flashing in slow motion, so that it actually made a rather pleasing, pulsing pattern in her mind. She knew she should probably stand or move his hands, but it seemed an awful lot of effort to make. And she kind of liked how it felt where his fingers were, lightly massaging her, just enough to be noticeable.

"You have a beautiful smile," he said.

She never knew what to say when men said things like that. Was she supposed to return the compliment? He had a prominent forehead, a thick neck and broad shoulders. In the dark, he was handsome enough.

"A really beautiful smile."

"That's very nice of you to say," she said. And she meant it. He was making her feel good. He was making her feel attractive and wanted. That's what she had come for. That's all she had come for.

"You slay guys with that smile. And you know it. Don't you? You know that I'm defenseless."

"You don't seem so defenseless." She was Lana Turner. Or Lauren Bacall. Someone svelte and sophisticated. Someone whose nose didn't hook. Someone whose hair didn't frizz. Someone who didn't do Spin classes till she was ready to faint without ever getting rid of the last roll of fat around her waist.

If she were thinner, Tad would have treated her better. She didn't care about Tad. She didn't care where he was or whom he was with. She was with Al. Or Hal. She was having a good time.

She must have closed her eyes for a moment, because when she opened them, he was much closer. He spread her knees and stood between them. His hands were now under the hem of her skirt. She remembered kicking off her jeans at home and wriggling into the skirt, and she remembered thinking, hoping that someone would want to put their hands exactly where Hal's hands were now. She decided his name was Hal. She didn't really like the name Al.

He was kissing her, and he was better with his hands than with his mouth. But what he lacked in technique he made up for with enthusiasm. This was probably the point when she should tell him that she wasn't going home with him. But it wasn't like she was making a commitment to him just because she was letting him put his tongue in her mouth.

"What do you want?" he asked, coming up for air.

That was the million-dollar question, and much too complicated to answer after twelve hours of primate observation in a basement lab and four bourbons.

"What do you like?" he rephrased the question. His hands were now sliding up the inside of her thighs. She kind of liked that. But she didn't necessarily want to say it out loud. She curled a forefinger under the waistband of his jeans, hoping it would make the point that he should just continue doing what he was doing.

"What do you like?" he asked again.

He was like a dog with a bone. Well, a dog with a boner. She smiled again, hopefully playfully, but more likely goofily. "I don't know."

"You're a woman alone in this kind of bar after midnight on a Saturday night. You know what you like."

She liked Tad. But where did that get her?

"Do you like to be tied up?" He whispered in her ear. "Do you want to tie me up?"

She kissed him again, partly to make him stop talking. She didn't want to talk. She didn't want to think. She wanted to forget she even had a brain. Just a body. Fingers. Nails. Teeth. Tongue.

"Do you want to go down on me? Do you want me to go down on you?"

So many questions. It felt like a quiz. She was losing some of her buzz. "What would *you* like?" she finally said, turning the tables on him.

He slipped one of his fingers inside her, and she gasped. She felt the wetness of his breath on her left ear. "I'd like to tie you spread-eagled to my bed and eat your pussy for hours."

That was a shame. Because he was better with his hands.

CHAPTER FIVE

Austin kissed the back of Naomi's shoulder.

He wanted to wake her. He was afraid that each moment she slept was a moment they didn't get to spend together. Well, technically they *were* together. But he wanted to be talking. He wanted to be kissing. He wanted to be inside her.

What he didn't want to do was sleep. He could do that when he was back in Michigan, which was going to be all too soon. The clock on the nightstand said it was 8:10 a.m., which meant he had less than four hours to spend with her before he had to get to the airport.

He felt like a kid on Christmas morning wanting to open his presents but having to wait. Except it was the person he was waiting for who was the present. Or maybe not a present so much as an amusement park. Was that a sexist thought? Or just a sign of how much he enjoyed being with her?

In his mind, he was already rearranging his call schedule to go to Miami as soon as possible. The next weekend was out, because there was no way Len was going to let him have two weekends off in a row. But the weekend after was a possibility, if Austin was Len's bitch until then. That was assuming Naomi would even want him coming to Miami, which was a big assumption given that he barely knew her.

But he didn't feel like he barely knew her. He felt like he had always known her. Always known how to make her laugh. Always known how to make her moan. At that moment, if someone had offered him the presidency of the United States, he would have insisted there was no power he could be granted that was greater than the power to make Naomi Bloom smile.

He leaned over to see if her eyes were still closed. They were. He yearned to see the warm azure pools beneath her delicate eyelids, but he forced himself to let her sleep. The question was for how long: thirty minutes? Sixty? It was impossible to believe he had missed out on twenty years with her. Not that he would have been "with" her in elementary school. He had a vague recollection of a short girl with thick eyeglasses and a shy smile who sometimes came over to his house to play with Mandy. He wondered what would have happened if he had kissed her back then. Would everything in his life be different? Would he have lived in Italy and played guitar in a rock band?

As if. He wasn't interested in kissing girls when he was ten years old. He was interested in winning swimming and tennis trophies. He wondered if Mandy might have ever showed Naomi his trophies. They were hard to miss, sitting on the mantel in the living room of their three-bedroom condo. He wanted Naomi to know about his athletic prowess. He wanted her to know everything about him. And he wanted to hear the details about every place she'd ever lived. Every meal she'd ever cooked. He felt like his heart was going to burst through his skin. He reminded himself that was physiologically impossible, but it didn't stop the sensation.

He had never felt like this. Whatever "this" was. He didn't know what to call it. Lust, yes. But more than lust. He leaned over again. Her eyes were still closed. He checked the clock. It was only 8:14. He lifted the white duvet and nestled closer beside her, listening for a change in her breathing. No such luck.

Part of him wanted to wake her and proclaim everything he was feeling. But that was the impulse of an overtired and overstimulated mind. There were chemical reactions going on in his brain that had nothing whatsoever to do with the real feelings one has in a real relationship. It hit him how much he wanted a "real" relationship with her, and he didn't want to skip over the introductory steps. Like finding out where she went to college and whether she was gluten tolerant. She was a pastry chef, so she was probably gluten tolerant. But again he was assuming things. And assuming things was precisely what he didn't want to do. The biggest thing he didn't want to assume was that she was feeling the same way he was feeling. If he blurted that he was falling for her, it could totally freak her out. It was already freaking *him* out.

But if he didn't say something to her, then he'd never know what she was feeling. There was something to be said for taking a risk. For throwing caution and scientific protocol to the wind and just saying out loud what he was thinking.

"I'm sorry," Naomi said, startling him. He hadn't noticed that she had opened her eyes.

"What are you apologizing for?" he asked, nervous that she was somehow privy to his inner thoughts.

"What I said yesterday," she said softly. "About you choosing to become a doctor when you were so young. I forgot your father was a doctor." She paused, seeming hesitant. "And I forgot about the accident. I mean I forgot at that moment."

"I wouldn't expect you to remember," he said.

"I definitely remember. I wrote you a card. At the time. I don't know if you ever got it."

He remembered a bunch of cards from kids at the elementary school. Some in crayon. He didn't remember if he had responded to them.

"I remember wanting to give it to you in person and being very upset when my mother insisted I had to mail it. Isn't that silly?"

"It doesn't sound silly." It sounded sweet. He traced the outline of her shoulder blade with his pinky. Then he cuddled closer.

"What are you doing down there?" she asked as he pressed against her.

"Just saying good morning."

"Good morning or wood morning?"

"Can it be both?" He kissed the nape of her neck, detecting a salty scent that was part her, part ocean breeze wafting through the diaphanous curtains at the open window.

"Why did your family move away so quickly after the accident?" she asked him.

Because his mother was having a breakdown. Because his sister freaked out every time she saw the ocean. And it's hard not to see the ocean when you live in a beach town. "Just seemed the thing to do," he said.

"I never got to say good-bye," she said. He hadn't said good-bye to anyone really. Other than Stu. Naomi turned around to face him. "Is that when you decided to become a doctor?" she asked, her burgundy velvet lips only inches from his own.

"It wasn't a final decision, but yeah." He kissed her again, a deep kiss, like he was immersing himself in her. When he finally pulled away, there was less space between them.

"So when did being a doctor become a final decision?" she asked, rubbing her nose against the stubble on his chin.

"The day I graduated medical school," he said. He loved the way her smile spread across her face and then curled upward, catching the corners of her eyes. It was like her eyes were also smiling.

"What about the day before you graduated?"

"What about it?" he asked, rolling on top of her.

"What were you planning on doing with your life?" she asked.

"Stu was trying to convince me to partner with him on his start-up," he said, while delivering small kisses down her neck in between every few words.

"No way. On EZstreets?"

"That wasn't the name at the time, but yeah. I've loved computers since I was a kid. Stu and I even took a computer programming class together when we were in the fourth grade. Total geeks. Right?"

"I took a computer programing class. Am I a geek?"

"Maybe you should team up with Stu," he said, licking the nook above her clavicle.

"I failed the course," she said with a throaty laugh.

"You don't seem like the type of person who fails courses."

"Okay, I got a C, but in my house that was considered failing."

"Hey, in my house, all it took was a B. And a B-plus usually invoked a sad sigh," he said, starting to gently rock against her.

"I know that sigh," she said, joining in the rhythm of his movement. "It's like you're letting down generations of ancestors, who are sitting around in heaven playing mah-jongg and waiting to see what you do next to disappoint them."

"I can't see you disappointing anyone," he said, and she blushed. He couldn't deny he was trying to score points, but he also meant what he was saying. He couldn't imagine anyone being disappointed with someone so talented and beautiful. He looked around for where he'd left the condoms.

"My mom's kind of the queen of disappointment," Naomi said, turning her head away. "Mostly with my dad, but there's plenty to go around. I'm sorry. That was a stupid thing to say. And I'm making my mother sound much worse than she is. She just cares too much. About too much. And says *way* too much. Now you're thinking I take after her."

"I wasn't thinking that." He was thinking how vulnerable she looked and how much he wanted to protect her. "What about your dad?"

Naomi got quiet. "I don't know," she said, examining her thumbnail. "Fathers and daughters are tricky. Don't you think?"

"My father pretty much adored my sister," Austin said, surprising himself by talking about his father, which was something he rarely did. "Mandy could do no wrong."

"I'm jealous," Naomi said, then winced. "No, not jealous. Sorry. What I meant was it's great she was able to have that kind of relationship with her father."

"In some ways," Austin said, wondering if the opposite were more true. He didn't want to go there. But it was too late. His brain had shifted gears. Synapses were firing in the wrong region. "There are things you can't control in life," he said, rolling off her.

Naomi nodded as if he had said something meaningful, but it wasn't meaningful. It wasn't even coherent. And he wanted to be coherent. He wanted her to understand who he was. Which was expecting a lot, since he wasn't even sure he understood.

"My point," he said, "is that there are also things that you *can* control. And I think it behooves you, I mean, it behooves me, to take responsibility for the things I can control." He had never said that out loud before. He had thought it many times, but he hadn't shared it with anyone. Naomi nodded again, but she didn't say anything. So he kept talking.

"Every endeavor in life has an odds ratio associated with it. So while people say you can't predict the future, it's not entirely true. You can predict your probability of success. Which means you can choose to do things with a high probability of success. Or you can gamble, and I'm not a gambler. I don't even play poker."

"Huh." She sat up. He immediately regretted half of what he'd said. But he wasn't even sure about which half. "I'm trying to figure out if I've ever before slept with a guy who didn't play poker." She smiled mischievously. "I'm guessing I could whip your ass in a game."

Great, he thought. One more thing they didn't have in common. But there was no point in pretending to be someone he wasn't. "I'm never going to be a billionaire, but I'm also never going to lose everything. I could never do what Stu's doing."

"You never know."

"Not going to happen. In every career, there's a ladder you have to climb, but Stu not only has to get up the ladder, he also has to build it. The great thing about medicine is that the ladder is already there, and it's not going anywhere. It may not always be easy rising from step to step, but it's usually clear what the next step is."

"Does that get boring?" she asked.

Austin stopped and thought about it. "No," he said. "It's comforting. I'm a junior partner in an established practice. And I know that when the senior partner retires we'll buy him out, the same way he bought out the senior partner before him. And the same way someone will buy me out when I'm ready to retire."

"Wow. You have it all worked out."

What had he just done? He'd just mapped out the next thirty years of his life without leaving room for including someone else's plans. Someone like her. "But it's not like everything's set in stone," he assured her. "More like sand," he said, trying to undo the damage. "In fact, we recently lost our other junior partner, and we're scrambling to find a new one. So things can get pretty wild and wooly."

"Wild and wooly?" she teased. *Oh God.* He sounded like a character from *Ice Age 2.*

"My life is just so different," she said. Meaning their lives were so incompatible. "I could be fired tomorrow. Technically, I'm on a contract, but that doesn't mean much in the restaurant business, especially when the owner's making noises about going in a more Latin-fusion direction. And I'm kind of overdue for trying something new. Someplace new."

"In Miami?"

What he really wanted to know was if moving to Michigan was even a remote possibility, but it seemed presumptuous to ask. And he doubted someone who had lived in Miami, Rome, Los Angeles, London, and Vienna would want to settle down in a suburb of Detroit.

"I'm not married to Miami," she said. That was the opening he'd been waiting for. He took a deep breath.

"Oh my God," she exclaimed, looking at the clock. She jumped out of the bed. "I've got a plane to catch."

And that was it. He had just wasted their last remaining minutes together talking about retirement plans.

"Would it be okay if I used your shower?" she asked.

"Depends," he said, thinking fast. "Would it be okay if I joined you?"

She giggled as she scurried into the bathroom, and he took that as a yes.

They were late getting to the post-wedding brunch. Naomi accused Austin of dawdling as she briskly traversed the Crystal Cove main lobby to the terraced dining room. He had to hustle to keep up with her.

There was a lavish buffet in the coral-colored room, and a couple dozen people milling about. By this point Austin was inured to the scrutiny his clothing inspired, but this time around people seemed mostly amused by the return engagement of his one and only outfit. Naomi hugged two women who looked vaguely familiar from the night before. But Austin hadn't paid much attention to anyone besides Naomi. He waited for her to introduce him, but she didn't.

She was standing just out of his arm's reach. He'd been dreading this moment, this inevitable feeling of "separating," of becoming two individuals again after having felt briefly melded together as one. He wanted to go back. He wanted to cling to the memory of their last embrace in the steaming shower and would have happily skipped the brunch, but Naomi had stymied his effort to stall their arrival.

As it turned out, they had made it down before Steffi, who was giving a new meaning (or possibly an old one) to wedding crashing. The bride had imbibed more than was wise and was having trouble staying vertical. However, Stu was having no trouble piling up a buffet plate with a lofty mound of waffles, eggs, bacon and corned beef hash.

"I think they'll let you come back for seconds," Austin joked as he and Naomi made their way over.

"This is seconds," Stu said. "I didn't eat anything last night other than the chocolate volcano. I'm starved."

"I don't think I have time to eat," Naomi said, looking at her watch, which made Austin gaze at her slender wrist, which made him yearn to be touching it.

"The car service isn't picking you up for another half hour," Stu told Naomi.

"I thought it was earlier."

Austin did a double take. "You didn't rent a car?" he asked.

"Steffi picked me up at the airport."

"I can give you a ride!" He realized he had spoken much louder than he had intended when several guests looked up from their meals.

"They already hired the car service," Naomi said in a hushed voice.

"We can cancel it," Stu offered.

"You can't cancel this late," she said.

"What's a few more dollars at this point?" Stu said as he moseyed over to the omelette station.

"I can take you," Austin told Naomi. "I'd like to take you."

"You don't have to do this," she said, lowering her voice again.

"Do what?" he asked, not sure what they were keeping secret.

"The whole polite morning-after thing."

He was being many things, but polite wasn't one of them. "I'm going to the airport. You're going to the airport. I'm not being polite. I'm being practical." *Practical?* Could he be less romantic? "And environmentally friendly," he added, which had a distinctly more flirtatious intonation in his head than when it came out of his mouth.

"I just don't want to make things uncomfortable," she said.

Did she mean uncomfortable for him or for her? Because the only thing making him uncomfortable was having to say good-bye. Well, the only thing other than her seeming to be okay with it. Or was she just being self-protective? He needed to let her know how much he wanted to see her again. But he needed to find a low-key way to do it.

"So, has Austin asked you out for New Year's yet?" Stu's voice boomed across the buffet table.

"New Year's?" Naomi was confused.

"Stu!" Austin squawked.

"Austin used to have this obsession with finding a New Year's date."

"It wasn't an obsession," Austin objected. If Stu thought he was being funny, he wasn't.

"In college, he used to count the days remaining until New Year's. Do you still do that?"

"No!" Austin avowed, a little too strongly.

"He used to start counting from a year out."

"You're exaggerating."

"Was it someone else I lived with junior year who announced on January second, 'Only three hundred and sixty-four days to find a New Year's Date'?"

"I did that one time," Austin said, "and it was meant as a joke."

Naomi was laughing as she headed toward the fruit sculpture at the far end of the buffet. It was unclear if she was laughing with him or at him. He grabbed a plate and started digging into the corned beef hash.

"You son of a gun," Stu said, socking Austin in the arm.

"What are you trying to do to me?" Austin asked.

"What are you talking about? I totally have your back."

"Why the hell did you bring up New Year's?"

"Women eat that stuff up," Stu said. "Makes you look sensitive. I'm betting you're going to be the next one going down the aisle."

Typical Stu. Whatever he was doing, he wanted Austin to do. That was how Austin had ended up taking the computer programming class. It was also how he had ended up joining a fraternity. "Well, lay off," Austin said. "She hasn't even agreed to let me drive her to the airport."

"That's cause you move too slow."

"I don't move too slow."

"Like, turtle speed."

"I don't think that's exactly accurate," Austin said, his voice doing its characteristic rise in pitch.

"What's not accurate?" Naomi asked, returning with a plate of blackberries. Austin didn't know what to say.

"Austin's opinion of Silicon Valley," Stu replied, confirming he had Austin's back. "Did he tell you I asked him to be my partner on EZstreets?"

"He did," she said while procuring a buckwheat-pecan waffle.

Stu looked surprised. "Did he tell you I continue to ask him every week?"

"He didn't," Naomi said.

"It hasn't been every week," Austin assured her, inching closer to her.

"Just about," Stu insisted.

"Stu, I have a career. I have a job."

"You have a job in Michigan. Most people couldn't find Michigan on a map." *Was this supposed to be helping?* "It's like you're living off the grid. Come and join the real world."

"Since when is Silicon Valley the real world?" Naomi asked with a smile, seeming to also take a step closer.

"He's missing out on a gold rush."

"Gold rush or gold fever?" Austin said, his hand lightly grazing Naomi's waist.

"If this is an illness," Stu said, gesturing toward the expansive hillside view just beyond the elaborate buffet, "may I never heal."

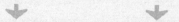

Austin had a sick feeling in his stomach. At first he thought it was the hash. But he'd had the feeling for almost fifteen minutes, which was roughly how long it had been since he'd last seen a familiar road sign. He wondered if Naomi already suspected what he was slowly coming to realize:

They were lost.

Well, not lost, because there weren't many roads in the mountains, and there was only so far they could go before hitting a freeway or the ocean. But for the moment, Austin had no idea where they were.

"I think I made a wrong turn," he said. He had been paying too much attention to Naomi and not enough to the road, and they had very little time to spare.

"You know I don't believe in wrong turns," she said, smiling.

"You're really serious about that?" It was one thing to make a philosophical point. It was another thing to be running late to the airport.

"Turn there," she said, pointing to a small road branching off on the right.

"Do you have any clue where it goes?"

"Let's find out."

He looked at her like she was crazy. A good crazy. "But what if we miss our planes?"

She put her hand on his. "Then we miss our planes."

He turned. And when that road came to an end, he turned again. And then again. He didn't know what direction they were going in anymore. No, that wasn't true. With her hand in his, he knew exactly in what direction they were going. He just didn't know which way the road was headed. But it didn't matter. They skated along serrated hilltops of green and yellow brush and basalt outcroppings, with the vastness of the Pacific to their right, which was not the side it belonged on, and yet he wouldn't have wanted it any other way.

They talked nearly nonstop, shouting to be heard over the sound of the wind from the open windows as they compared their favorite episodes of *The Wonder Years* and shared their mutual fondness for Duran Duran. Austin cranked an eighties station on the radio, and, under duress, Naomi confessed to having once attended a Milli Vanilli concert. But it was Austin who had seen Madonna's Blond Ambition tour. He insisted he went only as a chaperone for Mandy, feigning indignation as Naomi laughed and watching her caramel-colored hair dance in the breeze. He was disappointed when they inadvertently came upon Route 73 slashing across the pristine landscape.

As he was about to turn onto the concrete thoroughfare, there was a moment when he thought about taking off in the opposite direction. It was an irrational thought, but a compelling one. All it would take was one turn of the wheel and a press on the gas pedal to set off into the unknown. He glanced at Naomi and tried to read her face. She was looking out the windshield with a pensive expression. Was she having the same thoughts? Was she hoping he would do something extraordinary? Or was she just admiring the late-season wildflowers?

"He'd never know."

He made the turn onto Route 73. He traded the two-lane byway they'd been traveling for the eight-lane highway and closed the windows as he did so. He followed the signs to the 405 freeway and then to the airport. Well, to the Thrifty rental car return, where they boarded a shuttle bus to the airport.

They were no longer alone, and it felt odd. Like they should have had a significant interaction before boarding the bus. But it had all happened too quickly, pulling the car into the Thrifty lot, removing their luggage, well, her luggage and his carry-on computer bag, and then running to catch the shuttle before it left. And here they were, in the company of a newlywed German couple, three backpackers, and an elderly couple from Nebraska with three oversized vintage suitcases.

The shuttle bus came to a stop at the Delta terminal. Austin helped Naomi with her bright red compact suitcase and the Nebraskans with their battered, bulky ones before going inside and inquiring about his own, which he was happy to hear had finally arrived. He was less happy to hear it was in transit to the Crystal Cove Resort.

The security line was mercifully short. Or short by LAX standards. Austin would have relished extra time with Naomi. But Homeland Security protocol didn't provide for a particularly romantic atmosphere. Soon enough, he was putting his shoes back on and accompanying Naomi to her gate.

If he was going to say something, it was now or never. But he didn't know what he should say. And it felt forced and uncomfortable to say something intimate under the glare of fluorescent lights and the gaze of harried strangers. He wanted to convey what he was feeling without sounding false or foolish.

"It was great meeting you," he said, which accomplished neither. "I mean, re-meeting you." He corrected his words but not their tone. He wanted to hold her, but not standing in public at an airport gate. He wanted a private moment. A special moment. But their lips were already meeting before he had come up with a strategy, and the moment passed stillborn.

There was a quick good-bye, and he walked away. The internal re-criminations commenced immediately. He couldn't believe he had fumbled the moment so completely. As he was jostled by anxious travelers, he replayed the scene over and over. Halfway to his own gate, he stopped in the middle of the crowded corridor, telling himself he should go back. And do what? Proclaim his love for her? People didn't fall in love in the course of a few hours. Not rational people. It deprived love of any real meaning if you labeled every transitory desire "love." It diminished love. And it diminished his feelings. Which were real, if undefined.

But if he wasn't going to tell her that he loved her, what could he say to her? "Don't go." He groaned. Or "This isn't the end. This is only the beginning." Everything he came up with was hopelessly clichéd and a bit preposterous. He wasn't good at this kind of thing. As many an ex-girlfriend would have happily concurred. Well, not so happily. But there were several women on the planet who could attest to how inept he was at saying what he was feeling.

He needed time to think. Of course, he could have been thinking on the drive from Crystal Cove or on the shuttle bus or in the security line. But all that time was spent simply enjoying being with Naomi, not thinking about her. Well, he *was* thinking about her. Nonstop. But not about what he wanted to say to her. That was a different kind of thinking.

He veered into a men's room, where he paced back and forth until an older man washing his hands began to eye him nervously. Austin entered one of the stalls, put down the toilet seat, and sat himself down to mull his options.

Option one: e-mail her. They had exchanged contact information. And an e-mail would allow him time to collect his thoughts and express them effectively.

And it was a complete wimp-out.

Option two: tell her what he was feeling. But that brought him back to the bigger question: what exactly was he feeling? The thrill of a great night. Or was he feeling something more? It had to be something more. Didn't it? Because as much as he wanted to kiss the inside of her thigh, what he mostly wanted right that moment was to hold her hand or just sit beside her. In fact, there was a tightness in his chest at the thought of not being beside her for the next hour. And worse, for the next day. And every day after that.

That's what he needed to tell her. And he needed to do so immediately. He looked at his watch. He still had time. Her plane didn't take off for another twenty minutes. He grabbed for the stall door. But it didn't open. He pulled again. It seemed to be jammed. He shook it once. Twice. Three times. The whole stall shook, but the door didn't budge. It was stuck. And so was he.

"Hello!" he called out. He pounded on the door. Nothing. The older guy must have already left the restroom. Austin reached his hands over the top of the door and tried to jimmy it. Still nothing.

So he tried to pull himself up and over. He slowly lifted himself upward, his shoulders and biceps straining the seams of his shirt. He was glad all those chin-ups at the gym were finally paying off. He could feel the physical strength of his body. And he liked the feeling.

The problem was that once he had his chest up to the top of the door, he really didn't have any leverage to do much of anything else. He just kind of hovered there, trembling slightly from the effort. What he needed to do was to get a leg over the top of the door. But his legs weren't anywhere near the top of the door, as he struggled to remain suspended just a couple of feet above the ground. Sweat was already trickling down his neck as he tried to swing his legs up and over, smashing his left kneecap into the side of the stall. By which point the tendons in his fingers were crying out for mercy.

He slumped down to the floor and thought about crawling under the door. But that seemed terribly unmanly after the previous stalwart, though unsuccessful, effort. He stepped up onto the toilet to see if it would give him a better angle, but it wasn't high enough or close enough. Hearing a final boarding call for Naomi's flight got his adrenaline flowing, which might explain why he leaped off the toilet seat and tried to vault himself over the stall. But he didn't really have time to figure out the physics of what he was attempting to do before sailing briefly through the air—and then body slamming into the door.

He tried the latch one more time, in the dim hope that his strenuous efforts had loosened the mechanism, but no such luck. It was looking like crawling was the only viable option. So he got down on his hands and knees. However, the walls of the stall were too low for that to work. The only way he was getting out was on his belly. And even that was tricky because the toilet was in the way. To get his head under the door, he had to go into a modified downward dog yoga pose. More like a downward puppy. Or just a plain sad puppy. He slowly shimmied forward, until his ass got stuck.

If someone had taken a video of him at that moment, they would have captured him at his nadir. Sprawled on the floor of an airport bathroom, wriggling his tush underneath a stall door, feeling something wet underneath his left thigh and not wanting to know what it was.

And then he was free. He grabbed his computer bag and stood up. There was a wet stain in a compromising place on the front of his jeans, but otherwise he wasn't too much the worse for wear. He sprinted through the terminal, weaving around pedestrian traffic and dodging oncoming electric vehicles with his bag banging against his back. He arrived at the gate just in time to watch an airline employee shut the door to the Jetway.

Austin refused to accept defeat. He could think of only one thing to do, and it seemed to work in movies.

"This is an emergency," he declared, trying to control his agitation, which just made him seem more agitated. "You have to open the door."

"What's the emergency?" the gate agent asked with skepticism.

"There's a passenger on board who forgot something. I mean, she left something behind," Austin said, making it up as he went along.

"What did she leave?" Austin suspected saying "me" wasn't going to have the desired effect.

The gate agent waited for a response, and Austin racked his brain to come up with one. It wasn't that he had believed the ploy was going to succeed, but there was nothing he wouldn't have done to see Naomi again.

If he didn't know better, he might have thought he was in love.

CHAPTER SIX

Naomi didn't know what to make of Austin's kiss good-bye. It wasn't even a kiss. It was more like a peck. As if he couldn't wait to get away from her. Had she entirely misread him?

He had been so attentive and tender all morning, and he had listened to her. Really listened to her. He disagreed with half of what she said, but he did so in a way that showed her opinions were truly being heard. She couldn't remember the last time she felt a man had really *heard* what she was saying.

Maybe she should be happy with the time they had together. Maybe for once she should be content with what she had rather than wishing for something more. But she did want more. And she was almost sure they wanted the same thing.

She decided there was only one explanation for Austin's abrupt departure: he was coming back. He probably had a very specific plan. It was so clear that he was someone who always had a plan.

He was going to come back to the gate with a goofy gift like a Dodgers T-shirt or an LA snow globe. And she was going to ask him to be her New Year's date. That was the line she'd come up with. And she thought it was pretty clever. She was looking forward to seeing the expression on his face when she said it. And she was going to say it as soon as he showed up. She was absolutely certain Austin was going to show up.

Right until they announced the final boarding for her flight.

She reluctantly got in line. She couldn't believe she had been so wrong. About Austin. About their connection. Maybe he was intimidated by her. She wouldn't want to be with a man who was intimidated by her. But she seriously doubted that she could intimidate anyone. In culinary school she'd been steered toward pastry work when it became clear she didn't have the bravado necessary to run an entire kitchen.

She wanted to go back to the way things were before they'd gotten to the airport. Something had shifted around the time they had pulled into the car rental lot. There was a nervousness or a distractedness that hadn't been there earlier. Things had felt so easy and effortless. There was a moment when they were driving along the crest of the Santa Rosa foothills with the Pacific laid out like a carpet and their fingers intertwined, and what Naomi recalled feeling was complete serenity. Just a sense of being exactly where she belonged. She rarely felt like she was where she belonged, and it took so much effort pretending.

She wished there had been some way to stay in that moment. But moments end. Roads turn. She remembered Austin turning onto the highway. She remembered having the urge to stop him. "Keep going," she had wanted to say. Keep driving. Just the two of them and the road and the sunshine. Like Thelma and Louise. But without the canyon and the suicide. Or Brad Pitt. So it wasn't really like Thelma and Louise at all.

But the point was she hadn't told Austin to keep going. And she regretted it. She regretted it the moment they turned north on Route 73. And she regretted it even more as she took her window seat on the plane.

She should have told Austin how she felt about him. She'd just assumed there would be plenty of time later. It seemed impossible that she had found Austin Gittleman after all these years. And lost him so quickly.

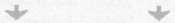

Naomi emptied her crayon box onto her drawing table. She drew one letter in each color. First magenta, because it was her favorite. Then periwinkle blue, because it was her second favorite. Burnt orange was last, because it reminded her of dried apricots, and she didn't like dried apricots. She wanted the card to look like a rainbow. And she hoped that all the colors would cheer Austin up.

She had made him a Valentine's Day card the same way. But she hadn't given it to him, so she didn't have to worry about repeating herself.

So far she had written only one sentence. "Austin, I am very sorry you are sad." When Naomi was sad, she liked to lie next to her cat, Cleopatra. So she drew a picture of Cleopatra. Just Cleopatra's head and whiskers, because Naomi wasn't good at drawing paws.

She wanted Austin to feel better and come back to school. She missed seeing him on the bus. She missed Mandy too. But she missed Austin more. The first time she ever saw him was at the bus stop, and she thought he was the cutest boy she had ever seen. She thought he was even cuter than Ricky Schroder. Mandy said she needed new glasses.

But Mandy had still given her one of Austin's school pictures. Naomi had taped it on the face of her Ken doll, and she put on a poolside wedding for Barbie and Austin/Ken. But the photo kept falling off, and Naomi was worried it was going to fall into the pool. So Naomi had taped the photo above the fireplace in her Barbie Dreamhouse. She had wished she had miniature trophies she could put next to it.

She picked up the goldenrod crayon. She liked goldenrod, but it was hard to see on the page. So she had to press hard. She made a capital "I." Then color by color she wrote out, "I hope you are happy again soon. Because you are very nice and I like you very much."

Her mother had entered her bedroom. Naomi could hear the swish of her Donna Karan pleated pants. Naomi curled her shoulders forward, trying to shrink herself into the smallest amount of space possible so her mother wouldn't notice her. But no matter how small Naomi tried to make herself, her mother could always see what was wrong with her.

"You can't say that," her mother said, picking up the card from the table. "You can't tell a boy you like him."

It's a private letter, Naomi thought. *You can say things in private.*

"Naomi," her mother said, "there are very few powers girls have over boys. But the one power every girl has is the power to keep a boy from knowing if you like him. It's a magic power. Did you know that?" Naomi shook her head while keeping her shoulders hunched. "Do you know what happens when you give magic away?" her mother asked.

"What?"

"You can never get it back."

Naomi was pressing her nose to the window of the plane, the way she had often done as a kid. She used to look forward to watching the plane fly through the clouds, imagining what it would be like to touch them. But there were no clouds at the moment, and she was looking down at the parched mesas below. The day had started so promising, but now it seemed as arid as the desert landscape. Even the upgrade to a business-class seat wasn't giving her any pleasure. It was going to be a long flight.

"Would you like a complimentary drink?" Naomi heard the attendant ask.

"This depends on who is giving the compliment," was the response from her seatmate. There was a slight accent. Maybe Italian. Definitely a flirt.

The flight attendant giggled. Maybe she was flirting too. Though she was probably young enough to be the man's daughter, from the little Naomi could see of him when she turned around.

"Or is there something you would like with alcohol?" the attendant asked.

"There is something I like with alcohol, but I will settle for a gin and tonic."

Naomi snorted unintentionally.

"Are you okay?" he asked, turning his tanned and stubbled face in her direction.

"Allergies," she quickly said.

"Are you allergic to flirtatious jokes?" he asked, and again the hint of a southern European accent.

"Only bad ones," she responded.

His eyes crinkled in an appealing way when he smiled. He looked familiar, but she couldn't say why. Until the flight attendant brought him his drink.

"Here you are, Chef Gil."

Carlos Gil had restaurants in Miami and Madrid. Several years back, Naomi had applied for a job as a sous chef at Sevilla, one of his first restaurants in Miami. She hadn't even gotten an interview. But Gil would have to be much older than he looked. Though his thick hair was salt-and-pepper, his unlined brow and ruddy complexion didn't suggest a man in his fifties.

"Can I buy you a drink?" he asked Naomi, quickly adding, "To make up for, how you say, attack of allergy."

"No, thank you," she demurred.

"*Salud,*" he said before downing his entire cocktail.

Naomi watched with mild concern. She didn't want to have to

deal with a drunken Spanish chef for the long flight cross-country. "You might want to pace yourself, cowboy. It's a long flight."

"Then is good I sit next to a tall glass of water," he said. Naomi blushed. "I hate to fly," he said. "I have, how you say, fear when you fly?"

"Fear of flying?" Naomi suggested.

"I thought there was a word."

"Not that I know of." Was there? She wasn't sure. She also wasn't sure if he was flirting or just making conversation. Well, she was mostly sure, but she wasn't sure if she should encourage him or, if she did, what her motives were. She wanted to tell him she was a pastry chef, but she was afraid it would look like she was angling for a job. And maybe she was.

"Oh," he said, falling silent. He opened his black buttery leather carry-on and took out a paperback book. Something thick and Spanish.

Naomi's opportunity had passed. She looked back out the window; the topography below was now a parade of sawtooth sienna slopes. She'd have a good story for the guys in the kitchen, how she'd met the trendsetting Carlos Gil and shut him down in less than five minutes. It was a winning weekend all the way around.

"Do I really look like a cowboy?" Carlos asked.

"I didn't mean it like that," Naomi said, turning quickly around.

"My grandfather was a cowboy. *Vaquero.* In Andalucía. He was very good with a lasso. This is how he catch my grandmother."

"How do you know she wasn't waiting to be caught?" Naomi asked.

"*¡Salud!*" he exclaimed, tossing back the dregs of his drink. "Señorita," he said, calling out to the attendant. "Another gin and tonic."

"Maybe I'll join you," Naomi said, "if the offer's still good." After all, it was a long flight. She could spend it crying over Austin Gittleman. Or she could choose to do something else.

CHAPTER SEVEN

There was a man's head buried between Mandy's legs, and she was trying to remember the man's name.

She was tied to an antique four-poster bed that wouldn't have been out of place in *Martha Stewart Living*. Though the Velcro straps would have been.

The man adjusted the straps, hoisting her legs higher off the bed before returning his attention to her nether region, sliding the side of his thick forearm against her and pressing it deep like a freighter ship plying an undulating sea. Mandy wouldn't have minded if he kept doing that, for the next week.

But eventually he switched things up, burrowing with his knuckles and then with his tongue. She wanted to call out his name, but she was afraid she'd say the wrong one. She seemed to remember the name Hal. But she wasn't sure. So she had been calling him "Baby," and now he was calling *her* "Baby." (Well, not at the precise moment, because he was otherwise engaged.) Mandy usually disliked being called "Baby." But she wasn't complaining. She felt like she was nearly levitating. For a bound woman, she felt incredibly unrestrained.

The sordid truth was she was enjoying herself. More than she deserved to. She was smart enough to know when she was being stupid. And going home with a man who fingered her in public was dangerously stupid. For all she knew, he could have had homicidal tendencies. Or herpes. Which was arguably worse. It was still possible he had some kind of STD, though he showed her a clean bill of health from his doctor and seemed a little perturbed she couldn't produce the same.

Leaving the bar, she had feared he lived in some basement lair in a ramshackle house north of Main Street. She'd imagined some kind of hoarder's hovel with an excavated pit in the back like something from *The Silence of the Lambs*. She had kept her hand around the mace on her key chain the entire walk over, ready to make a run for it. But he actually lived in University Towers, one of the only high-rise buildings on campus. And he had impeccable taste in home decor.

She luxuriated in the feel of the expensive slate-gray sheets while chastising herself for her recklessness. And she wasn't just being reckless; she was . . . she was quivering. No, she was making bad choices. She was also quivering. But that didn't mean this wasn't a bad choice. She belonged home working on her dissertation proposal. She needed to keep track of what was important, and the most important thing in her life was coming up with a way to convince her adviser that she was on track and on schedule, though she was currently neither. She was playing with fire, because she was already at risk of academic probation due to the two incompletes on her transcript. After twelve months those would change to failing grades if she didn't hand in final papers, which was in addition to writing her dissertation. So she had more than enough work to occupy a Saturday night without a date.

But it was like a fever had come over her. Sitting alone in her apartment hours earlier, her skin had begun to itch, and she'd felt an intense craving. Not necessarily for sex. Or danger. Though she was self-aware enough to realize that must have been part of it. What she'd craved was attention. Validation. And, oddly enough, peace.

There was something so peaceful about being wanted. About knowing a man wanted something very specific from her, and knowing she had control over whether or not he got what he wanted. She so rarely got what she wanted. And it was the next best thing.

There was an increasingly fast rhythm between her legs. She felt a vibrating sensation, like when her dentist gave her laughing gas. "Oh God," she called out. "Oh, Hal."

The rhythm stopped. A red and wet chin came into view. "What did you call me?"

"Hal?" Mandy said softly, and when that didn't get a response, "Al?"

He laughed. "My name is Phil."

She was mortified. She pictured someone videotaping this moment and submitting it to an X-rated version of *America's Funniest Home Videos*. "I'm sorry," she said. "I'm so sorry, Phil."

"Don't be," he said. "I kind of like Hal."

"What?"

"I want you to call me Hal."

And then he went back to work on her clit, before untying her and fucking her. They spooned for an hour or so afterward, which might have been her favorite part. She liked how it felt having his dense body draping hers. It made her feel smaller. Thinner. And, strange as it seemed, protected.

CHAPTER EIGHT

The tennis ball went wide. But Austin hit it back anyway because Len was unbearable when he lost. However, Austin had intended to hit it back deep. Instead, it sort of plopped down just short of the service line, and Len was all over it with an inside-out forehand to the far corner of the court. Austin went racing for the ball, but the point was over before he made it even halfway there, putting Len ahead for the set by four to two.

"Yes!" Len exclaimed. "That's the way to do it!"

Missing the ball seemed to be the metaphor for Austin's life since his trip to LA the previous week. But there was something about losing to a man close to thirty years his senior that was particularly demoralizing. Initially, Austin had been losing on purpose, but he hadn't planned to fall so far behind. His goal had been to give Len an extra point here and there, not let Len run roughshod all over him. It wasn't good for Austin's ego—or their working relationship.

As Len prepared to serve, Austin tried to loosen up by running in place. He was determined to get back in the set and even out the score. However, he still had to be careful not to actually win, because whenever he did, Len ended up in a snit the rest of the day, criticizing

Austin at the office in front of the staff and purposely delegating to him the least desirable of the patients. Playing tennis with Len was a lose-lose proposition. Austin had tried passing on their weekly matchup at the Franklin Athletic Club, but that also put Len in a foul mood.

They weren't even supposed to be playing for points. But Len got bored, as he did every week, and said, "You know what would make this more interesting? If we had a little wager going." It wasn't like Len was much of a gambler. All they ever bet was a coffee or a bagel. But . . . There always was a "but."

"That means we have to play for real points," Len said, as if he was having the thought for the first time. "You up for the challenge?"

And what was Austin supposed to say? "No, I prefer not to be challenged. I prefer you not use our tennis game as a place to work through the aggression you feel toward your wife."

Austin thought he was being pretty clever about letting Len win without making it conspicuous. It actually took a fair amount of mental calibration, finding ways to give Len a few line calls in his favor and purposely flubbing the occasional volley. But being two games up was bringing out Len's inner Agassi. Years seemed to be melting off his gait and his swing. His footwork was smoother. His shots were deeper and stronger, requiring Austin to hustle around the court in a way that was completely in conflict with the nonaggressive game he had been previously playing. Meanwhile, Len's serves were increasing in speed and spin, with the latest skidding off the court at an obtuse angle before Austin could get his racquet on it, bringing the set's score to five-two as they both approached the courtside water cooler.

Austin was now one game away from losing his dignity along with the one-set match. He was frustrated with himself for caring and more frustrated with Len for taking advantage of his conscientiousness. But Len didn't know Austin was being conscientious. Len probably just thought Austin was playing crappy. And he was. Which wasn't solely because of Len. Austin was having a hard time focusing his thoughts on anything but Naomi.

"You look like you're a million miles away," Len said. More like eleven hundred. "Have you called that girl in Miami?"

Of course Austin had called Naomi. Numerous times. But he always got her voice mail. He had also e-mailed, and she had replied. But her replies were somewhat delayed and never more than a few words. She seemed distant. Or evasive. Or both. He couldn't tell if she was mad at him or waiting for him to make the next move, and he wasn't sure what the next move was if he couldn't even get her to engage in a conversation. If she lived in town, he would have just asked her out to dinner. But she didn't live in town.

It was possible she simply wasn't interested in him. But, ego aside, he had sensed a connection between them, and he refused to accept that it was all in his head. Then again, if he was so convinced she wanted something more, he should have acted on it when he had the chance.

"Your problem is you live your life the way you play tennis," Len said between gulps of water. "No follow-through."

Austin had a terrible problem with follow-through on his ground strokes. It seemed so easy and obvious when he watched professional players. Just let your arm keep on moving after you hit the ball. Let the momentum carry the racquet head up and over your shoulder. But when he was on the court his racquet often stopped immediately after hitting the ball, like a train coming to an abrupt halt right after leaving the station. Not only did it deprive Austin's game of topspin; it did nasty things to his right shoulder, which took the brunt of all that acceleration coming to a quick stop.

"You always seem like you're holding back," Len said, picking up his racquet again. "You need to leave everything on the court. You should have nothing left to give."

As Austin prepared to serve, he silently vowed to show Len just what it looked like when he didn't hold back. But the problem was Len was right.

Austin was the king of holding back. It was what he did. With Naomi. With everything. When he craved potatoes au gratin, he'd order a plain baked potato to save calories in case he wanted something decadent for dessert. When he yearned to stay at an Embassy Suites, he'd book the Marriott Courtyard so that he'd have extra room in his budget if he decided to stay an extra day. He made a habit of keeping things in reserve: time, money, calories—and emotions. It was like an emergency kit for his psyche. No matter what unpredictable circumstance he found himself in, he wanted to know he had the resources to handle it. He never wanted to feel as helpless as he had when he was ten years old. The problem was that he was prepared for disaster but not for success.

He needed to change that. He needed to risk putting everything on the line, he thought as he tossed the tennis ball high in the air and whipped his serving arm in a circular orbit before pummeling the ball for a clean winner.

Len looked perplexed. "I wasn't ready," he said as he trudged across the court to get in position for the next point. He must not have been ready for that serve either, because it was another winner.

Austin managed to bring the score to a more respectable five-four. He felt galvanized and decided he needed to take the same aggressive approach off court. He decided right then to send Naomi a bouquet of roses. Two dozen. What the hell, three dozen. But he didn't have an address for her. He wondered how inappropriate it would be to ask Steffi while she was still on her honeymoon. Based on the texts he'd been receiving from Stu, it probably wasn't a good idea. From the scowl on Len's face, winning the last two points might not have been a very good idea either.

"I think I twisted something in my knee," Len said with the most exaggerated grimace Austin had ever seen on someone over the age of six. "Not sure I should keep playing," Len said, meaning he preferred to lock in his one-game lead rather than risk losing the set, which was fine with Austin.

But winning by default didn't seem to offer the same palliative effect on Len's mood. "I'm not getting the response I expected from the job ad," he grunted on his way to the locker room.

Len had placed an ad for a new junior partner more than a month back. "No one you want me to meet yet?" Austin asked.

"Not really anyone to meet, period. A couple nibbles, but no one's come in for a first interview."

Maybe Len's reputation as a micromanager was preceding him. It had given Austin some trepidation before he jumped on board. And he probably wouldn't have, if Len hadn't guaranteed that he would be retiring in five years, which meant he would be retiring in the coming year, which meant Austin would soon be a senior partner. Having a job with long-term security had appealed to Austin, but now he wondered if it was unappealing to Naomi.

"You're a million miles away again," Len said. "Why don't you just go down to Miami already? Just not on Labor Day weekend. I'm taking Cindy to Hilton Head."

While Austin showered and changed, he replayed Len's words in his mind. The truth was Austin had been thinking about going to Miami since watching Naomi's plane depart LAX. He had considered buying a ticket on the next plane, before deciding it was a bit crazy.

Instead, he left her a voice mail while she was still in flight, telling her how much he'd enjoyed their time together, and his intention had been to bring up coming to Miami when she called him back. He had even contemplated the possibility of pulling off an additional visit or two before the holiday season. And not that he wanted to get ahead of himself, but since Naomi knew Mandy and his mother, he figured if things went well, it wouldn't be out of line to invite her to join his family in Michigan for Thanksgiving. And once they were talking about Thanksgiving, it would be a very natural progression to asking her out for New Year's.

But none of that was happening. The entire scenario seemed to have crashed and burned after his initial phone call. Now he wished he had waited to call until after she had landed in Miami. Maybe he would have reached her instead of her voice mail. But that didn't happen. And they hadn't spoken. And it seemed presumptuous to invite himself to Miami without even asking her opinion.

As he was leaving the sports club, he texted Mandy for *her* opinion, and he noticed he had three texts from Stu.

The texts had started coming the first day of Stu's honeymoon. While Hurricane Bethany had been a significant inconvenience for Austin, Hurricane Cordelia and Hurricane Daphne had wreaked major havoc on Stu and Steffi's trip to St. Barts. Though Cordelia never hit St. Barts, it delayed their arrival by a day, which was what prompted the first texts from LAX. Then when Stu and Steffi finally arrived in the Caribbean, everyone was battening down the hatches for Daphne, who took her time before besieging the island with pelting wind and rain.

The forced indoor seclusion could have worked out nicely on a honeymoon, except that Steffi was suffering from some kind of yeast infection. Stu had been sending missives describing in graphic detail the cauliflower-like eruptions from his wife's vagina, under the mistaken belief that Austin's ophthalmology training made him knowledgeable about gynecology—and immune to nausea.

"She's shopping again," Stu wrote in his latest message. The storm system had moved on, but the yeast infection had not. "She loves to shop. She can shop twelve hours a day. Who knew?"

"You would," Austin wanted to say, "if you had married someone you'd known longer than a baseball season." But instead he typed, "All women like to shop. I think it's genetic." He didn't really believe that all women liked to shop, but he thought the sentiment would improve Stu's mood.

"Oh, first you get upset when I ask you for gynecological assistance," Stu texted, "but now you're a geneticist."

Or not.

Stu was about the only person Austin hadn't asked for advice about Naomi. It didn't seem appropriate, given what Stu was going through. And so far, being a newlywed wasn't exactly bringing out his romantic side.

Another text arrived: "I never thought I'd be beating my meat on my honeymoon."

Stu was definitely not going to be of help, and Mandy hadn't responded. Austin tried calling her on his way to Ford Hospital, where he was giving a lecture to first-year medical residents. It was something he did a couple of times a year. He didn't have the patience for a career in academia (he didn't know how Mandy put up with the byzantine bureaucracy), but he enjoyed the give-and-take with students and felt the interaction kept him sharp.

His call went straight to voice mail, which was becoming a recurring event for him when contacting women. Except he didn't imbue it with any particular significance when it happened with Mandy, so why did the same outcome elicit a different response when Naomi was involved? This was the danger with straying from the scientific method. Emotions got in the way of clearheaded logic. And you could end up seeing what you wanted to see. Or what you feared to see. Rather than what was really there.

Turning onto the Southfield Freeway, Austin noticed the lack of traffic, which was odd for almost nine a.m. He remembered as a kid, the six-lane highway would be bumper-to-bumper at rush hour as hundreds of thousands of auto industry workers commuted to manufacturing plants and sales offices and executive suites. But now there were so few vehicles on the road, Austin could have been doing doughnuts if he'd wanted to.

It was unsettling to think about where all the people had gone. It was possible they had relocated to the same places the jobs had migrated. But that was unlikely, given that so many of the auto jobs were now in places like Mexico and China. This was one problem that couldn't be blamed on the 1967 race riots, which were responsible for much of what was dysfunctional about Detroit.

The problem was the city wasn't adapting to changing circumstances. It was a city trapped in old ways of thinking. Austin wondered if he was also a product of that thinking. Could a city's political impotence have an environmental impact on an individual's psychological development? He wondered if anyone had ever done a study on the subject. He'd have to look it up. More important, he needed to counteract any such effect by taking bolder action. Like going to Miami. If Naomi approved.

"Just tell her that you're coming," Mandy said, sounding tired of the topic within seconds of answering his third call.

"But isn't that being pushy?"

"Sometimes women like guys to be aggressive," Mandy said.

"I don't want to come off as abrasive," Austin said. "Or a stalker."

"How about annoying? Are you worried about being annoying?"

"Do you have some other brother who has put up with *all* your relationship and pseudorelationship drama for twenty years and never asks for your help in return?"

"Never asks for my—"

"*Almost* never," he corrected himself.

"Don't tell her that you're coming," Mandy said, reversing herself.

"You mean don't go?" Austin liked that suggestion even less than her previous.

"No, I mean the opposite," she said. "Just go. Don't try to figure out the right thing to do. Just do it. Whether it's right or not. Maybe there isn't a right thing to do. Maybe there are just things that feel right."

⬇   ⬇

"You're *where?*" Naomi asked, sounding a little breathless.

"I'm at the Miami airport," Austin said again. Actually, he was in a room at the Miami airport Marriott Courtyard, but that didn't go with his cover story. "I'm attending a medical meeting in Miami, so I figured I'd give you a call and see if you'd like to get together later."

"I'd love to get together," Naomi said. She had no idea how good it felt to hear that. "It's just a total surprise. I'm actually on my way to the airport."

Austin thought he'd heard wrong. "You're on the way to the airport?"

"It's a crazy day. Crazy week. Totally crazy."

He got the crazy part. What he was missing was why she was going to the airport. "Are you picking someone up?"

"I'm catching a plane." His heart sank. "But we can meet up now, unless you have some symposium to attend, because I'm going to be sitting at the airport with nothing to do. They make you check in ridiculously early for international flights."

"You're going abroad?"

There was a pause on the line. He thought they lost their connection. "To Madrid," she said. There was another pause. "Crazy, right?"

They made plans to meet in an hour at La Carreta, a popular Cuban restaurant at the airport, which would have been more convenient *if* he had actually been at the airport. Since he wasn't, he went down to the lobby to catch a shuttle. And had perfect timing, because he saw one pulling up. He also saw a line of people waiting for it—with suitcases! He had left his suitcase in his room, and it would be odd for him to meet Naomi without it, since as far as she knew he hadn't left the airport.

He went back upstairs to retrieve the case, contemplating that even a little dishonesty takes a lot of effort. *There's a lesson in that somewhere*, he thought, as he lugged his case outside to wait for the next shuttle.

Bad idea. He was in Miami in July. It wasn't a city, so much as a swamp with million-dollar condos. Austin remembered studying Siberia in ninth grade and wondering why people would choose to live in such a climatically challenged place. He conjectured that those people were so cut off from the rest of the world, they didn't realize there were better options out there. But what excuse did Floridians have? Don't they get the Weather Channel? They couldn't even make California's claim of a "dry heat." This was wet heat wrapped in a drenched blanket inside a steam bath. This was what hell aspired to be.

By the time the shuttle arrived, he was sopping. There was a reason he hadn't waited inside the lobby, but the reason wasn't coming to him. It could have been due to sudden-impact heat stroke. Or just the humidity short-circuiting his neurological system.

The shuttle's air-conditioning was set to a subarctic level to counteract the external torridity. Austin imagined small icicles forming in the wet patches underneath his arms and in the small of his back.

For some reason, it wasn't until he was getting off the shuttle that it occurred to him the restaurant wasn't *at* the airport but *inside* the airport, meaning he was going to have to get past security. He had no idea how, but begging came to mind. Begging actually seemed to be the beginning and end of his list of options. He could claim he had left something behind at the gate, since he had left the airport less than an hour ago. It didn't seem unreasonable to ask a security agent to pretend he hadn't left, and by pretend, he meant let him reenter. He also figured there had to be a romantic soul or two working for the TSA.

There wasn't.

What he considered a reasonable and even heartwarming request was met with a threat of incarceration from a snappish supervisor with short-cropped hair and a shorter temper. Austin was informed that *no one* crossed the security checkpoint without a valid ticket (with a strident emphasis on the "no one"). That stumped him for a minute, but there was an obvious solution.

He had only one question when he reached the front of the line at the American Airlines counter. "What's the cheapest flight I can get leaving today?"

"Where do you want to go?" the ticket agent inquired.

"Doesn't matter."

She looked up at him suspiciously. But he convinced her his motives were amorous, not felonious, and twenty-five minutes later he was striding toward the restaurant booth where Naomi was sitting, with a boarding pass for a flight to Tampa in his pocket—and relief that he was only ten minutes late.

She stood up, and when they embraced he felt something electric. His arms found their natural place around her waist, as if her body had been designed with the dimensions of his in mind. They lingered in each other's arms until she pulled away.

"I was beginning to think you were standing me up," she said.

"I got a little lost," he replied with a sheepish grin as they sat down. There was a cafeteria tray on the table with a plate of several fried items and two Coronas.

"Is this restaurant okay?" she asked. "There's a fancier place called Top of the Port. But this place is tastier."

"This is great," Austin said. "Tasty is great." Just looking at her was great.

"So what are you doing here?" she asked.

"A medical convention," he said. He was pretty sure he'd already told her that. Was she testing him?

"Oh, right," she said, playing with her fork.

It dawned on him that it sounded like he'd purposely not told her about his supposed convention while they were in California. "Very last-minute," he said.

"The convention?"

"My attendance." And this was how one lie begets another. "My partner was going to come, but he wasn't able to." It was a white lie. To make her feel better. "He's taking his wife to Hilton Head." That part wasn't technically untrue (or wouldn't be in a few weeks' time).

"Take some food," she said, pushing the tray toward him. He appreciated the offer, but he had wanted to treat her to a meal. "I picked up some appetizers while I was waiting. The yucca fries are particularly good." She speared one with her fork. "I also got *croquetas* and a *pastelito*. It's a pastry with guava and cheese. I make a version with Gruyère and fig jam."

"Where can I get one of those?" he asked, taking a couple of fries.

"I could have cooked up a batch if you'd given me any advance notice," she said, gently chastising him. "But there's probably plenty of food at the convention."

"Of course." It was getting hard to remember all the things he was making up. He wanted to tell her the truth, but instead he said, "So you're going to Madrid?"

"Yeah," she replied, nodding.

He waited for her to say more, but she didn't. "Any particular reason?"

"You don't *need* a reason to travel."

He'd stepped right into that one. "I just meant you hadn't mentioned anything about Madrid while we were in LA."

"You didn't mention anything about a convention." She seemed prickly.

"I wasn't planning on going," he said, "until my partner canceled." Oddly, saying it a second time made it feel more true.

"Right," she said, biting into a croquette. "Sorry. It's actually a potential work thing."

"You're thinking about working in Madrid?" He tried not to sound as disconsolate as he felt.

"It's a possibility," she said. She took a healthy swig of her beer, and he followed suit. "It's an opportunity. Maybe. It's a vacation. How about you?"

"I'm not going to Madrid," he said with a smile.

She laughed. "No you're going to be partying down with the doctors. Hitting the hot spots."

"I don't know about that," he said. "Little too hot out already. Maybe the lukewarm spots."

She took another gulp of her beer. "I wish the timing was better." He wasn't sure what she meant. He only knew what he hoped she meant.

"It would be nice to spend more time together," she said, and something deep inside him ached at the words. "But you probably have a jam-packed schedule."

Tell her, he told himself. *Tell her that there is no convention.* But to what end? She was getting on a plane to Madrid. And all he'd be doing was admitting to being a liar. Which he wasn't. Well, except for the very ill-thought-out machinations of his current situation.

"Not so jam-packed at the moment," he said.

She seemed to ruminate a bit about this statement. She looked at her watch. Then she put down her beer. "Come with me," she said, abruptly bounding from the table.

"Where are you going?" he said, racing after her with his suitcase in tow.

"It's a surprise." They sped through low-ceilinged corridors and down slow-moving escalators. As they neared the terminal exit, Austin became even more confused.

"Don't you have a plane to catch?" he asked.

"I'm checked in and so is my luggage. All I have to do is go through security again when I get back."

"Get back from where?"

"That's the surprise," she said with an impish grin, before dashing through the glass doors and flagging a taxi.

"Earlington Heights Metrorail," she told the driver.

"They have trains in Miami?" Austin asked. It was news to him.

"You'll see," she said.

The taxi zipped along a different expressway than the shuttle had taken earlier, depositing them at what looked like a commuter rail station. Austin was paying the driver as a locomotive pulled in.

"Run!" Naomi commanded.

She emptied a handful of quarters into a turnstile, and they managed to scramble up a stairway and on board just before the train's doors closed. They laughed as they caught their breath, like truant teenagers playing hooky. Standing close beside her, he felt like he would follow her anywhere.

Less than fifteen minutes later, they disembarked and she led the way up an escalator to what looked like another train platform. But instead of a train, what came along was called a Metromover—a bright blue electric vehicle that looked like a hybrid of a monorail and a bus.

"There's a good chance you're going to think I'm ridiculous," Naomi said, "but this is one of my favorite things to do in Miami."

They got on board, and she pulled him to the front of the tram as it emerged from the station on a curving elevated track that swooped its way around and through the high-rises of downtown Miami. It was like Chicago's El with a touch of the Jetsons. And Austin was a like a kid on a carnival ride as the Metromover hugged sleek glass buildings and pastel-colored edifices. But the best part, the part that made him feel giddy in a childlike way he'd rarely felt when he was truly a child, was when the Metromover plunged through the façade of a glittering tower, tunneling through to the other side as if the track's path had been designed by a drunken engineer or a denizen of Toontown.

Naomi was watching him watching the Miami skyline whiz by. "Isn't it great?" she asked, beaming like the eight-year-old he dimly remembered. He nodded. "My friends make fun of me, but I think it's awesome."

"It *is* awesome," he said, taking her hand in his and feeling a surge of adrenaline as she gripped his fingers. They rode the entire downtown loop. And then they did it again. She pointed out places of interest, like the Freedom Tower and Bayfront Park. He tried to pay attention to her words, but her words were flowing from her mouth, and her mouth was a work of art made of mesmerizing curves and crescents.

He noticed her check her watch again, and he died a little. It seemed that before any time had passed they were exiting the tram into the sticky late-day air. He could feel the heat rising as they descended an escalator to the rail platform below. Naomi was giving him directions to the convention center, which wasn't particularly useful, since he wasn't really staying there. She was saying she was glad he had called. He was saying he was glad she was glad. And then he did what he'd come to Florida to do.

He kissed her.

On the lips. Tenderly. But fervently. Everything he felt for her was in that kiss. He left everything on the court. And he held her to him like he was never going to let her go.

But he did.

CHAPTER NINE

Mandy was sweating. She knew her faculty adviser liked to make her sweat, but this time it was literal.

The air-conditioning was on the fritz in West Hall, where she was explaining, no, defending her dissertation proposal. The amazing thing was she was actually excited about it, but excitement is less valued in academia than levelheaded gravitas. And she had no gravitas. What she had were her notes from thousands of hours of watching chimpanzees have sex. Often violent sex. And she had evidence that the violence was often linked to self-destructive and unpredictable female behavior. Something Mandy knew a thing or two about. And her hypothesis was that primates had as hard a time comprehending each other's actions as their *Homo sapiens* cousins.

"There's been so much focus on sexual coercion by male chimpanzees," Mandy said, coming to the conclusion of her presentation, "but what if there's also an element of confusion?"

"I think not," said Dr. Lola Peña-Punjabi.

"You don't think there's confusion?"

"I do not think there has been too much focus on sexual coercion."

"I didn't say *too* much," Mandy said, mindful it was a primary focus of the department's research.

"I do not think I can support you using university resources to rationalize rape."

"Are you serious?" Mandy asked in disbelief. But Dr. Lola Peña-Punjabi was always serious.

"Rationalizing rape" was in no way what Mandy was suggesting, but it was pointless to argue. Mandy knew there were few job opportunities for someone with a PhD in primatology, and even fewer for someone without a PhD. Or without the support of her department. It was a very small and incestuous world. And the narrow pathways to success had numerous toll bridges that were guarded with a tenacity that put Homeland Security agents to shame.

"Isn't it worth considering that a female's actions may not always be to her benefit?" Mandy asked. "And isn't it really empowering females to give them permission to make mistakes?"

Dr. Peña-Punjabi regarded Mandy in a way that suggested she was the one making a very large mistake.

"Amanda," her adviser said. No one ever called her Amanda. Dr. Peña-Punjabi claimed that formality was a way of showing respect, when really it was a way of showing condescension. Mandy looked nervously at her wristwatch. "Amanda," she repeated, "is there something else you would prefer to be doing?"

"No," Mandy assured her. "I've been prepping for this meeting for the last week."

"What I meant is, is there something you would prefer to do other than a dissertation?"

"I'm very excited to get started writing a dissertation." Mandy dreaded the thought of it. "Unless there's some other option I don't know about." She gave a quick laugh to show she was joking, but she wasn't.

"You do not *have* to get a PhD," Dr. Peña-Punjabi said in her cautious, soft-spoken way. Her toffee-complexioned face remained almost inert, with her lips making the bare minimum motion. "You also do not *have* to get one in this program. Perhaps it is not a good match."

Mandy's throat constricted. Being told you're "not a good match" was the ivory tower equivalent of Donald Trump saying, "You're fired."

Mandy's first thought was that a decade in academia had given her no employable work skills. Other than possibly typing. And she had no place to live outside of student housing. And no way of paying back her student loans. But she was getting ahead of herself. She couldn't be kicked out without first being put on probation. And even that was a long and time-consuming process that she suspected Dr. Peña-Punjabi would prefer avoiding.

"I will do whatever it takes to complete this program and earn my degree," Mandy said.

Dr. Peña-Punjabi sighed. "If that's what you really want," she said. "But I do wonder if you are making things unnecessarily difficult for yourself." If she were a man, Mandy thought, she would be a total manstrosity.

Before Mandy left the office, she received a two-week extension to come up with "a more suitable proposal." Those were Dr. Peña-Punjabi's precise words. But when had Mandy ever been attracted to anything "suitable"?

She found herself thinking about Hal. He had texted her several times, but she hadn't responded. Though she had thought about it, more than once. If she responded, it meant she wanted to see him again. And she didn't. She refused to be *that* person. The person who, well, wanted to be with a person like Hal. The whole point was that she wasn't emotionally invested in him. He was the antidote to Tad. He had cleared the toxins out of her system and helped her stop obsessing about Tad. She finally had been able to focus on work without checking her phone for texts every five minutes.

And because nature abhors a vacuum, the moment she no longer needed to hear from Tad was when she started hearing from him incessantly. Phone calls and texts and e-mail. She hadn't responded to any of his messages. She hadn't even opened his last e-mail, which he'd sent more than a week back. Though she supposed that she should. Out of politeness. Or curiosity. Everything she felt about Tad, she now viewed from a distance. Like watching some video documentary and wondering, Who is that woman, and why doesn't someone stop her?

She supposed she owed Tad an apology for her blog post. Though it wasn't like she'd named him, and it was unlikely he would have seen it. They didn't have any friends in common, to the best of her knowledge. The advantage of meeting online. But the least she could do was open his e-mail and read it. So that's what she did on the corner of State Street and South University. If she'd had any inkling about the length of the e-mail, she would have chosen a spot with a bench.

> Mandy, I'm writing because you won't answer my calls or my texts, which makes it kind of hard to have a conversation. Obviously, you're still upset we didn't get together a couple weeks ago. You seem to have some idea that since I didn't meet up with you I must have been "doing it" with someone else. And while I appreciate your faith in my libido, the truth is the reason I wasn't able to get together with you was that my parents were in town. And the reason I didn't tell you that my parents were in town is that I didn't really want to introduce you for a lot of reasons that really have nothing to do with you and a lot to do with me (and my parents, who being parents, come with a lot of operating instructions). And, yes, I kind of thought it was a little soon for the whole "meet the parents"

thing. My concern was that if I told you I didn't want you to meet my parents you might get insulted. You might have a hissy fit. You might run off and give me the silent treatment. Kind of like what you're doing now. I know I should have just told you the truth. But I didn't. Because I'm human. And I do stupid things. And I make mistakes. But I think that's the definition of being human. I don't know. You're the anthropologist. Here's what I do know. I like you. A lot. And it's really upsetting to me that you're so angry you won't even speak to me. Because I really thought we were getting along pretty well. But that's my perspective. You might have a different one. It would be nice to know what it was. Maybe you could share it with me. Like in an e-mail or a phone call. Or maybe over pizza at Cottage Inn? Just throwing it out there. And I'm sorry. For what I did (not telling you about my parents). And also for whatever you think I did (but I assure you that I didn't). I hope you're okay. And I hope to hear from you soon. Miss you. Tad

She read the e-mail twice to make sure she didn't imagine what she read the first time. Her heart was beating fast. All the feelings she had pushed aside came rushing back. She could see his slim wrists as he sat typing the e-mail. She could see his eyes squinting at his computer screen as he tried to come up with the right words. He said he liked her. She felt like she was twelve, when her best friend told her that Jimmy Barkin liked her. Except that was only a rumor, and Jimmy had denied it when she saw him at his locker. But Tad Emerson liked her. Tad Emerson with the sensitive face and the silly sideburns. Tad Emerson who played "Kokomo" on his trumpet for her. Tad Emerson wanted more than booty calls. And it terrified her how much it meant to her.

CHAPTER TEN

Naomi gripped the handrest as the FASTEN SEAT BELT sign was illuminated. No matter how many times she flew, she never had acclimated to turbulence.

"Please return to your seats and prepare for landing," the doe-eyed flight attendant instructed in a tense voice that implied the landing might be an immediate and fiery event.

The plane dipped and dropped. "Please, God, not before I have my own restaurant," Naomi whispered under her breath.

It was a ritual thing she said to herself on planes. But she wondered if it was really what she wanted most in the world. And what it said about her if it was. She claimed to be looking for a long-term relationship, yet it didn't seem to be her priority.

She supposed she could have said, "Please, God, not before I'm married." But there was something desperate and demeaning about thinking that way. Thinking that marriage was some kind of brass ring and that her life had value only once she attained it. She bridled at the notion. She had slaved for too many hours in front of too many hot stoves. She had been tongue-lashed by too many sadistic egomaniacs.

Yet it turned out she could take the girl out of the OC, but she couldn't take the OC out of the girl. She still wanted the old-fashioned hearth and home, though preferably in a renovated London flat rather than the suburban sprawl of Southern California. She wanted the hubby and the kids in footie pajamas. She was jealous of Steffi. Steffi! Who practically had a countdown clock going to her thirtieth birthday and, when the alarm went off, grabbed the first single man in sight. Okay, maybe not the first one. But Stu was the kind of man-child Steffi had always steered clear of in the past. Naomi wished she could have said the same for herself.

But she was making better choices now. Or she was making less frequent bad choices. She wasn't sure which of the two categories Austin belonged in. Until twelve hours ago, she would have simply categorized him as MIA. Sure, he had diligently followed up after their night together. But he had never told her he wanted to see her again. He implied it. Or he allowed her to think he implied it. But he never came out and said it. While Carlos was picking her up when her shift ended at midnight and wining and dining her at South Beach hotspots, all she was getting from Austin were laconic voice mails saying "Hope you're having a great day. Call me if you have time."

She supposed she could have called him, but she didn't see the point. If he had something to say, he should have said it. And one thing he most definitely didn't say was "I'm coming to Miami, and I'd love to see you." Or even "I'm going to be in Miami on business this week. How about a drink?" Instead, he showed up with no advance warning and seemingly little interest in whether or not he saw her.

But he did see her. And she saw him. She saw his eyes light up like a five-year-old's when the Metromover zipped through the inside of the Knight Center. She saw him share her goofy enthusiasm and match it with his own.

And then there was that kiss. It had caught her by surprise. She hadn't necessarily expected him to kiss her. And definitely not like that. She tingled when she thought of it, and she'd been thinking of it a lot. She had thought she was over him. She had certainly tried to be. If you can't get over a schoolgirl crush by the time you're thirty, well, what does that say about a person?

But she hadn't told him about Carlos, and she couldn't pretend it was unintentional. Not that there was much to tell. Other than she was flying halfway around the globe for a guy. No, for a job. For a job interview. She was going for the job interview. She was almost sure of it.

The plane pitched to the left, and she braced herself for a tempestuous descent. Another quick prayer. A simpler one. *Let Austin kiss her again.* That was even worse than the first. *Damn, Austin.* He was messing with her mind. Again. One of the reasons she was going to Madrid was to get over him. But there was nothing to get over. They weren't in a relationship. They weren't even dating. Carlos was the one who was pursuing her. Carlos was the one who'd begged her to come visit. Carlos was the reason she was going to Madrid. Well, Carlos and the job interview. And the adventure. Though she was getting a little old for adventures. No, one was never too old for adventures.

Naomi joined the applause when the plane's wheels made abrupt but steady contact with the ground. She followed the crowd into Terminal Four of the Madrid-Barajas Airport, flowing down ramp after ramp along the glass-sheathed building, past candy-colored steel beams that called to mind the vertebrae of gargantuan exotic birds.

She took her place in a line at passport control and turned on her phone to check the time, but her phone didn't turn on. She tried again. Nothing. With growing panic, she realized she had forgotten to turn it off before the flight. She'd been distracted, thinking about Austin. No, the problem was she *hadn't* been thinking. And now she was out of battery. And the hotel reservation number was on the phone. And the address! It was okay, she told herself. Any decent taxi driver would know the hotel's location. *If* she could remember the hotel's name. But Carlos had made the reservation, and she was blanking.

Though Naomi prided herself on her ability to navigate through airports, she somehow got turned about after customs and couldn't find the right baggage claim. The arrival hall's soaring height and rippled bamboo ceiling had given way to brutalist columns and row after row of low-hanging, wok-shaped fluorescent fixtures. The minimalist signage seemed contradictory or her limited Spanish was failing her, and she seemed to be going in circles.

As she raced to and fro, she grew increasingly aware of being a small, solitary figure in a vast, indifferent place. Where was she running? Why was she always running? She stopped and leaned against a column, taking a few deep breaths. Arrivals were the hardest part of traveling. She knew that. If she could just get to her hotel, everything would be fine. But at the moment nothing was fine. And she couldn't help but think it was a sign.

She spied a flash of red on a distant carousal. There was a reason she traveled with red luggage. She hurried toward the revolving bag, thinking she was more competent than she gave herself credit for being. She needed to remember that. And she needed to remember to never pack her charge cord inside a checked bag again. She retrieved it from the zippered pocket where she had stuffed it, but she couldn't find an electrical outlet.

She groggily headed for the exit, dragging her wheeled case behind her, not really sure what to do next. She could take a taxi downtown and try to get online at a Starbucks. Did they even have Starbucks in Madrid? The morning light was disorienting. It was four a.m. in Miami, and she was starting to feel the time difference and her lack of sleep. She felt drugged and dreamy, as if she'd been smoking weed and drinking espresso simultaneously.

"Buenos días," an overeager taxi driver called out to her as she weaved through a line of cars. Everyone seemed a little too loud and too close to her. She kept imagining that she recognized people's voices, even though they weren't speaking her language. She even thought that she heard her name. "Naomi!"

She saw his chin first. His cleft chin with salt-and-pepper stubble that matched the disheveled thatch between his ears. He was leaning against a Mercedes limousine.

"You came to pick me up?" she asked, incredulous.

"¡Por supuesto!" he replied with a wide grin, as if it was the most foolish question he'd ever heard. And she was running again. To Carlos. Into his arms.

CHAPTER ELEVEN

Someone's elbow rammed Mandy's pelvis. And not in a good way.

"Sorry about that," Gordon called out to everyone from the driver's seat of the mustard yellow jalopy. "Hit a pothole."

"Are you okay?" Tad asked.

Mandy didn't know how to answer that question. She was sharing the cargo compartment of a 1972 Volvo hatchback with two guys and four trumpet cases.

"We'll be there in less than an hour," Gordon said.

"We'd be there in less time if you took I-94," said Drew, who was snaked across Mandy and Tad and the likely possessor of the offending elbow.

"Taking the 96 is a mile shorter," said Omar, the designated navigator, who occupied the front passenger seat. "I checked on the map."

"But there's more traffic on the 96," Drew said.

"We should have left sooner," Tad said. "We're going to be late for the gig." Tad rarely got nervous, but he sounded nervous.

"We're not going to be late," Gordon said, exuding the confidence of a man with more than six inches of personal space.

"Is there a reason we're not using the backseat?" Mandy asked, wondering why they hadn't unfolded it and worrying that the question made her sound prissy.

"The floorboards," Gordon replied.

"They're bad?" she asked.

"They're missing," Tad said.

That didn't exactly add to Mandy's sense of security. She was already concerned about the unsettling vibration of the low-riding vehicle, which seemed to be held together with duct tape. She wanted Tad's friends to like her, but she also wanted to make it to 2008. As she gazed straight ahead out the back window, it felt like she was lying only inches above the roadway, with the headlights of the cars behind them shining directly in her eyes.

"But Betty drives great, doesn't she?" Gordon enthused. The first half dozen times Gordon had referred to Betty, Mandy had mistakenly believed "Betty" was his girlfriend. "Listen to that baby purr." To Mandy it sounded more like the coughing of a consumptive patient. But maybe that was a good thing for an engine.

This wasn't how she'd intended to spend New Year's. But at least she was with her boyfriend. Well, technically Tad wasn't her "boyfriend," since he didn't like labeling things. But they had been seeing each other almost every weekend except when he was playing gigs or hanging with "the guys." Since Gordon and Omar rarely dated and Drew's idea of a relationship was paying for dinner before sex, time with "the guys" was usually an estrogen-free zone.

So Mandy was surprised when Tad asked if she wanted to come along to the New Year's gig in St. Clair Shores. She had been grateful he wanted to spend the holiday with her. Or to be more accurate, she was grateful after she got over being resentful that the issue had been in doubt. But Tad had left out the part about cramming clown-style into a compact clunker. In fact, he had left out that they'd be spending the entire evening with the guys. But she didn't want to complain, because Tad didn't like when she acted needy. Or obsessive. Or crazy. She was working hard at being the new Mandy. The cheerful and emotionally stable Mandy. It was a lot of effort. And more so when her body was folded like an origami crane.

"There's a lot of traffic," Tad said, half under his breath.

"That's because we're on the 96," Drew said.

"It's shorter!" Omar insisted.

"Have I ever missed a gig?" Gordon asked.

"Yes!" Drew responded.

"Let me rephrase that," Gordon said. "Have I ever missed a gig in the last year?"

"If we had just left on time, we'd be fine," Tad said. Mandy was feeling guilty for making them go out of their way to pick her up. She should have offered to go to Tad's place when she found out they were running late. She wondered if Tad was blaming her for the extra delay.

"The problem is we're hitting all the northwest suburbs during rush hour," Drew said.

"Did you know the Detroit suburbs have more highway per capita than anywhere in the world?" asked Omar, who had a habit of spouting random factoids. When Mandy first met him, she thought he was autistic.

"Detroit has more highway than Los Angeles?" Gordon sounded skeptical.

"Per capita," Omar corrected him. "Because the suburbs became like independent cities after the riots, and the car companies pushed zoning laws promoting single-family homes."

"Why does everyone blame the car companies for everything wrong with Detroit?" Drew asked.

"Because they controlled the city," Omar replied. "Why do you think Detroit has almost no public transit? They literally tore out streetcar lines."

"Did the car companies tear out the streetcar lines?" Drew asked. "Did Henry Ford go out with a pickax and start digging up train tracks?"

It was odd to Mandy how much people in Ann Arbor talked about Detroit and how rarely anyone went there. Maybe in the New Year Tad could take her to the MGM casino that had just opened downtown. Maybe they could have a date that involved leaving his apartment and didn't include enough people for a basketball team. She reminded herself how happy she was that she and Tad were together. And they couldn't be closer together. She was developing a contusion from where his belt buckle was stabbing her thigh.

"Are you really defending the car companies?" Mandy asked Drew, trying to engage in the conversation and appear to be an easygoing girlfriend (who didn't need the label of "girlfriend").

"Not defending them," Drew said, "but not blaming them for doing what corporations do, which is make money, not make cities work."

"But they're not making money," Omar pointed out.

"Maybe we're the ones to blame," Tad said, shifting his weight. She realized that though they were pressed against each other, he hadn't once intentionally touched her. There was no caressing. No stroking her skin or her ego. Maybe it was because of the guys being around. But that didn't make her very optimistic about the prospects for the evening.

"What are you talking about?" Drew said.

"I had to call the club to confirm stuff for tonight," Tad said. "And when I recited the facility director's name into some automated directory, it hit me that not long ago that was someone's job. Someone looked up the number for the person you were calling and connected you. You don't see many telephone operator positions in job listings anymore. And think about the bank teller jobs that vanished once we started getting cash from ATMs. We just take for granted that we get cash from a machine. We take so much for granted. ATMs. Voice mail. E-mail. E-books. Maybe e-cars are next. We keep gobbling up new technology without thinking about the people we're making obsolete. And what happens to all those people? Do they evolve? Or do they fly planes into buildings? Or do they do something even worse we haven't seen yet?"

Now Tad was depressing Mandy. If she wanted to be depressed, she would have stayed home and worked on her dissertation.

"That's a bogus argument from Socialist Economic Theory 101," Drew said.

"No," Tad said, "that's how things look to someone who's had to actually face the reality of the job market."

"You mean all two weeks since you got your degree?"

"I'm just saying there's a lot of people out there who are no longer needed," Tad said. "It's not just the car companies having trouble. They're just the canaries in the mine."

Mandy was impressed by Tad's passion, but she couldn't help wondering why he wasn't as passionate when it came to his feelings for her. Unless he didn't have equivalent feelings for her.

"Those are some big-ass canaries," Gordon said.

"The car companies suck," Omar opined. "Michigan is fucked."

"You don't think the same thing could happen to the rest of the country?" Tad asked.

"Right," Drew said, "because you entered the work force, the whole country is gonna have a cataclysmic economic meltdown."

Gordon slammed on the brake, sending Mandy's head slamming into the back of the front seat.

"What the fuck?" Drew said.

Mandy lifted her head and saw a sea of red lights when she turned toward the front of the car. At first she thought it was some kind of dizzy aftereffect, but she realized it was brake lights. And there was a long line of cars at a standstill. In the distance she could see flashing emergency lights.

"Must have been an accident," Gordon said. "Probably someone was drunk."

"It's too early to be drunk," Omar said.

"It's never too early to be drunk," Drew said.

Cars weren't moving. At all. And it looked like they hadn't in some time. There were silhouettes of people standing between the lanes of traffic.

"We are so screwed," Tad said. Mandy felt herself being bodily rearranged as he scrambled up and over her. He lifted the latch on the hatchback and got out of the car.

"Tad?" Mandy called after him. "Where are you going?" He didn't say anything, just shoved his hands deep into the pockets of his leather jacket, pulling it tight around him. She followed after him, walking between the stopped cars. "The party's going to be going past midnight," she said to his hunched back. "If you guys end up being late, you can play later."

"They hired us for the cocktail hour," he said without turning around. "They don't want a trumpet quartet playing on New Year's at midnight."

It felt weird to be walking down the middle of an expressway. To be moving freely past hundreds of cars that were unable to do so. There was something exhilarating about it. Mandy felt a frisson of nervousness, wondering what would happen if those cars started rolling forward again. But there was safety in numbers, and there was a fairly large crowd up ahead. "Accidents happen, Tad," she said, knowing firsthand how useless those words could sound, but hoping they would also be helpful. "There's nothing you can do."

"That's exactly the problem!" He moaned. "There's, like, no jobs. And there's nothing I can do. The guy who hired us tonight has a connection with the Detroit Symphony Orchestra, and he was going to help me get an audition."

That explained his agitation. "Maybe he still will," she said gently, bracing for another eruption. Tad just sighed. "Or you'll get an audition someplace else."

"There is no place else. Unless I leave Michigan."

The thought of his leaving gave her a queasy feeling as they reached the periphery of the crash site. Halogen headlamps from the waiting vehicles spotlighted the area, like a movie set, but one where the starring actors had already departed.

There seemed to have been three cars involved in the crash, and none of them had fared too well. An SUV was accordioned against the concrete divider. The other two cars had somehow ended up head to head with their innards splayed across the lanes amid broken glass and blood. In the backseat of one of the cars were two crimson New Year's party hats.

No one in the gathered crowd was saying much of anything as grim-faced policemen kept them yards away from the debris. A teenage girl with ironed blond hair was sobbing softly, and a freckled boy in a leather jacket was rubbing her back. Mandy longed for Tad to put a comforting arm around her waist, but he wasn't even looking at her.

"If we had left Ann Arbor on time . . ." Tad let the thought hang in the air.

"But we didn't," Mandy said.

"It could have been us." Tad seemed genuinely disturbed by the notion.

They stood in the chilly air, watching and waiting like the others around them. Though it was unclear precisely what they were waiting for.

"It was nice of you to come tonight," Tad said softly, still not looking at her.

"It was the only way I was going to see you," she said, being much more honest than she intended. Tad was silent, and she wished she could take the words back.

"If you lived in my apartment, you'd see more of me," he said, or seemed to have said. She found it difficult to believe she had heard him correctly. "Seems kind of dumb that we're both paying rent."

She felt like the ground was tilting, like she was sliding downhill and unable to get any traction. Her feelings for Tad were like a mudslide. They came all at once and left her gasping for breath. "You want me to move in?" she managed to ask him.

"Only if it's what you want," he said.

And then what? she wondered, knowing she shouldn't. But what happened after he discovered she wasn't as easygoing as she'd been pretending. What happened after he discovered just how neurotic and damaged she was?

"*Is* it what you want?" he asked.

There were so many things she wanted. "Yes," she said.

"I'm glad," he said, slipping his hands around her hips. They kissed in the pulsing light of the emergency flares. "Don't worry."

CHAPTER TWELVE

It was just a day like any other day. Austin kept repeating that to himself while he examined the watery eyes of Harvey Fishman.

"Better One or Two?" Austin asked, adjusting metal dials on the phoropter while Harvey leaned in against the machine, focusing on the eye chart on the far wall.

After a long pause, Harvey said, "Can I see One again?"

"Absolutely." Austin flipped the lens. "Better One or Two?"

"One," Harvey said hesitantly as he ran his hand through the thin gray strands covering his scalp.

"Good," Austin responded.

"No, Two."

"Also good," Austin said with a smile. "Now, neither of these may be very good, but is it better A or B? That's A?" He switched back and forth between the optics. "Or B?"

"Can I see the previous one again?"

"A?"

"No, One."

"You said Two was better."

"I'm not sure," Harvey answered, sounding anxious. "Can we start over?"

Naturally, the last patient on a holiday was going to be a difficult one. No, not a holiday. Just a workday like any other workday.

Austin pushed away the phoropter, deciding he had a better chance of coming up with an accurate prescription if he did the refraction exam manually. He pulled out a polished mahogany case from under his desk, wiping away an invisible film of dust before flipping open the brass clasps. It had been his gift to himself when he finished his ophthalmology residency and one of his prized possessions. Inside were 266 glistening lenses with metallic rims, meticulously placed in labeled slots on a black velvet base. He put on a pair of thin plastic gloves before removing a lens and holding it in front of Harvey's left eye. For the next half hour he slowly and painstakingly held up lens after lens, sometimes in combinations of two or even three, with Harvey vacillating every step of the way.

The tediousness of the task soothed Austin. It kept him from dwelling on less productive topics, like where he might have hoped to spend his New Year's Eve. Once Austin had confidence in the prescription, he proceeded to put drops in Harvey's eyes. It was while waiting for Harvey's pupils to dilate that Austin's mind began to churn, and he left the examination room to check his phone for messages. He had this crazy idea that Naomi might call. It was right up there with expecting a call from the state lottery board, but, like they say, hope is the thing with feathers, or in Austin's case, with rocket propellant.

He had one voice mail, but it wasn't from Naomi.

It was Len, calling from Cabo, to remind Austin to contact Inteflex after the holiday. Austin had offered to reach out to his former medical school program to see if there were any alumni looking for jobs. Len and Austin hadn't yet filled the junior partner position, and

Len was getting increasingly nervous, though Austin was the one bearing the brunt of the additional workload.

Austin was about to put the phone back in his pocket, when it buzzed. His first thought was that it could be Naomi. But it was Stu.

"Do you have plans tonight?"

"Yes," Austin said. He was lying, as he had done many times over the course of the last week. Though it easily could have been true. A friend had invited him to a party at his home. But it was going to be married couples and their kids, and the party was going to end at eleven, which seemed to make it less of a New Year's party than an old year's party.

"I don't believe you," Stu said.

The fact was that Austin didn't want to go out for New Year's just for the sake of going out. There was too much pressure to have a good time, and he was actually looking forward to picking up some Buddy's Pizza, staying in and catching up on episodes of *Lost*.

"How about joining Stuffi and me?" Stu asked.

"In California?"

"In Detroit, wise guy. We're staying at the new MGM Grand."

"Thanks for the advance warning."

"Don't be a girl about it."

"You text me practically every time you blow your nose, but you don't mention you're coming into town on New Year's?" Austin was kind of relieved, because he would have felt too guilty to say no.

"Last-minute thing. Got a meeting with a venture capital guy here on Wednesday. So decided to spend the holiday in Detroit. You in?"

"I'll come see you tomorrow," he said.

"Don't be lame. Come tonight."

"I told you I have plans."

"And I told you I don't believe you. Come on. It'll be fun."

Right. Loads of fun. Being a third wheel with a newlywed couple on New Year's Eve. A bickering newlywed couple at that.

"I think you and your bride probably need some quality time together, just the two of you," Austin said.

"If it's just the two of us, we may kill each other. I'm serious, dude. She started kickboxing, and she's a little scary when she gets mad."

And that was supposed to entice Austin? "I'll see you tomorrow."

"Don't put off till tomorrow what you can do tonight. And get here by nine. We're going on the midnight riverboat cruise."

There was no way Austin was going on a river cruise. Being trapped at a floating New Year's party he couldn't leave was his idea of hell.

He returned to Harvey and continued with the eye pressure part of the exam, positioning Harvey's chin on the ledge of the tonometer.

"So, Doc, do you have plans for tonight?" Harvey asked.

Austin was tired of lying and no longer saw the point. "Not really," he said. "Probably just going to stay in."

"You and me both," Harvey said. "New Year's, Shnoo Year's. Right?" Harvey was more excited than Austin about discovering their common bond.

"Try to stay still," Austin said. "I'm measuring the pressure inside your eye." He hoped that the tonometer's probe approaching Harvey's eye would silence him, but no such luck.

"People pay through the nose to go to some shmancy party with bad food and loud music. Who needs that? We got a better plan, right, Doc?"

Austin was growing uncomfortable with the idea of being simpatico with Harvey. He was a nice enough man, but he was also a sixtysomething man, with a thick paunch, mismatched clothing and Coke-bottle glasses. Austin didn't believe in judging a book by its cover, but Harvey's personality was no great shakes either.

"I got myself a nice piece of sirloin from the butcher," Harvey informed Austin. "Not too fatty 'cause I gotta watch my cholesterol. But

I got some nonfat vanilla ice cream, which tastes just as good as the real stuff. Swear to God. Gonna make myself a root beer float, broil up that sirloin and watch a video on my thirty-two-inch flat-screen TV. There's not a party out there that can beat that. Am I right?"

Austin gazed at the downtown skyline as the riverboat drifted down the Detroit River. The party cruise wasn't as bad as he had anticipated. But he had anticipated it being pretty bad.

The faux Mississippi steamboat traveled back and forth along a two-mile stretch of the river, which seemed to Austin like the boating equivalent of paddling in place. The prime rib on the buffet was dry, but the lasagna was tasty. And the band was enthusiastic, though they sang with more volume than skill, straining to reach high notes and landing too often in the crevices between pitches.

Austin took a swig of his third Scotch and soda and looked down at his phone. Still hoping for a message from Naomi. But not expecting one. He could have been home contentedly watching episodes of *Lost* if Harvey hadn't shown up as the ghost of New Year's Future. Austin wished he could go back to pretending it wasn't New Year's. But it was. And he was alone. Alone with people. Which was somehow even worse. But he wasn't going to meet anyone new sitting in his living room. Though he wasn't entirely convinced he was going to meet anyone on the boat either.

Stu had failed to mention it was a swing dance party, and the people on board were pretty serious about their dancing. There were men in zoot suits and women in polka-dot dresses doing dips and flips. A guy in a white fedora did splits, and Austin's groin muscles hurt just watching. But it was hard not to, because the guy was dancing with a striking woman in a red dress with dark skin and long, darker, curly hair.

"You should ask her to dance," Stu said, noticing that Austin was gawking.

"Right," Austin said, looking away.

"Why not?" Stu said, tossing back a shot of Stoli.

"I can't swing dance," Austin said. "I can barely regular dance."

"That doesn't stop Stu," Steffi said, finishing her drink as well.

"And she still dances with me."

"She doesn't have a choice," Austin said.

"Who says?" Steffi said.

"Are you looking to find some other guy to dance with?" Stu asked her.

"Who knows?" she teased. "The night is young."

"See, Austin, this is why you don't want your wife dressing hot and sexy."

"You think this dress makes me look hot?" Steffi was wearing an iridescent purple dress with a plunging neckline. Stu touched her thigh with his index finger and made a sizzling sound. "I'm glad you like it," she said with a contented smile, "because this is the dress I bought in St. Barts."

Stu's mood shifted the moment she mentioned St. Barts. "Are you trying to make a point?" he asked.

"Just stating a fact," she said.

"I said you looked nice."

"And to look nice I need to buy nice things," she said. "Unless you want me walking around naked."

"That would be a whole lot cheaper," Stu responded. It was the first time Austin had witnessed them bickering in person, and it was a lot easier hearing about their spats via Stu's texts.

"You're disgusting," Steffi said, getting up from the table.

"Hey, it was your idea to walk around naked," Stu called out as she walked away.

"You should go after her," Austin said.

"Do you know how much that dress cost?" Stu asked. "Take a guess."

"A thousand dollars."

"Five thousand dollars," Stu said. "Who pays five thousand dollars for a dress? I could get a sixty-inch plasma TV for five thousand dollars."

"I thought you were in the middle of a gold rush."

"I am. I will be. Once the VC deal goes through, she can buy a ten-thousand-dollar dress."

"Are you worried it's not going to go through?"

"No, I'm not worried," Stu said. "But other people are worried about Google Maps, now that they added satellite view and street view."

"That seems like a good worry."

"Those are just pretty pictures. We're not living in the picture age. We're living in the information age. EZstreets is the only 3-D mapping service that includes fully integrated white-page listings for every residence and every commercial business."

"What's to stop Google from also adding that?"

"Let them. Because Yahoo and MSN will have to follow suit, and it takes too much time and money to build it from scratch in-house. One of them will buy us up in a flash. That's what the VC guys are counting on, which is why I've got this meeting on Wednesday. These money guys in Detroit are hungry for the next big thing. They're hungry to put this city back on the map and want to get in on the deal. Come with me to the meeting."

"What for?"

"I don't need you to build the Web site with me. I don't need you to give up years of your life. I just need you now while I'm in the home stretch."

"You don't need me."

"I'm a software guy. I go into these meetings, and I've got my

CFO and my VC people, and it becomes an alphabet soup. I need someone in the room I can trust. Take a year off and work with me. Take six months off."

"Stu, I can barely even get a day off. We're still short one partner."

"Listen to yourself. I'm begging you to let me hand you part of my company, and instead you're working your butt off for a guy who takes advantage of you. Where's your self-esteem? And where's your sense of adventure?"

Austin wondered if that was what Naomi would say if she were there. It would be so easy to take Stu up on his offer, but Austin instinctively distrusted anything that was too easy. He felt more comfortable going uphill than down. And that was a problem. It suddenly seemed like he was putting up unnecessary resistance to the natural path lying before him. He could feel a surge of momentum pushing him forward. Or was that just the rolling motion of the boat combined with the alcohol running through his bloodstream? He needed to figure out the answer. No, he needed a sign. He snuck a glance at his phone, willing a message from Naomi to appear.

"You keep looking at your phone," Stu said. "You got a booty call lined up tonight?"

"Right."

"Whatever happened with Naomi?" Stu asked.

"Nothing much," Austin said, acknowledging the unfortunate truth. "Why?" He tried to sound nonchalant. "Do you ever hear from her?"

"I haven't," Stu said, "but I bet Steffi has."

"You bet Steffi has done what?" Steffi asked on the defensive. She was back at the table, gripping a fresh drink.

"Have you talked to Naomi?" Stu asked her.

"I told you Naomi's in Spain," she said. "Do you ever listen to anything I say?"

"What's she doing in Spain?" Stu asked.

"She met a celebrity chef from Madrid. On the plane coming back from our wedding."

"From your wedding?" Austin asked.

"Can you believe it?" Steffi said.

"No," he replied. He absolutely couldn't believe it. He tried to calculate the odds, but his brain started to hurt from the effort.

"Are you going to dance with me, or do I have to find someone younger and cuter?" Steffi asked Stu.

"Only if Austin comes with us," Stu said, pulling Austin up from his chair. Steffi joined in, and though Austin protested, he found himself being dragged onto the dance floor, where he felt marooned among the dancing couples. He tried to return to the table, but he was like a pedestrian trying to cross an intersection against the light, as flashy dancers spun by him in every direction. Standing still was about all he could do to avoid becoming dance-floor roadkill.

The band was cranking out Barry Manilow's "Bandstand Boogie," and Austin swayed to the music, hoping he didn't look half as ridiculous as he felt, before deciding it didn't matter if he looked ridiculous, because he didn't know anyone there. He needed to meet people. He needed to make an effort to meet people. But for the moment, he just let his head bob from side to side as the lights blinked on and off, or maybe it was his eyes blinking, but in either case it resulted in a soothing, strobe-like effect.

Stu seemed to be coming toward him in slow motion, and with him was the dark-haired woman in the red dress. "Austin, this is Bianca. She's from Brazil." Stu had a Cheshire grin on his face. "Do I come through for you or what?"

"Happy New Year," Austin said to Bianca.

"Happy New Year," she replied, putting her hands on his shoulders as her hips continued moving to the beat. Austin put his hands on either side of her taut waist. He had an inappropriate memory of going horseback riding for the first time and of the excitement he felt touching the horse's flanks. He also remembered falling from the saddle and breaking his arm.

"So you're from Brazil?" Austin asked.

"No," Bianca said leading Austin in a small circle.

"No?"

"My family is from Brazil. I grew up in Kalamazoo."

"Did you dance a lot in Kalamazoo?"

"You're cute," she said, lifting one of Austin's arms and twirling herself underneath it. She was a swirl of hair and color. She was more than cute. She was beautiful, and she smelled of cinnamon. Yet Austin couldn't help thinking he would prefer to be dancing with Naomi.

Maybe Bianca sensed that, because when Stu and Steffi shimmied by, she smiled broadly at them. "Your friend is also cute," she said.

"He's married," Austin said.

"It's New Year's," Bianca replied. "Everyone's fair game on New Year's."

As if to prove her point, she grabbed Stu by his collar and planted a full-mouthed kiss on him. Austin thought Steffi would blow a gasket. But she was laughing. She pulled Stu off Bianca, spun him around and gave him more of the same, giving literal meaning to the term "sucking face" while running her lacquered fingernails down the back of his head. Stu responded by gripping Steffi's five-thousand-dollar-clad butt, and they started mashing on the dance floor as colored lights spun. Or the room spun. Or at least rocked gently to and fro.

Austin wobbled his way outside onto the deck. He leaned over the railing and watched the black waves lapping against the boat. There was something ominous about the dark water. But also peaceful. He liked the sound the water made as it sloshed against the hull. Was that the right word—"hull"? It seemed like an odd name for such a crucial part of a ship. He was on a ship. He was sailing into the new year. Sailing forward. But now the boat was turning again. He didn't want it to turn. He wanted the boat to keep going downriver to Lake Erie. Through the Erie Canal to Lake Ontario. Along the St. Lawrence River until they reached the Atlantic and then across the ocean to Spain.

He thought about what Bianca had said. "Everyone's fair game on New Year's." He had an impulse to do something stupid. He fumbled with his phone, hitting the wrong buttons several times before the right number appeared. He was going to regret doing this in the morning. But he would regret not doing it even more.

"Hi Naomi. It's Austin." He wasn't even sure what time it was in Spain. "I just wanted to wish you a happy New Year. And I wanted you to know that I'm thinking of you." He stopped himself before he said, "I'm always thinking of you."

CHAPTER THIRTEEN

Carlos was on top of her.

He said it was his favorite way to fall asleep. But he never asked Naomi if it was hers.

"You have such beautiful skin," he murmured.

He said it tenderly, but it irked her. What did it even mean? It wasn't like she was responsible for the quality of her skin. Sure, she used moisturizer and whatnot. But it was mostly a matter of genetics. And age. Of course, she was almost thirty-one, as her mother liked to remind her, and no longer quite the prize she would have been at, say, twenty-six. But he wasn't thirty-six. Or even forty-six. Sometimes she felt like he didn't love her so much as fetishize her.

And what about her? Did she fetishize him? Not for his age or his looks, though his grizzled chin and slate gray eyes could be darn near irresistible. No, the question was would she have been as attracted to him if he weren't a world-famous chef? Was she nothing but a slightly sophisticated star fucker? Not even all that sophisticated, given how quickly she had moved to Madrid. But wasn't it a good thing that she was seduced by his culinary skills, rather than his skills in the bedroom? Not that she was exactly complaining in that department. The sex wasn't revelatory (like his fried squid with black ink mousse), but he was pleasantly attentive, if a little more interested in the entrée than the appetizers.

Maybe she hadn't been immune to the perks of his professional success, but there was no shame in it. Everyone brings something to the table. And now, almost six months later, she had gotten rather used to her life of leisure. She enjoyed her daily walks along the Gran Vía or the Calle Mayor, stopping for a *Napolitana* pastry at La Mallorquina or a croquette at the Market of San Miguel. She enjoyed her afternoons at art museums, having the time to explore them slowly. She'd spent hours the previous day captivated by a black-and-white film at the Reina Sofía, and it was only a forty-second film. *Sortie d'Usine III* by Auguste Lumière. Her French was worse than her Spanish, but she had looked up the title when she got back to the apartment, and it translated as "Leaving the Factory III." Made in 1896, according to *Wikipedia* it was the first film ever made. Well, the third version of the first film.

And it was precisely what its name implied. A simple scene of workers leaving a factory. Mostly young women in wide-brimmed hats and floor-length skirts. Also young men. Some in dark three-piece suits and boaters. Naomi had flushed in her loose silk blouse as she imagined what it must have felt like to be wearing such garments in an un-air-conditioned factory on a summer day. The workers scattered in all directions. A woman gave a quick tug to her friend's skirt before they headed opposite ways. A dog cavorted with a man riding a bicycle. And just before the doors of the factory closed, a nervous man darted back inside, perhaps to retrieve a forgotten hat, though Naomi preferred to think it was a parcel for his paramour.

She watched the scene over and over. It all went by so quickly. And then it was over. Less than a minute in these people's lives. An unguarded moment. She wondered if the workers knew the moment was being captured on film. And even if they did, could they have possibly conceived of it lasting more than a century? Freeze-framing them in their flickering youth. It struck Naomi that everyone in the film must be dead, though some might have great-grandchildren or even great-great-great-great-grandchildren. Others might have perished young in one of numerous wars, or succumbed to heartbreak. Naomi yearned to know what they dreamed of doing. What were their ambitions? Did they succeed? She had this awful feeling that their lives were never as carefree as they seemed in those forty seconds. Why were they in such a hurry? Each time the film loop completed its cycle, she had an impulse to try to stop them. To warn them that this was all they had. In this moment, they would stay callow and luminous. Where were they going? And wasn't it about time she asked herself the same question?

Naomi hadn't worked in a kitchen since leaving Miami, unless she counted the effort she made in preparing confections for Carlos. Though she wouldn't accuse him of luring her to Madrid under false pretenses, the position in his restaurant never quite materialized. Her Spanish had improved, though it was still *malísimo*. She found if she smiled a lot, people tended to be patient with her. Or at least men did. It was one of the perks of being a young woman with attractive skin, even one who was almost thirty-one.

Her left arm was falling asleep. She gently rolled out from under Carlos. *"Cariño,"* he said softly. He called everyone darling. Even the busboys. She found it endearing. It just didn't have a lot to do with her. She glanced around the room. Nothing seemed to have much to do with her. The chrome and dark wood furniture. The aboriginal art. She had come with only her one suitcase. Though she had clothes in his closet and tampons in his bathroom, she wasn't sure she had a significant presence in Carlos's life. No, that wasn't quite accurate. There were numerous photos online that proved she had a major presence by his side at charity galas and restaurant openings. And, of course, in bed. No photographs of that. Well, none online. He draped his leg over her. She used to find it comforting. Now she felt imprisoned.

She often wondered what would have happened if she hadn't come to Madrid. If she had stayed in Miami. If Austin had showed up a week or even a day sooner, she very well might have. She had been confused by his mixed signals since Stu and Steffi's wedding. Of course he'd been ridiculously drunk that night, and she'd practically thrown herself at him.

She wished she knew what was going on in his mind. She suspected he had a girlfriend, and he was just too embarrassed to tell her. If she added up his hot-cold behavior, that was the simplest explanation. Steffi had thought he was single at the time of the wedding. But Steffi barely knew him. And Stu was completely unreliable about that kind of thing.

Which didn't explain why Austin had called her two weeks ago. And on *New Year's Eve*. Why would he do that if he was with someone else? And if he wasn't with someone else, why hadn't he once tried to talk to her about what he felt for her? Or if that was too much to ask of a guy, why hadn't he asked her out? Which seemed a reasonable question, as long as she disregarded the minor fact that she was living with another man on another continent.

But the bigger question was why was she in bed with her lover, thinking about another man? Carlos was passionate, creative, funny, kind, charming, generous and successful. It was like she had filled out a questionnaire in a women's magazine, and he had been manufactured according to her specifications. She lived in a multimillion-dollar Art Nouveau flat. Was lavished with expensive clothes and jewelry and was photographed at A-list events. Yet she was still unsatisfied. She was her mother's daughter.

She was also living in a fantasy. A beautiful fantasy, maybe from a Jacques Demy film. But in the real world, she didn't want to be someone's trophy wife. And Carlos wasn't the marrying kind. So trophy mistress was as good as it was going to get. He hadn't been encouraging her career, which was a subtle way of saying he didn't think she was good enough.

But none of that really mattered, because the crazy, stupid truth was she hadn't been able to stop thinking about Austin since she'd received his latest voice mail. Actually, since Miami. Oh, who was she kidding? Since their night in Crystal Cove. And her mother's rules be damned, it was time he knew.

"Cariño," Carlos called out to Naomi, "someone is at the door."

He had heard the doorbell as well as she had, but there was an assumption that she was both part-time lover and part-time housekeeper. Though that was unfair, because they actually had a full-time housekeeper. Naomi was just in an unsettled mood. She was feeling guilty. As if she had cheated on Carlos. And she supposed, in a way, she had. What had Jimmy Carter said about lusting in his head? Or was it his heart?

The doorbell rang again. *"Cariño,"* Carlos drawled from his office, which was closer to the front door than the bedroom, where Naomi was pacing back and forth. She had decided to call Austin the moment she had gotten up, but it was too early in the States. And it was too early in Madrid for visitors. Who could possibly be coming by before ten? And why wasn't Carlos concerned that the concierge hadn't buzzed them?

Naomi was out of sorts as she clomped to the door, so it was hard to say if she was more or less irritated when she saw it was her mother standing in the vestibule.

"Happy birthday!" Lila Bloom trumpeted.

"It's not my birthday," Naomi said to her unexpected guest. Though nothing her mother did was ever truly unexpected.

"I'm one week early," Lila said, kissing her. "So sue me." Naomi hated celebrating her birthday early, and if she remembered correctly, she'd gotten the trait from her mother.

"*¡Sorpresa!*" Carlos said, coming up behind her. Naomi hated surprises. Something Carlos didn't know. But her mother certainly did.

Lila breezed into the apartment, her lithe body within pounds of her daughter's despite the twenty-two-year age difference. Her mother stood a tad taller, which was due to either an actual difference in height (as Naomi had claimed since puberty) or better posture (her mother's verdict). They also wore their hair in the same side-swept, shoulder-length style, but that was where the similarities ended. Lila was immaculately put together, with nails and lipstick in a nearly identical shade of coral and an ivory wool suit that looked like she had never sat down in it, despite the fact that she had just gotten off a plane. Naomi's nail polish was chipped and her lips were chapped. She was wearing one of Carlos's old sweatshirts and little else.

"I was in New York, visiting Noah, and Carlos thought it would make a wonderful surprise to pop across the pond."

She hated that her mother was the kind of person to say "pop across the pond."

"I thought you were maybe a little homesick," Carlos said to Naomi, rubbing her back.

Guilt. Guilt.

"She should be," her mother added. "She hasn't visited in a year."

And more guilt.

"How's Noah?" Naomi asked. She hadn't spoken to her brother in more than a month. He had said she was living like a modern-day courtesan, which she didn't like. What she particularly didn't like was that she agreed.

"He's dating a nice African man."

"'African American' is the preferred term," Naomi corrected her.

"I know what to call an African American," Lila huffed. "But he's dating an African. A Nigerian. Skin as dark as tar. But very buff. That's the word people are using now, right? Buff?"

"I wouldn't know," Carlos said with a wink, while making her a mimosa.

"So you liked him?" Naomi asked.

"I didn't say I liked him. I said he was a nice man. I didn't understand a lot of what he said. He speaks with a British accent."

"Ah," Carlos sighed, as he handed her a drink. "That could be very difficult," he said, rolling his "r." Naomi had to stop herself from laughing.

"Carlos, I understand everything you say," Lila assured him. "I have a Mexican gardener, and I talk to him every day without any problem whatsoever. It's the British accent that throws me."

Naomi was beginning to wonder how long her birthday gift was staying.

"Carlos, this mimosa is the most fabulous mimosa I've ever had in my life. Naomi, you're a lucky woman."

"She knows," Carlos said as he handed Naomi a mimosa.

She did know. That was the problem.

"Naomi, don't tell your father about the African. He's going to shit bricks. He already thinks that Noah is dating men just to spite him."

"What if they get serious?" Naomi asked. "Are you just going to keep it from him?"

"Of course not," Lila said. "I'm going to tell him when I get back. I just want to be there to enjoy his reaction."

Naomi didn't know what to say. Carlos did: "I must go to the restaurant."

"Don't leave me alone with her," Naomi wanted to scream out.

"For dinner," he said, "I think tapas on Cava Baja, *¿sí?*"

Naomi had doubts she would survive until dinner, but she nodded. Within minutes Carlos was out of the apartment, and she thought she detected him moving faster than usual.

It was only after he was gone that the full magnitude of the inconvenience of her mother's visit hit Naomi. There was no way she was going to be able to call Austin. Her mother didn't understand the meaning of "privacy" or "personal space."

However, Naomi knew it couldn't have been easy for her mother to have schlepped to Madrid, especially given how little she liked flying, which was something she and Carlos had previously bonded over. Naomi also knew her mother loved her, and deep down her mother meant well. The problem was her mother wasn't all that deep.

"So has there been any talk about a ring?" Lila asked.

"That's not on my agenda," Naomi said.

"Well, it should be, because men don't move unless there's a fire in the belfry." Her mother had this habit of saying things that sounded like common knowledge but were in fact nonsensical statements she made up on the spur of the moment.

"Carlos isn't really looking to get married," Naomi said.

"Neither was your father. It's amazing what a pregnancy can do." Her mother had always been regrettably straightforward about the order of events surrounding Naomi's birth.

"You want me to get pregnant to get Carlos to marry me?"

"No, I want you to get pregnant so I can have grandchildren. I'm just pointing out that sometimes people need a little extra motivation."

"Maybe I'm the one who needs extra motivation. Maybe I'm not convinced that Carlos is the right man for me."

Lila took Naomi's hand in hers. "Can I give you some advice?"

"No."

"Don't be a dope." This was advice? "There isn't much I can give you in this world, but by the grace of God you have my looks. You have your father's eyesight and stubbornness. But you have my looks. And you can do so much more with them than I did."

"They're not some kind of currency," Naomi said with distaste.

"Oh, honey, that's exactly what they are. I know it's not politically correct to say so. But it's true. A pretty girl gets things that other people don't. So get yourself those things while you can. Because it doesn't last long."

This was why Naomi lived an ocean away from her mother. "Have you ever considered that everything you think about the world is wrong?"

"Every day."

"I'm serious."

"Yesterday I had dinner with an African man who *shtups* my son," Lila said, her voice getting brittle. "Everything I think about the world is upside-down. But what am I going to do? Give up? Cry? I'm a fighter. Like my mother was. And like I taught you to be."

"Not everything has to be a fight," Naomi said.

"If your grandmother thought like that, she'd have ended up in a German oven, and then you wouldn't have anything to worry about."

Naomi felt a familiar surge of guilt and rage. "Why do you say things like that?"

"Because it's the truth. And I always tell my children the truth."

"Well, stop!" Naomi protested, and Lila did in fact stop. Naomi put her hand to her head, wondering if she'd also inherited her mother's migraines. "You can't barge into my life and presume to know 'the truth' about my relationship."

"I didn't barge in," Lila sniffed. "I was invited."

"You can't possibly know if Carlos and I belong together. I don't even know. And I'm the one who lives with him." Naomi realized she was sounding shrill, which was not the way to get through to her mother. "What I do know is that fighting isn't the only way to prove your strength. In fact, sometimes the strongest thing you can do is to walk away."

"You walk away from *everything*!" Lila threw her hands in the air as if her emotions were too big to be contained inside her body. "You were going to be a lawyer. You were going to be a psychologist. You were even going to be a ballet dancer at one point. And now what do you do? You bake cookies."

"I'm a pastry chef!"

"Where? Where are you a chef?"

This is what her mother did. She knew exactly where Naomi's weak spots were—because she was the one who helped create them—and she'd stick her lance in as deep as she could where it would do the most damage.

"I'm not marrying Carlos!" Naomi brayed, feeling like she was sixteen years old again and battling with her mother over a prom dress.

"Well, I tried my best," Lila said. "I knew this was a losing battle from day one."

"What's that supposed to mean?" Her mother was baiting her, but she wasn't going to let her get the last word.

"You were never going to be able to hold on to a man like Carlos."

Now Lila was trying reverse psychology on Naomi. But it wasn't going to work. "I don't want to 'hold on' to Carlos. I want to move on. I'm the one thinking about leaving him. Not vice versa. He's still here."

"Is he here? I don't see him."

"He's at work!"

"Everything's a choice."

Naomi groaned. Sometimes she wanted to strangle her mother. "Carlos is very happy with me," she said. But was he? The truth was there had been a slight detachment recently. A carelessness in his caress. An occasionally distracted look in his eyes. His lovemaking had become a little less vigorous. A little less frequent. She had written it off as his age, but was it really his waning interest? And was that the real reason Naomi had been thinking about Austin?

"Naomi, I'm not trying to hurt you. Anything that hurts you hurts me. I just don't know how to help you." There were tears in Lila's eyes, and she was not the crying type. "How many times are you going to do the same thing? How many men are you going to run away from?"

Naomi hadn't looked at it as running away. She was looking at it as running toward something. She was just a little vague about precisely what. No, that wasn't true. She was running toward Austin. Austin Gittleman. Someone she had dreamed about since she was eight years old. Someone destiny had brought back into her life. And someone who hadn't once expressed any deep feelings for her or in any way suggested anything more than a passing attraction. Oh God, her mother was right. And she hated when her mother was right.

"Don't run away, Naomi," her mother said. "Fight."

Naomi thought of the young women in the Lumière film, running off the screen to unknown futures. In a hurry to get someplace else. Heedless to the laws of nature and collagen. Approaching thirty-one, could Naomi really afford to do the same? As soon as she had the thought, she silently chastised herself. It was ridiculous to be thinking of herself as old when she was still young. She knew better. She didn't know why she did this to herself.

"Fight for Carlos," her mother was saying. "If you don't fight, you're going to lose him, because he's a successful man with options. And you're a woman over thirty."

That was why! *She* was why.

Naomi wasn't going to fight. But she also wasn't going to run away. She was going to "hold on" to this moment in her life, and she was going to hold on to Carlos. Because he was good to her. Because he was good *for* her. And because there was no way she was going to give her mother the pleasure of being proven right.

"I don't know why things are so difficult for my children," Lila said, forgetting herself and sitting down in a way that was doomed to put deep creases in her slacks. "Maybe it's all my fault."

"You think?" Naomi gibed. Sometimes she wondered if she could have had a worse possible role model.

"Maybe it's because of the names I gave you and your brother."

"What are you talking about?" It was typical for her mother to go off on some crazy-ass tangent. And Naomi was out of patience. She was out of energy.

"They say that in the Bible Noah gets *shtupped* by his son," Lila said, seeming much older and wearier than when she arrived. "And Naomi is a bitter woman without a husband or children."

CHAPTER FOURTEEN

"I'm getting divorced," Stu said over the phone.

"You're not getting divorced," Austin replied, holding his BlackBerry to his ear while searching for his room key. He had the paper key sleeve with the name of the Chicago Millennium Park Hotel imprinted on it. But no key.

"How do you know I'm not getting divorced?"

"Because you've been saying it since your honeymoon."

Austin looked behind the bureau to see if it had fallen. Nothing. He had entered the chic wheat-and-basil-colored room only an hour ago. So the key had to be there. Somewhere.

"Some honeymoon," Stu harrumphed as Austin emptied his suitcase onto the bed.

Austin had become accustomed to the roller-coaster ride of Stu and Steffi's relationship. Their routine was several weeks of nuptial bliss, followed by a knock-down, drag-out fight, usually ending with Steffi crying and Stu storming out, which was when he would call and say he was getting divorced. This was quickly followed by apologies and shockingly good make-up sex, to hear Stu tell it. They were not a positive advertisement for marriage.

But marriage wasn't Stu's primary problem. His IPO had been canceled and investors were heading for the exits. It turned out Google was going in direct competition with them. And Yahoo was laying off employees, not investing in new products. But Stu wasn't giving up hope. He kept saying that 2008 was going to be a great year for IPOs, but, for the moment, the money train had stopped rolling.

"I can't even afford to divorce her," Stu said. "Isn't that pathetic? Of course, she can't afford to divorce me either. She messed up. If she had divorced me a month ago, she could have bought herself a Sub-Zero freezer full of Manolo Blahniks." Stu laughed, either picturing a freezer full of shoes or taking glee in Steffi's loss.

Usually, Austin let Stu vent. It seemed to help him, and Austin didn't really mind listening. Frequently he was tempted to remind Stu that the qualities in Steffi he found so objectionable, her bursts of emotion and extravagance, were precisely the qualities that had drawn him to her. Less frequently, Austin was tempted to ask about Naomi.

She had never responded to his New Year's call, which had been two months ago. For the first few weeks he had remained optimistic, but she was probably living with the guy in Madrid Steffi had mentioned. Austin could have asked Steffi for more details, but he didn't want to know. He desperately wanted to know. He didn't want to know.

"Here's the thing," Stu said. "I'm not sure the problem is Stuffi. I think it might be me. I think I might not be cut out for marriage."

This was new. "What are you talking about?" Austin asked, throwing his clothing back into his suitcase, still keyless.

"I'm not one of these people who dreamed of having a life partner. My idea of a fun night isn't cuddling up with someone and watching *Project Runway*. I'd prefer to be sitting in my boxers watching *Family Guy*. I sometimes really resent having to accommodate this other person. She says I forget about her. And the truth is I do. There are sometimes hours that go by or even a whole day when I forget I'm married. Just entirely forget. Like it never happened."

Austin didn't understand how that was possible. He wished he could forget about Naomi. He wished he could figure out precisely what it was about her that stuck in his mind. Was it her spontaneity? On one hand, he thought she was flaky, but on the other, he wished that he were more like her. If he could just identify and analyze the parts of her that had burrowed so deeply into his brain, they would have less power over him. And *then* he could forget about her.

But even being in Chicago was partly because of her. He was at an ophthalmology conference. Or late for an ophthalmology conference. It was precisely the kind of medical ghetto that he usually avoided, but after the Florida fiasco, it occurred to him that instead of lying about attending conferences, he could actually start going. It would be a way to meet people. And potentially a way to find a new partner for his practice. Which was critical. Len hadn't been exaggerating about there being a dearth of interested applicants. The Inteflex office hadn't even bothered calling Austin back. Which was not a good sign.

It seemed that no one wanted to move to Michigan. And the people who were already in Michigan, oddly enough didn't want to be in private practice. When Austin was in school, seventy percent of the graduating class went into private practice, and most of the rest went into academia or research. HMOs were the enemy back then. Nobody wanted to be an "employee," working for a "corporation," where profits took priority over patients.

But now he was being told the statistics had completely flipped; seventy percent of the medical school graduates *wanted* to work for a corporation. They didn't want the call schedule, the malpractice liability, the insurance paperwork or any of the other responsibilities that came with a private practice. They wanted to put in their hours and go home. At first, Austin had thought it was an anomaly, but after ten months of searching for partner candidates, it was no anomaly.

"Well, if worse comes to worst, we can be roommates again," Stu said.

"Huh?" Austin was on his hands and knees, searching for the key under the bed.

"Unless you already have a roommate," Stu said. "Have you been holding out on me? Have you got something regular going on?"

"No, nothing regular," Austin said. Nothing irregular either. Every time he was on a date with someone, he found himself comparing the woman to Naomi. Which was foolish, since she was probably living with some Spanish dude. New Year's had come and gone. Three hundred and twenty-five days until the next one. The situation was ridiculous. He was ridiculous. And Stu was ridiculous. "Stu, you're spending too much time thinking about what's wrong with your life rather than what's right about it. Get Steffi a box of Godiva and go home."

"Have you not been listening to anything I just told you?"

"Just do it."

Austin checked his pockets for what he thought was the umpteenth time, but there it was, a slip of shiny plastic caught inside his wallet. He'd had the key all along.

"Cataract Surgery and the Compromised Cornea" sounded vaguely titillating to Austin—he thought it would make a good title for a book of ophthalmologic erotica, if such a thing existed. But the seminar was actually rather dry, which he found amusing given that dryness was a major cause of a "compromised cornea." Mandy accused him of having ophthalmologist humor. She didn't mean it as a compliment. The moderator promised she'd be broaching controversial topics, and then went on to talk about ecstasia, which despite the promise of its name, refers to a bulging of the cornea and not any other anatomical parts.

Austin ducked out early and wandered into the conference reception area, where there were a large number of people sampling bland appetizers under poor lighting. Not the ideal atmosphere for finding a business partner. Or a date. The men at the conference outnumbered the women by a three-to-one ratio since there were so many more male ophthalmologists than female. And the number of single attendees was infinitesimally small, but Austin entered with a hopeful attitude. And it seemed to be rewarded.

"Austin Gittleman?" a woman called out. She was petite, with a birdlike face. She looked familiar, and he realized they had gone through Inteflex together. Her name was Eleanor, but he couldn't remember her last name. What he did remember about her was that she had been a total gunner in school. The type who did nothing but study every night and every weekend and then complained about how unprepared she was before acing every exam.

But he had to admit she was much more attractive than she had been in med school. Her brown hair was pulled back less severely from her face, and she was wearing a dress, which he couldn't recall her doing in the past. He also noticed there wasn't a ring on her left hand.

"Eleanor!" he exclaimed.

"I saw your name on the registration list," she said. She seemed to sound happy about it.

"What are the odds?" he said.

"It depends whether you're doing a one-way ANOVA analysis or a chi-square," she said, as if she had said something incredibly amusing. Austin had a new understanding of what Mandy meant by ophthalmologist humor.

"Don't forget to factor in the unlikely qualitative variable of us both being single."

"Why are you assuming I'm single?" she asked, sounding displeased.

"I noticed you weren't wearing a ring," he said, backpedaling.

"Because I'm not someone's property," she snapped.

Austin tried another approach at civil intercourse. "You might be amused to know, I recently called the Inteflex office."

"For nostalgia's sake?"

"No, to see if they could help with a job search."

"Well, you need a lot of help if you're calling Inteflex." He chose to believe she was making another poor attempt at humor.

"Not sure why you would say that," he said with his most ingratiating smile.

"Because there is no Inteflex."

Not the response he was expecting. "What do you mean there is no Inteflex?"

"Gone. Finito. It's been over a year now."

Austin couldn't comprehend what Eleanor was talking about. "How could it be gone?"

"Very easily. They stopped funding it. All that pie-in-the-sky seventies idealism met up with twenty-first-century realpolitik, and the realpolitik won. Let's face it, people aren't really screaming for healthcare reform these days. That kind of ended with the dead-on-arrival Clinton health plan. Don't you read your alumni newsletters?"

"Not often, I guess," he said, still reeling from the news.

She looked at him with disdain. "Well, if I was trying to find a job I would try to stay more up-to-date."

She strode away before he could inform her he was the one hiring (or ask if she knew anyone looking). He had rarely repelled someone so completely, and he couldn't wrap his head around what she'd said about Inteflex. It was like saying the English Department was gone. Or the entire university was gone. It didn't seem possible that an institution could vanish. He had graduated only eight years earlier. It was like his diploma was written in disappearing ink. Although, the medical school was still there. Or he hoped it was.

Lost in his thoughts, Austin didn't realize how long he had been staring at a woman standing beside the punch bowl. She was in her mid-thirties, with long scarlet bangs, and she was picking up finger sandwiches one after the other, eating the inside and putting the bread back on the table wrapped in a napkin. "I haven't eaten carbs in three years," she said when she noticed Austin looking at her. "I'm Dallas." She wiped a hand on her slacks and extended it toward him. "But I'm not from Texas."

Austin was thrown by the coincidence. "Neither am I," he said, feeling a little tongue-tied as he briefly clasped her surprisingly warm hand.

"Is your name also Dallas?"

"Austin," he replied. "But I also never lived in Texas. I was conceived there. My parents went to grad school at University of Texas."

"My mom just liked the sound of Dallas. It was between that and Sassafras. My mother thinks she's a poet. But really she's just fond of tea." She smiled. He couldn't tell if she was pleased to be enlightening him or proud of her cleverness. Most likely, a little of both.

Or maybe she was flirting.

"You're the third Austin I've ever met," she said, "but the first one with dentures."

So much for the flirting. "I don't have dentures," he assured her.

"Are they dental implants?" she asked.

"They're my real teeth."

"But they're so perfectly symmetrical. Like a movie star. You have Brendan Fraser's teeth. You must have heard that before." Austin shook his head, befuddled. "Well, I don't understand why. Unless it's because you're not as tall as Brendan Fraser. And your nose is a little less proportional. However, the resemblance between your teeth is remarkable."

She was nearly Austin's height, with narrow shoulders curving slightly inward in a vaguely defensive posture. Her hands meandered through the air as she spoke, and her flyaway red hair seemed eager to head off in multiple directions. But her gaze was locked in place on him. Or his teeth. "Do you always . . ." He searched for the right words.

"What?" she asked, jumping in before he could complete his thought.

"Say everything you're thinking?"

"Always. That way I don't have to remember anything."

"You don't want to remember what you're thinking?"

"The opposite," she declared, her eyes widening. "I want to remember everything, but I have a terrible memory."

There was something endearing about her unmitigated candor. She reminded him of a child running barefoot through the rain, and he had the urge to run after her with a pair of yellow rubber boots.

"Are you a doctor?" she asked. "Of course you're a doctor. I'm not. I'm a conference crasher. I live about ten blocks away. No, I was invited. I do live ten blocks away, but I was definitely invited. Really. I'm speaking on a panel about practice management. I have a name tag in here somewhere." She started searching in her oversized leather purse. "Well, you'll have to trust me on it. But never trust anyone wearing orange."

"You're not wearing orange."

"Exactly." She smiled again. It was a warm and enthusiastic smile. But also short-lived, like the sun poking out from behind thick clouds, unsure about the effort required to burn through. "I never wear orange. I wrote all about it in my book."

"You wrote a book." Austin was impressed. He had written one paper for a medical journal, and he had found it one of the hardest things he'd ever done in his life.

"It's on my name tag. I really should find my name tag. I'm supposed to be networking. Are you networking?"

"I'm networking with you."

"How do you know I'm worth networking with?" she asked slyly.

"You wrote a book," he responded, straight-faced.

She laughed, but only momentarily. "I did," she said. "It's called *Managing Your Minutes: How to Get the Most Out of Your Cell Phone and Everything Else in Your Life*. It's self-help. But not touchy-feely. Because self-help can be very touchy-feely. Which is not to say the book doesn't have an existential aspect to it. But it's mostly about taking control of your life. Making emotional decisions like they're business decisions. So that you're being more 'joyficient.' That's a term in the book for getting the maximum joy and efficiency out of everything you do. And I can't believe I'm going into my whole shtick. Though you have no way of knowing if I'm just making all this up. Are you a gullible person? I have no name tag. I could have come in off the street."

"You could be a conference crasher," Austin said.

"Do you want to get a drink?" she abruptly asked him.

"You're standing next to the punch bowl."

"A real drink," she said.

"With an umbrella in it?" he asked, though he had no idea why.

"Exactly," she said, smiling broadly.

Austin was glad he had sprung for the room with the king-sized bed. Even with the extra space, they had almost rolled off a couple of times already.

Dallas treated the bed like a playground, and he was the jungle gym. She was different than he had expected. For starters, she barely talked, which was a surprise given the fact that she barely stopped talking until they took their clothes off. And she was calmer, slower. All the bravado fell away as she lay there beneath him, smiling and laughing.

"What are you doing?" she asked.

"Nothing," he said.

"It doesn't feel like nothing." She laughed again. It was a rich, joyous laugh, like it came from the deepest part of her.

"What does it feel like now?" he asked as he lifted her leg over his shoulder and leaned down to kiss her mouth, her neck, her breast.

"It feels good," she said.

And then they both stopped talking.

It was almost an hour later when she got up to go. He held on to her wrist.

"Do you want me to stay?" she asked.

He did.

She sat down again with her back to him, shoulders bent forward, her scapulas pressing up against her skin like small wings. "I have a kid," she said.

"Do you need to get home?"

She shook her head. "He's with his dad tonight," she said, picking at a fingernail. "I just think it's good to express these things early."

He looked at her sitting there. The tumble of wayward hair. The delicate arc of her freckled back. "I like kids," he said.

She turned around. Her eyes seemed to scan his face, searching for something or a lack of something. Then she lay down and rested her head against his chest.

"I'm glad," she whispered.

CHAPTER FIFTEEN

No one told Mandy the weekend was going to be a multigenerational event.

Well, it was Mother's Day, so two generations were implicit. But three were not. Austin had invited his girlfriend, Dallas, who came in from Chicago with her four-year-old son, Coal.

Mandy didn't know what kind of woman wanted her son's name to remind people of environmental degradation. Would you name a kid "Diesel" or "Methane"? Actually, Diesel sounded like a pretty cool name.

"Be nice to her," her mother said, handing Mandy a freshly washed bath towel.

"I'm always nice," Mandy said, tossing the towel onto her bed.

"You're always passive-aggressive. It's not the same thing."

In thirty years, the only time her mother seemed to put her master of psychology degree to any use was when she was analyzing her children. Penelope Gittleman was a puzzle to her daughter. But one that Mandy had stopped trying to piece together many years back. Mandy felt the pieces had been jumbled and some were missing. Well, one crucial piece was missing.

Her mother never dated anyone after she was widowed. Or not anyone that Mandy knew of. Mandy had often thought of asking why, but she always chickened out, not really wanting to know. She imagined her mother was lonely. But Mandy was learning that living with someone could also be lonely. So maybe her mother was on to something.

"Did Austin tell you about Dallas's book?" Penelope asked.

He had sent Mandy a signed copy. "I think he mentioned something."

"It's interesting," Penelope said.

Her mother described things as "interesting" only when she was being diplomatic, so Mandy wasn't the only one put off by Dallas. "What didn't you like?"

"I didn't say I didn't like it," Penelope said. "Don't tell your brother that I said I didn't like it."

"You didn't," Mandy said with a mischievous smile. She was glad they were on the same side. She had forgotten how much she enjoyed the feeling.

"I thought the book was clever," Penelope said. "I just prefer someone be trained in psychology if they're going to give out psychological advice. But I'm biased. And some of the worst advice I ever received was from people with years of training. So maybe it's better to have people like Dallas on TV giving out their five cents' worth of guidance."

"Twenty-four ninety-five in hardcover," Mandy said.

"I'm sure it's cheaper online," Penelope said with a chuckle.

She seemed more relaxed as of late. More subdued. Maybe she had adjusted her meds. Whatever she was doing, it seemed to be working, though she still occasionally cried in her sleep. Something Mandy had discovered on her last visit. But it was more like gentle weeping. Not the kind of crying jags Mandy had heard when she was a child. Mandy remembered Austin tiptoeing into her bedroom late at night and turning on her radio to try to muffle the sound.

Coming home brought up so many complicated feelings for Mandy. She wished Tad had accompanied her as he had promised he would before their most recent breakup. She had stopped keeping count. Or even keeping score. Which is why she didn't hesitate to call him after her mother left the room.

"Hey," he said, "aren't we on a break?"

"Was that my decision or yours?" she asked, truly vague about the details of their last conversation.

"I think it was mutual."

"We can't have mutual decisions if we're not living in the same state."

"We're living in the same apartment."

"No, I'm living in it, and you send rent checks once a month."

"My orchestra tour is what's paying the rent."

They had been through this a hundred times. If that was possible. It was like putting two and two together over and over and hoping that it will eventually add up to more than four. He had taken the touring gig so they could stay together. But they were never together. He was out of town most of the time. And she got lonely. And she got texts from Hal.

"How's the dissertation going?" he asked.

It had been nine months since she had proposed a new thesis about the sexual coercion of female chimpanzees in estrus, which happened to be the subject of Dr. Peña-Punjabi's research. Unsurprisingly, she approved.

The only problem was that Mandy had little interest in writing two hundred pages on a topic that had been done to death and to which she had nothing to add. In nine months she had written less than nine pages. Sometimes after hours of staring at her blank screen, Mandy would type line after line of platitudes: "Sexual coercion is bad. Sexual coercion is an act of aggression." And if she did it long enough, questions would start to percolate in the back of her mind.

How do male chimps learn to be coercive? Is it passed down from father to son or is it something in their genes? And if adaptive evolutionary principals apply, why don't females adapt to protect themselves? Or was it their adapted behavior that had resulted in the male coercion? But whenever Mandy raised these questions with Dr. Peña-Punjabi, her faculty adviser would suggest Mandy focus her attention on better-documented areas, and by that, Dr. Peña-Punjabi meant areas documented by her. It wasn't that she was an egomaniac; she just played one in the lab.

"What if I got a job?" Mandy asked Tad.

"You have a job."

"I mean a real job."

"It wouldn't change anything."

"Meaning you like living in second-rate motels?"

"Meaning I think we made a mutual decision to take a break."

If Mandy couldn't even remember the conversation, it hardly seemed likely that something sacrosanct had been decided.

"I really need you here this weekend," Mandy said, hating pressuring him as much as she hated admitting how dependent she had become on him. But what she hated even more was feeling like a fifth wheel in her own home, the spinster sister on her way to turning into her mother, who at least got a man to marry her before losing him.

There was silence on the other end of the line. She could hear Tad's breathing, so she knew he hadn't hung up on her. Not that hanging up was his style. No, he would usually say something like "I'm hanging up now" before cutting himself off from the tentacles of her insecurities.

"Mandy," he said, "even if I thought it was a good idea to ignore everything we had agreed on—"

"We don't agree on anything," she interrupted.

"That's pretty much what we agreed on," he said. "But putting that aside. If I was to rent a car and drive straight there from Minneapolis, I wouldn't get there until tomorrow morning, and then I'd pretty much have to turn around and come back. It doesn't make any sense."

"What if you took a plane?"

"A last-minute flight would cost a fortune."

"I'll pay for it. I don't care." Given the balance in her bank account, she knew that she should care. But this wasn't about being practical. This was about wanting him there and wanting to make things right between them.

"I care," he said. "I care about wasting money and time to do something stupid."

She gasped. "So making me happy is stupid?"

"That's not what I meant."

"You promised you would come!"

"I shouldn't have said that."

No, he shouldn't have, and now the floodgates were opened. "You promised I could trust you. You promised I wouldn't regret it. But I do. I regret moving in with you. I regret ever meeting you." None of it was true, and what she really regretted was saying any of it.

Again, there was silence.

"I'm hanging up now," Tad said.

She shouldn't have called him. She had made everything worse. Much worse. She thought she could trust herself, but she lacked the required discipline. It was like buying a carton of ice cream on a Saturday night and pretending there would be any left on Sunday morning. Thinking about ice cream made her hungry. She slumped into the kitchen and stood in front of the Frigidaire with the doors open, seeking clarity in its frosty embrace and craving a pint of Häagen-Dazs rum raisin, but she knew the closest she was going to come in her mother's home was some sugar-free, fat-free, taste-free soy dessert.

"You're destroying the ozone," her mother said, padding in behind her.

Mandy stopped for a moment to figure out if that was even true, and she concluded that it was but only in the most tangential of ways, before grabbing a bowl of grapes and closing the doors.

"Is your friend going to be joining us?" Penelope asked.

Mandy's shoulders tensed. She wished she hadn't mentioned Tad to her mother. And she never would have done so if he hadn't said he was going to come with her. *Never again.*

"No," Mandy said. "No friend coming."

"I thought you said you were bringing a friend."

Mandy kept her eyes focused on the grapes. "You must have misunderstood." She heard the edge in her voice and the soft sigh that escaped her mother's lips. Mandy felt both angry and guilty, but the guilt won out. "Have you decided where you'd like to go tomorrow for brunch?"

"I was thinking I could cook something here."

"You're not cooking on Mother's Day."

"I like to cook."

"Since when?" Mandy wanted to ask, but she held her tongue. Her mother probably wanted to make a good impression on Dallas and Coal.

"We could take you to one of your favorite places," Mandy suggested, "like the Original Pancake House."

"That was always your favorite place, not mine," her mother said, smoothing a strand of Mandy's hair.

Mandy remembered that as a kid she could never decide what she most wanted to order, so Austin would offer to share with her, and they'd get both the skillet-sized baked apple pancake and even bigger Dutch pancake. "I bet Coal would like it," she said.

"He's a sweet kid," Penelope said, gazing out the kitchen window.

The backyards in Southfield seemed to have shrunk since Mandy was young. Yet the trees were larger. She didn't remember any trees taller than the houses when she was growing up. But now there were two in her mother's backyard and several more in the neighbor's. Oaks and pines. Mandy remembered loving the weeping willow trees at her elementary school. She felt comforted by the idea of a tree that cried.

Austin was chasing Coal around one of the oak trees. When Austin caught Coal, he lifted him over his head, then let go for a split second, pretending to drop him, before swooping him back up skyward. Coal laughed uproariously, screaming out, "Again! Again!"

Mandy watched her mother watching. She saw the tear form in the corner of her eye. Mandy knew her mother was thinking about her father. Mandy somehow always knew when her mother was thinking about her father. She felt a stone pit in her stomach. Every time she took a breath it nestled deeper into her flesh.

Dallas was also outside with Austin and Coal, her copper red hair blowing in the light wind. Mandy only dreamed of having bangs that shiny and straight. Dallas was snapping pictures with her phone while holding an umbrella over her head with her other hand, despite the cloudless, sunny day.

"What's with the umbrella?" Mandy asked.

"She has very sensitive skin," Penelope said. "She's half-Armenian." As if that explained it.

"And half-vampire?" Mandy asked. She heard her mother sigh again before leaving the room. Mandy knew she should have kept that thought to herself. Better yet, she shouldn't have had it in the first place. She was still tense from the call with Tad. She needed some time to herself to unscramble her emotions. But that wasn't going to happen, because the brood was heading indoors. As she heard the door to the garage open, she thought of making a run for it. But there was nowhere to go. Her mother had gone upstairs. Austin, Dallas and Coal were now downstairs. And Mandy was trapped.

"Okay, Monkey," Dallas said as they entered the kitchen, "time for your nap."

"Monkeys don't take naps!" Coal responded.

Mandy considered offering data to contradict that hypothesis but restrained herself. She kind of liked his spunk, even if his facts were a little wobbly.

"No nap, no ice cream," Dallas said. At the words "ice cream" Mandy perked up a bit. Maybe they had brought contraband with them.

"Can we go swimming in the lake after?" Coal asked.

"We're not in Chicago," Dallas said as she unzipped his navy fleece jacket, leaving him to squirm the rest of his way out of it. "No lakes here."

Actually, they were surrounded by lakes, but Mandy had to admit that none were as close by as in Chicago.

"But we can go to a pool," Austin offered. "How about that?"

"Is it a big pool?" Coal asked, seeming unconvinced a pool compared favorably with a lake.

"A very big pool," Austin said.

"Will you come swimming with us?" Coal asked, turning to Mandy. She didn't know if she was more taken aback by Coal's interest in her joining them or the notion of her going swimming.

"Mandy doesn't swim," Austin said, covering for her.

Coal nodded in a sympathetic way. "You can borrow my floaties," he said.

Mandy had never fallen for a boy so quickly. She wondered if he would consider dating her in twenty years.

"That's very nice of you," she said, "but I'm allergic." That's what her mother had written for years on her phys ed notes, and it still worked.

"I'm allergic to peanuts," Coal volunteered.

"That sucks," Mandy said.

"Mandy!" Austin said as Dallas glared.

"I mean, that means no sucking on any peanut butter Popsicles for you," Mandy said, thinking fast but not quite fast enough to make much sense.

Coal looked at her skeptically. "Yuck! There's no such thing as peanut butter Popsicles."

"Is Mandy being silly?" Dallas asked Coal in a singsong voice, shepherding him away from Mandy before she could do more damage. "Coal is proud of his peanut allergy. Aren't you?" Dallas said, and Coal nodded. "Because it makes him special."

Mandy was glad there were no peanut butter Popsicles around, because she was afraid of what she might be tempted to do with one.

Dallas and Coal headed upstairs, with Coal negotiating the required length of his nap. Mandy noticed that Dallas didn't retrieve his navy fleece from the kitchen floor where he had discarded it.

Once they were out of earshot, Austin sat down across from Mandy and asked "So?" Like Mandy was supposed to be able to read everyone's mind in this family. They were too interdependent. Their roots were too entwined. It inhibited photosynthesis.

"So what?" she responded, feigning obliviousness.

"What do you think of Dallas?" he asked in a low voice, picking up Coal's diminutive jacket and folding it over the top of a chair.

"The question's what do *you* think of Dallas?"

"I asked first," he said, smiling.

"I hear she's half-Armenian."

"She is," he said, scrunching his brow as if trying to see where Mandy was going with that. "She's also half-Jewish."

"I think it's a little weird that you're dating someone with the same color hair as me."

"I wouldn't really call it the same color," Austin said, using his cautious, don't-disturb-the-sleeping-lion voice.

"Do you mean she has vibrant-colored hair and I have mousy-colored hair?"

"No—"

"Because we both have red hair, don't we?"

"So now I can't date a redhead or I'm secretly wanting to have sex with you?"

"Ew," Mandy said, recoiling. "Don't be gross."

"You're the one who brought it up—"

"I said it was weird. I didn't say it was sexual." Mandy shuddered. "I think she has a nice kid."

"She does," he said. "And?"

"And what, Austin?" Why was he pushing her? She wasn't in the mood to be pushed. "I barely know her. And what I do know about her, frankly, is a little odd. I mean, she named her son 'Coal.' Was 'Nuclear Waste' too many letters for the birth certificate?"

Now she was just being ornery. She needed to get away from her family. She needed to get out of this house. She needed ice cream. Surprisingly, Austin smiled. "It just so happens, I asked her about the name. And she chose it because coal is a source of power. Both positive and negative. It's a name with responsibility. It's also a pretty common name when it's spelled 'C-O-L-E,' which has exactly the same meaning, and Dallas is big on transparency."

Transparency? Really? Then she should have named her kid Saran Wrap. Mandy wanted to be supportive. She truly did. But Austin was pissing her off with the infatuated way he was talking about Dallas. What irked her was that not long ago it was Naomi he'd been talking about. And talking about. He had carried on nonstop about Naomi for more than eight months, and then simply switched horses. Was it really that easy for guys?

"I'm thinking of proposing," he said.

For the second time in an hour Mandy found herself gasping. "You've only known each other a few months."

"We're not going to get married right away, but going back and forth to Chicago is exhausting. I'd like her to move here, and with Coal involved, I feel like I need to make a commitment."

"You feel or she feels?"

"Same thing," he said, looking down at the floor.

"It's not the same thing at all." This woman seemed to have her brother twisted around her finger, and what Mandy wanted to know was how she'd done it. "Proposing is a big deal, Austin."

"She doesn't want to uproot her life and her kid's life unless the plan is to get married. And I don't blame her."

"Do you love her?"

He rummaged through some utility bills lying on the table. "You're better at discussing that kind of thing than I am."

Were all men clueless when it came to expressing their feelings? "What about Naomi?" she asked.

"Naomi's not an option."

"Do you still have feelings for her?"

"It doesn't matter."

"That's not an answer."

"For God's sake, Mandy!" Austin bolted up from the chair. "I'm talking about Dallas, not Naomi."

"No, you're not talking about her at all. You're asking me to talk about her. Am I supposed to tell you what you feel about her?"

"Do you mind?" He gave her the same sheepish grin she remembered from childhood, and he was once again the geeky boy who was embarrassed to buy his own hair gel. "I like being with her," he said. "I like the way her mind works. I like not always understanding how her mind works."

Was that enough? And if it was, why wasn't it for Tad? Why wasn't she enough for Tad? She started to tear up.

"What did I say?" Austin asked, seeming both baffled and guilt ridden. He looked at her like she had lost her mind. And maybe she had. "We don't have to talk about Dallas. Okay? We can talk about your new boyfriend. When do I get to pass judgment on him?"

"I don't have a boyfriend," Mandy mumbled.

"Mom said you were seeing someone."

Everything was too intertwined. Everything was everyone's business. They weren't a family. They were a group therapy session. "I made him up."

"She said he was coming for the holiday."

"He's my imaginary boyfriend, so he's here standing next to me."

"Mandy—"

"No, actually, he isn't here. Because even my imaginary boyfriends abandon me. Because that's what men do. They leave."

The moment she said it she knew she shouldn't have. Not because she didn't believe it. It was the one thing she fervently believed. In fact, it was the cornerstone of everything she believed. But she made a point of never saying it out loud. And if there was one person she shouldn't have ever said it to, it was Austin. He stood there, looking sad.

"You can't go through life thinking like that, Mandy." Now he was going to comfort her. She felt like she was seven years old again. And the worst part was she felt like crying on his shoulder, exactly the way she did back then. "It's not true," he said, "and it's not good for you."

She wiped her nose with the back of her hand. "I know," she said. It was just sometimes hard for her to remember.

CHAPTER SIXTEEN

Everything took so much effort.

Carlos could see how hard Naomi was working on her *feuilletée*. Or *hojaldre* as his mother used to call puff pastry. He would have offered to help Naomi, but it would just have upset her. He would have offered to have someone do it for her at the restaurant, but that would have upset her even more. She had already spent days making gazpacho, *tortilla española*, *croquetas*, *almendrados*, and flan. She wanted to impress her friend from America. But it was more than that. It was what she did. She worked hard at cooking. She worked hard at their relationship. She worked hard at everything. So much effort. So American.

It wasn't that Carlos didn't work. But work was fun for him. Work was passion and fire. Smoke and sweat and magic and tantrums. But it wasn't hard. It had never been hard for him. Maybe when he first started out. But by twenty-five, he had his own restaurant. He worked eighteen-hour days, six days a week to make it happen. It was exhausting. But it wasn't hard. Life should not be so hard.

He watched her fold the butter into the dough on his grandmother's pastry board, the way her small but strong hands pressed into the dough.

The way her pink fingernails skimmed its surface as she sprinkled more flour. She pushed a strand of her shiny hair behind her ear. And the motion was perfect. He could spend hours watching the light play on her hair. He still wanted her. Although the sex had never been all that great. She was a little too inhibited. That was not an American thing. That was her. But Carlos had found in his life, the better the sex, the less interested he was in having a relationship. Something about completely letting loose and devouring a woman in bed made him uncomfortable around her out of bed. It would be easy to analyze some Catholic guilt thing in there. But he didn't really go for all that.

Naomi was rolling the dough with his great-grandmother's wooden pin. He wanted to tell her she was rolling too much. Too much rolling and the butter would leak. But she knew that, as she undoubtedly would tell him if he interfered. So instead he watched as her entire body moved back and forth. Her slender shoulders. Her delicate breasts. He watched the way she clenched her jaw, the way she often did when she was concentrating on something. He studied the tight, unblemished skin along the edge of her jaw. Yes, he wanted her. She made him feel young. She made him remember what it was like when his stomach did not hang over his waist. And his shoulders did not curve forward. Lying with her in bed, he dreamed a young man's dreams. And then he woke up in an older man's body.

Ah, there was the rub. She also made him feel old. The velvet texture of her skin made his feel parched. When he looked in the mirror his hair looked grayer. His face hung lower. He saw how people looked at him when he was standing next to her. First there was envy. And then there was pity. Because no matter how tightly he held her to him, he could not reverse the years. They were not equals. He could never again have what she had.

"Are you going to get dressed?" she asked, her face glistening from her efforts. A smidge of flour on the bloom of her cheek.

"I am dressed," he said.

She looked at him with disapproval while continuing to roll the dough. He noticed butter leaking out as he headed to the bedroom to change.

No, he would never again have what she had. But she would *never* have what he had.

He picked a linen shirt and a pair of jeans before washing up. He hoped Naomi wouldn't be annoyed if he wore jeans. But why shouldn't he be comfortable in his own home? He would put on loafers rather than sandals. That should make her happy.

He was not looking forward to the evening. The friend visiting from America sounded like a bit of a twit. But that was unfair. He only heard one side of the conversation when Naomi spoke with her on the phone. And Naomi said the same thing over and over: she told her friend to remember that she loved her husband. If she had to be reminded so many times, it was more likely that she didn't, Carlos thought. But it was none of his business. He would be a pleasant host for his bourgeois American guest, and he would act as if it was his greatest privilege. He was good at that. It came with running a restaurant—and with being Spanish.

What he wasn't good at was spending hours listening to two girls talking about relationships, especially since he was a participant in one of those relationships. They would be speaking English all night, *por supuesto*. It took so much effort to follow along. He had lived in America for more than a year, and he was proud of his English. But it was hard to think and talk in English while following two other people talking. He wasn't used to it anymore. He spoke English now only with Naomi, and when he thought about it, he realized they didn't really talk so much. They didn't need to. He had hoped she would have learned more Spanish. It was almost two years. But to talk to her in Spanish was more effort than talking in English.

The phone rang. It was probably the concierge announcing their guest, so Carlos let Naomi pick it up while he went into the kitchen and opened a bottle of Rioja Reserva he had brought back from the restaurant. Good enough for an American he had never heard of before. In two years, he didn't remember Naomi mentioning her name, which didn't suggest they were very close friends. He could smell the *palmeras* baking in the oven. He wanted to add a pinch of cinnamon, but he resisted the temptation. He took a quick peek. They looked good. Maybe the leaked butter wouldn't make a difference.

Naomi entered the kitchen. She was wearing a loose-fitting Adolfo Domínguez maxi-dress he had bought her. The light material floated from her body, making her look like Venus stepping out of a cloud. She looked bewitching in the dress, and he couldn't wait to take it off.

"What are you doing?" she said. "Steffi's on her way up."

"If we turn off the light," he said, "she won't know we are here." He wanted to taste the pinkness of her, the wetness of her, the tautness of her breasts and the give of her thighs. She let him fondle her, but when he went to kiss her she turned her head away.

"I just put on fresh lipstick," she said.

For a moment, she sounded exactly like her mother.

Steffi was not what Carlos expected. She strutted in wearing Manolo Blahniks from the new summer collection and a sleeveless dress that hugged her impressively full and firm breasts. She bubbled over with energy like a boiling pot of pasta on high heat. But her eyes were laser focused. This was no social visit. There was no talk about her husband, whom she may or may not have remembered when she held Carlos tight to her chest while greeting him.

She had a business proposition for Naomi. *Por supuesto*, of course, she was American. Everything is about work. Even when on vacation. He wondered if Naomi knew that was part of the reason for the visit. Was it why she had been so nervous? He had thought it was something else.

Maybe it was just his ego, but he thought it was about a man. He had a feeling, a fear, there was someone connected with Steffi. Someone Naomi was thinking about. Someone younger, no doubt. Carlos had taken Viagra every night for the last week. He had even tongued her butthole. An acquired taste. But he wanted to make her happy. He wanted to satisfy her. He wanted to prove he was not getting bored of her. He was getting old for such games.

Steffi had some kind of European import-export idea that she talked about incessantly as they ate. "Why should people have to come all the way to Europe when FedEx delivers everywhere?" she asked. Carlos guessed the question was rhetorical.

"What people need are middlemen," Steffi said. "Or middle-women. And that's where you come in. I want you to be my partner."

"In what?" Naomi asked.

"In the Web site I want to launch. It's called Steffi's Stuff." Carlos noted the company name didn't sound like a partnership. "And it would be stuff from everywhere. Stuff that people can't get easily. Or stuff that only a few people know how to get. And we curate that stuff. We pick and choose and put it all together in one place. Basically, we get paid to go shopping, and what could be more fun than that?"

The words poured out of her at a rapid pace, and Carlos was confused by a good many of them. He sipped his Rioja, letting the spicy wood and cherry notes swirl around his mouth. He noticed Steffi wasn't drinking any of hers. But Naomi had already filled her water glass several times. Americans could be so puritanical.

"For example, there's marzipan here people would kill for back home. And the chocolate. Oh my God, the chocolate."

"It sounds like Spanish Stuff, not Steffi Stuff," Carlos quipped. Naomi glared at him.

"We would start with Spain," Steffi said, "because you're here. But then we could expand." Naomi nodded encouragingly.

Carlos realized she was considering doing this thing. This tacky American thing. But why? The sum total of Steffi's business experience seemed to be a penchant for shopping. And he couldn't see Naomi getting creative satisfaction from packing up boxes of chocolate and marzipan. What would motivate her to even consider such a time-consuming and unworthy project?

And that was when he realized just how hard she was working at pretending to be happy with her life. She wasn't with him because of love. Or lust. Or even idolatry. Which he could live with. She was with him because of entropy. The work required to stay was less than the work required to leave. And the reason he understood this so clearly was because he felt the same.

He didn't want drama. He didn't want tears. He didn't want to sleep in separate rooms while she looked for another place to live. He didn't want to have to find someone new, and he didn't want to worry if they would be as forgiving about his back hair and his acid reflux. He didn't want any of it. But he also didn't want this. He didn't want to claim to love someone when in truth he was hurting her. And he was hurting her more than he liked to admit. He was hindering her ambitions. He was siphoning her youth. Every day they remained together left her with one day less vitality, and in time she would blame him for it, if she didn't already.

Steffi and Naomi were talking with increased animation. Naomi was taking notes. They discussed numbers and dollars and clicks and eyeballs. There were apps and aggregators and search engines and site optimization. There were unfamiliar words and words that came in unexpected combinations. They kept coming faster and faster. And it wasn't just the words; it was the world that was moving faster. Carlos felt less and less motivated to try to keep up.

It just took too much effort.

CHAPTER SEVENTEEN

"I know this isn't going to be easy for you."

"Jesus, Len," Austin said.

"But I don't see any other option."

"Jesus, Len," Austin repeated.

"The world is changing, and we have to change with it."

"You're not changing," Austin objected. "You're leaving."

"That's not fair," Len said. "The deal from square one was that I was going to retire by the time I was sixty. I'm almost sixty-two, and there's no end in sight. No new partner. No one to buy me out. This practice was supposed to be my retirement egg."

Austin looked in his hands at the literature Len had given him. Optimum Health Inc. There were glossy pictures of smiling patients and empathetic doctors. There were graphs of the "vast network" of devoted medical professionals. It was bullshit. This was a corporation. Plain and simple. Len was talking about selling their practice to a corporation and leaving Austin to be a drone working for faceless bureaucrats who could second-guess his medical decisions and fire him anytime they wanted. This was the antithesis of everything Austin planned for his life.

"Cindy's going to take me for everything she can," Len said. As if that made the situation better. "But it's worth it. Life is worth it. Being happy is worth it."

"I'm not happy, Len."

"You should be. You have a nice home. A nice girlfriend. And the practice isn't going anywhere. It's actually going to be a lot easier for you. Less overhead. Less responsibility."

"What if I took out a second mortgage on my house?" Austin said. "I could give you more money up front."

"I said you had a nice house. I didn't say it was worth anything. The housing market is shit in Michigan. The only good part for me is Florida is just as bad. Joanne and I have found a nice place only a few miles from the Bolletierri Tennis Academy."

"How long has this been going on with you and Joanne?" Austin asked. But what he really wanted to know was had they been having sex in the office.

"She's everything Cindy isn't."

"Meaning she's younger."

"Hey, she's not twenty-five." No, Joanne Friedman was a forty-something childless divorcée who was their vivacious, gourmet-cooking office manager. Austin wasn't only losing a partner and a practice. He was also losing a great coq au vin.

"Just meet with these people," Len said. "There's a woman, Hope Cassidy. She's a doctor. I think you'll like her."

"And if I don't like her?"

"Austin, I'm doing you a favor. Sure, if I wasn't cash starved at the moment, we could hold out for a few more years. But the writing is on the wall."

Austin wasn't sure about the writing on the wall, but the clock on the wall said he was already twenty minutes behind schedule, and he had a full docket of patients. If any of them were under sixty-five and on private insurance, he might even make some money for the day's labor. Maybe Len was right. Maybe it was better to just take his paycheck and let someone else worry if the numbers added up. He stuck the brochure in the pocket of his white coat. But he couldn't stop thinking it represented an evil empire and the end of medicine as a noble and humanitarian profession.

"You can't get hung up on doing things the old way," Len said. "Take it from someone who's been around a little longer than you. The past is always changing."

"Don't you mean the future?"

"Yeah, that too."

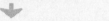

Naomi was reading an old copy of *People* when Austin came out. She had just picked it up to occupy her mind and to keep her hands from shaking.

It was stupid for her to be sitting there in his waiting room. Crazy-stupid. She didn't know what she was thinking. Other than she wasn't thinking. No, that wasn't true; all she was doing was thinking. She had spent the last four months thinking so much her brain hurt.

When Carlos broke up with her, she had at first been devastated. It was everything her mother had predicted. But worse. Instead of investing six months of her life, she had invested two years. And instead of walking away with her head held high, she had been kicked to the curb. No, not kicked. He was quite the gentleman about it, offering to sleep in the guest bedroom until she figured out what she was doing. He didn't even give her a reason. She said horrible things to him. Things she never thought would come out of her mouth. Things about his European snobbishness. Things about his performance in bed. And she had no idea why. Other than wanting to get a reaction out of him. Wanting some kind of emotional response to show that he cared about her. But he took it all with a sad expression and never fought back. As if she wasn't even worth the effort.

She had no friends in Madrid. No real friends that weren't also Carlos's friends. They mostly dropped her as quickly as he did, with even less graciousness. She was supposed to be scouting merchandise for Steffi, but she couldn't bear to stay any longer at Carlos's place and couldn't afford to get a place of her own.

She packed up her belongings, deliberating if she should keep the designer clothing and jewelry Carlos had bought her before deciding she had earned them. In the oldest way possible. She even let Carlos buy her one last gift: a Balenciaga suitcase to help get her stuff to New York, where she temporarily moved in with her brother. Actually, her brother and his fiancé, Godwin. Noah joked he had finally found God. The joke got old fast, as far as Naomi was concerned, but Godwin seemed to find it amusing.

It was Godwin who asked Naomi, on her third week in the Chelsea one-bedroom apartment, what her plans were. It had become a little too obvious that she didn't have any. Godwin had asked in a pleasant way. There was something about his very white teeth and British accent that made everything sound pleasant. But Naomi knew a clock was ticking. And not just on her days of free rent. As much as she hated acting like her mother, she caught herself lifting the skin around her cheekbones when she looked in the mirror. She kept reminding herself that thirty-three was young. But there were shadows under her eyes that didn't seem to go away. And a night in heels was followed by a morning with sore feet.

She had no idea where she was going or how she was going to get there. And then it occurred to her that she kind of liked that. For two years she had stayed in one place and had a steady routine, and what did it get her? A nice piece of luggage and an active Facebook account. For two years she knew every morning she'd have breakfast with

Carlos and a late dinner with him after he left the restaurant. She knew they would spend Christmas with his brother in Málaga. And she knew in August they would visit his sister in Barcelona. But she preferred not knowing. That was when she was at her best. It made her more spontaneous. And it made her brave. Brave enough to now be sitting in a suburban waiting room in Farmington Hills, Michigan. Brave enough to look up when Austin entered the room. And brave enough to ignore her beating heart and smile as if there wasn't a more natural place in the world for her to be. She wondered if she would have to tell him why she was there or if he would implicitly know.

And she wondered if he would kiss her again.

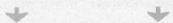

At first Austin thought he was seeing things. It had been a stressful day, so it was not ridiculous for him to think his mind was playing tricks.

But he blinked a couple of times, and she was still there. Naomi was sitting in his waiting room under the *Eyes Wide Shut* poster. And smiling as if she had been there all along and he just hadn't noticed her.

He escorted her along the grayish hallway, wishing they had repainted as Len had talked about doing for the last two years, and he followed immediately after her into his office with the old-fashioned eye chart on the wall, closing the door behind them. He didn't know where to let his gaze rest first as he watched her place her black shoulder bag beside her chair and cross her legs, one knee-high black boot over the other below her long gray wool skirt. He sat at his desk, wondering if he should wheel up next to her. But having the desk between them offered him some protection. Like a wooden moat to give him space and time to figure out what he felt about her being there. Shocked. Delighted. Confused. And so many more feelings he couldn't even put labels on.

"I happened to be in the neighborhood," she said with a small laugh. Her smile still swept all the way up to her eyes, but there were now a few tiny crinkles around them. "I don't know if Stu told you, but I've been working with Steffi."

Stu barely spoke about Steffi anymore. The divorce had just about destroyed him emotionally—and financially.

"We set up a store on eBay, and I'm scouting a vendor nearby," she said. "The Franklin Cider Mill. Do you know it?"

"I've gone there since I was a kid," Austin said. He almost said that he also took his kid there, but he stopped himself. For numerous reasons, not the least of which was that Coal technically wasn't his kid. Not even his step-kid, since there had yet to be a wedding, but there was a picture of him on Austin's desk. "They have great caramel apples."

"We want to get them to join us," she said. "We're creating this online international bazaar. The idea is to get specialty products only sold in one place, and make them available everywhere."

"Doesn't that go against your conviction about the importance of traveling?" Austin asked. He had meant it as a lighthearted question, but Naomi's smile disappeared. He had done it again. Put his foot in his mouth less than two minutes into their conversation.

"I never thought of it that way," Naomi said, her mood dimming. But then Austin noticed with relief that her face brightened. "I think it actually encourages people to travel and see these places in person," she said. "And it keeps the places in business, so that when people travel they won't find only Walmart and H&M."

There it was again. Her passion. Her optimism. He had looked into so many eyes, and no others had the incandescent brightness that hers possessed. And few could claim the color of a sunlit sea beckoning those in need of a warm embrace. "Are you still cooking?" he asked.

"No," she said, a little wistfully. "Not much. My ambition outpaced my ability."

"I don't know about that," Austin said. "I can still taste the chocolate soufflé from Stu and Steffi's wedding."

"That came out pretty good," Naomi admitted, seeming to relish the memory. "Maybe I'll make it for you again sometime in the future."

Was she just saying that or did she mean it? Did she plan to see him in the future? Was she flirting? He desperately wanted to believe she was flirting. But it seemed so unlikely. Then again, her being there in his office was equally unlikely.

"I'm really glad you came by," he said. Was that really the best he could come up with? He wanted to smack himself. And then he thought of Dallas and wanted to punch himself. Dallas deserved better than him making futile efforts at flirting with a past love. Then it hit him that he had never referred to Naomi in that way. His "love." He had been in love with her. He had avoided using that word. But there it was. Len was right. The past changes.

"Well, I couldn't come to Michigan without looking you up," she said. She was just passing through. That's all it was. Like a brief summer squall that comes and goes with little damage, freshening the soil. "No, that's not true," she said.

"What?" What wasn't true?

"I didn't just look you up." She wasn't looking at him anymore. She was looking out the window. He wished there was a better view than the generic parking lot. The pine trees were pretty, if plain. The sky was clouding up. There was a storm coming. Seemed to be the day for them.

"I came to Michigan to see you," she said. Austin wasn't sure he was hearing right. "I came because I never told you how I felt about you. And that was really stupid." She was tearing up. He handed her a box of Kleenex. "Thank you."

"You're welcome," Austin said, unsure what else to say.

"I think I was in love with you," she said. Austin was having difficulty breathing. "No, I know I was in love with you. I *am* in love with you. And I know it doesn't make a lot of sense for me to say. And it's not particularly fair of me to throw this at you. I don't know what I want you to say. No, that's not true either. I know what I want. But I have no idea what your feelings are or what's going on in your life."

"I'm engaged," Austin said. There were so many things he had waited so long to say, and that wasn't one of them.

"Oh," she said.

She seemed so sad. So disappointed. How could he let her feel that way when all he wanted was to take her in his arms and tell her how much he cared about her. How much he wanted her. How much he always had wanted her. And he might have. If he hadn't spied Coal's face looking up at him from a silver frame with a big, goofy, gap-toothed smile.

"She has a child," he said. "*We* have a child."

Naomi was standing up. She was leaving. "I'm so sorry," she said. She lifted her bag, inadvertently tipping it over and spilling lip gloss and credit cards onto the floor. A tin of mints broke open. Austin rushed to help her pick up the pieces.

"I had no right to come here and say stupid things," she said. "I can't imagine what you think of me. Actually, I can. You probably think I'm ridiculous. And rude. And a little emotionally unhinged."

"I don't think any of those things," he said, kneeling beside her.

He desperately wanted to kiss her. He knew it was wrong. But he couldn't help himself. He wanted to kiss her. He wanted to hold her. He wanted to take her back to his home and have one entire evening with her. Dallas had taken Coal to Chicago to see his dad. She would never know. Would it be such a terrible thing? To feel Naomi once more in his arms. They had been cheated of a lifetime together. What would be so wrong with taking just one night? As a keepsake. To have when he was older. To know that there was one night when he loved Naomi Bloom with all his heart and that she loved him back with all of hers.

But he couldn't do that to Dallas. Naomi was already on her feet and reaching for the door handle.

"I love you," he said, still on his knees. He was crying as he took hold of her other hand, and he saw she was also crying. "I love you so much."

She nodded, and then she fled.

CHAPTER EIGHTEEN

The leather swing was new. Hal held it steady as Mandy lay back into its hammock-like embrace and wondered if anyone had ever considered using one of these for a gynecological exam.

She was enjoying the relaxing sensation of being suspended in the air. Given her current emotional state, it seemed particularly appropriate to feel untethered from the earth. In fact, the more she thought about it, the more she came to believe she had responded to Hal's latest text specifically to untether herself.

As Hal adjusted the stirrups around her ankles, she felt like she was floating beyond the mundane reality of her life. Beyond laundry and Spin class and spell-checks and footnotes. This was the ultimate in postmodern, poststructuralist theory. She was the text. Her body was the text. And her body was far more physically comfortable at that moment than she had expected. Until he got on top of her.

No more floating. It was more a feeling of being squeezed like a half-empty tube of toothpaste. A rush of air was expelled from her compressed lungs as her pinched bladder groaned and the flotsam flowing through her lower intestine pleaded for release.

Hal was kissing her insistently. But his breath smelled of garlic.

And maybe oregano. She was guessing he'd eaten Italian food for dinner. It occurred to her that it wouldn't have killed him to treat her to a meal. Just because they were having kinky sex didn't mean he couldn't be a gentleman. At the very least he could have brushed his teeth. She was tempted to tell him so, but it would definitely be a mood killer. What kind of person didn't use a mint before kissing someone? Mandy had been carrying Tic Tacs in her purse at all times since she was sixteen, just in case.

She tried to turn her head to the side, but he was intent on open mouth-to-mouth action. She tried not to inhale, but that just made her feel like she was suffocating. They were rocking back and forth with his arms tightly wrapped around her. Or rather around the swing. She could feel the seams of the crisscrossed leather straps digging into her back.

She grabbed hold of Hal's shoulders and tried to readjust her position, but he lifted himself off of her, removing her hands and buckling them into restraints dangling above her head. His skin was oily. She didn't remember that. And he was flabbier than she recalled. He was standing between her legs, his soft flesh hanging from his broad torso with an endomorphic looseness. She missed the leanness of Tad. The compactness of his frame and the way his skin gripped his tendons. There was a utilitarian aspect to his physical being, as if he didn't take up any more space than absolutely necessary.

Thinking about Tad was a mistake. She imagined him seeing her, in this place with this man. She could picture the wounded expression on his face. No, worse, disappointed, and then relieved because she wasn't his problem anymore. She flushed with shame, which Hal took as excitement. He grabbed hold of either side of her waist and pumped her back and forth like she was a martini shaker in the hands of an overzealous bartender. She considered telling him to stop, but it didn't seem polite.

On her way home along the icy sidewalks, Mandy had a decision to make. And it wasn't whether she'd be seeing Hal again. There was no question about that ever happening. No, she had to come to terms with something more fundamental. She pulled her parka tighter around her to suppress the early-morning chill as she wrestled with the implications of her recent behavior. The way she looked at it, there were two options: either she was a damaged and depraved person— or she was merely human. Maybe it was self-preservation kicking in, but she chose to believe the latter. She was a member of a mammalian animal species that makes flawed choices. And she had been making some terribly flawed choices. But what would be cathartic for her, and what she believed would be cathartic for many people, was to find evidence that this trait was not limited to only one species.

And that was why on Monday morning, she was knocking on the door of Dr. Peña-Punjabi's office. Mandy had come to sweet-talk her. Literally. She had brought chocolate truffles.

"What is that?" Dr. Peña-Punjabi said when Mandy handed her the peace offering.

"Chocolate," Mandy said, stifling her urge to add "Something we earthlings enjoy."

"Thank you," Dr. Peña-Punjabi said stiffly while adjusting a strand of her glossy jet-black hair, "but I don't eat sugar."

Mandy chose to regard this as a sign of diabetes rather than anal-retentive behavior. Though either way, Dr. Peña-Punjabi could have just accepted the gift and given it to someone else. Mandy realized that was their problem in a nutshell. Dr. Peña-Punjabi was very linear in her thinking, while Mandy was more lateral in her approach.

"I've been reviewing my notes on observed incidents of sexual coercion," Mandy said, "and I'm still wondering if there's room for some element of confused or contradictory behavior."

"Amanda, we have already discussed this at some length," Dr. Peña-Punjabi said, removing her gunmetal eyeglasses.

"I know, but I'd like to discuss it more, because here's the thing: there's no question about sexual aggression in chimps, and you've done a fantastic job over the years of documenting that. But sometimes, and certainly not all of the time, the female chimps act in ways that seem self-destructive or at least not in their best self-interest. And sometimes the male chimps seem to act out of provocation and frustration as much as aggression."

"Amanda, I think I have made it clear that I find this line of reasoning to be muddled."

"I don't think it's muddled," Mandy said, holding her ground.

"I have no desire to continue this discussion."

"But I have a desire to continue it," Mandy said, attempting to match her adviser's formal tone. "It's years of *my* life we're talking about."

"We have also discussed that, and if this is not work you want to do, then you should consider going elsewhere."

"I want to do the work," Mandy said, emphatically. "But you're not letting me do the work I want to do."

"What you want to do is not objective scientific research. It is based on conjecture and emotion."

"That's not true!" Mandy said, getting emotional. "Look!" She retrieved a thick stack of freshly printed notes from her backpack and placed it on Dr. Peña-Punjabi's desk. "Pages and pages of scientific observation of chimpanzee interactions."

"You cannot assume chimpanzees have emotions." Now Dr. Peña-Punjabi was also getting riled.

"But you're assuming they don't."

"Because there is no way of knowing what is going on inside a chimpanzee's head."

"That's exactly my point! And that's what I keep telling you I want to write about!" Mandy slammed her hand down on Dr. Peña-Punjabi's desk, which was probably a mistake.

"Please leave my office," her adviser said.

"I'm sorry for banging your desk, but I'm not leaving until—"

"Please leave now, or I will have to call Security."

"You're going to call Security on me?"

"Please leave."

"You're going to call Security because I touched your desk. Give me a fucking break!" That was her second mistake. Dr. Peña-Punjabi picked up the phone. And Mandy figured she was entitled to a third strike.

"You aren't interested in what's going on in primate heads, because you don't have a clue what goes on in human heads. And you don't want to think about primates having feelings, because that would put them higher up the evolutionary ladder than you!" Mandy took her stack of notes and tossed them in the air so that they scattered across the office as a security guard appeared in the doorway. "Now tell me that primates always operate in their own self-interest!"

CHAPTER NINETEEN

It was the seventeenth time Coal played the same *SpongeBob* scene that put Dallas over the top, and, yes, she was counting. She turned off the DVD and took the remote away from him. That was the wrong choice.

"WHAT ARE YOU DOING?" he howled.

"Coal, I asked you to lower the volume."

"I did."

"No, you raised the volume."

"Because I can't hear. Because you're talking too loud."

"I'm talking to your father on the phone."

"I want to talk to him."

"Not until I'm finished."

"I WANT TO TALK TO HIM NOW!"

Dallas didn't understand those mothers who think the sun rises and sets on their children. Sure, there were days she was convinced Coal was the cutest, kindest, wisest soul on the planet, but there were other days she thought she had given birth to a demon child.

"I want SpongeBob!"

"No more videos, Coal. We're going to go see Penelope."

"I want SpongeBob!"

"You like playing with Penelope."

"I WANT SPONGEBOB!"

"Just let him watch the video," Jarrod grumbled over the phone.

"The problem is he knows that's what you would do," Dallas said to her ex, "and that's why he's throwing a tantrum."

"He's throwing a tantrum because you're taking something away from him," Jarrod said. "I know the feeling."

Instead of one child, she was stuck dealing with two. "I'm not taking anything from you," Dallas said. "I'm just asking you to switch one weekend in May."

"I look forward to my weekends with Coal. And I already bought tickets to a Junie B. Jones musical that Saturday."

"I'll reimburse you for the tickets."

"That's not the point."

"I WANT TO WATCH SPONGEBOB!" Coal wailed. Infuriated that he was being ignored, he jumped up and down, stomping his feet and clenching his fists as he puckered his lips into an angry fish face. Dallas was torn between wanting to laugh and wanting to smack him. Neither was an option.

"Coal, you're six years old now, and big six-year-old boys don't scream when they don't get their way."

"What about thirty-six-year-old women?" Jarrod asked.

"I'm not screaming, Jarrod. I'm politely asking."

"Okay, I will give up my legal right to see my son on my assigned weekend, *if* you let him spend the summer with me in Chicago."

"That's not going to happen."

"Then you've got a problem."

"WHO LIVES IN A PINEAPPLE UNDER THE SEA?"

blasted from the TV as Coal commandeered the remote Dallas had foolishly put down on the oak sideboard.

"No!" Dallas said, swiping the remote back from him.

"YOU'RE THE MEANEST MOMMY IN THE WORLD!" he screamed.

"Coal—"

"YOU'RE MEANER THAN GRANDMA!"

That was hitting below the belt. She was beginning to hate teacher in-service days.

"Coal," she said, summoning her best-modulated parental voice, which even she had to admit sounded more hostile than dispassionate. "You are going to stop screaming. You are going to put on your coat, and we are going to Penelope's."

"YOU NEVER LET ME DO ANYTHING I WANT TO DO!" Coal ran out of the room and up the hardwood stairs.

She had spent the entire day doing *everything* he wanted. First they went for a pancake breakfast at the Original Pancake House, which thanks to Mandy was now the only place he would eat pancakes. Then they went to the planetarium, which was followed by his favorite Coney Island hot dog for lunch and a visit to Paradise Park with two rides around the Kiddie Go-Kart track. And what was so unfair was that this squabble was likely the only part of the day he was going to remember.

"This is all your fault," Dallas said to Jarrod.

"How is it my fault?" he asked.

Dallas didn't know how it was his fault, but so many things were. "You're making everything difficult."

"Well, you know how I like making you squirm."

She wasn't sure if he was being typically immature or inappropriately sexual. Or both. "Jarrod, I'm asking for a small favor. I'm trying to get married, for God's sake. Can you cut me some slack?"

"Not my job anymore. You're confusing me with your fiancé."

"I'm confusing you with a human."

"You've been playing the wedding card for almost a year. If you put it off this many times, you can put it off another week."

It hadn't been a year, but it was getting awfully close. The original plan had been to get married the previous summer, but between the move, and work, and Coal, she had fallen behind with the planning, though it was beyond her why a wedding was solely a bride's responsibility. A Y chromosome didn't disable one's aptitude for calling caterers.

However, they didn't need a caterer, because they had decided on eloping. Well, she had decided. Austin had agreed in concept. Except he wanted to invite his mother. And his sister. Which meant Dallas needed to invite *her* mother. And her father. But her mother and father hadn't peacefully occupied the same city in more than twenty years, which was one of the reasons Dallas wanted to elope in the first place.

Just getting everyone to agree on a date had been exhausting. And then Len started working fewer hours, which meant Austin working more, which meant rescheduling yet again. And then her mother threw her back out, and Mandy had, well, her breakdown or whatever it was. And now Jarrod was being purposefully intransigent. She could hear Coal stomping around his bedroom. Like father, like son.

"Could you just compromise?" Dallas pleaded. She devoted her life to helping other people organize their lives. Why was it so hard handling her own? "It's very difficult to find a date that works for everyone."

"But it doesn't work for *everyone*, does it?" he asked, sounding more snide than necessary. "You just want me to be the bad guy."

"What are you talking about?"

"If you really wanted to be married, you'd be married already. You're having doubts, and you're looking for me to stop this train wreck."

"You're crazy."

"I lived with you for three years. I kind of have to be."

She hung up on him. It didn't solve anything, but it felt good. And *that* she had no doubts about. Jarrod thought he knew her, but he didn't. He just knew how to irritate her, and she wasn't going to let him.

On the one hand, it really didn't make a difference if she delayed the wedding again. Austin had made a commitment to her. He had bought her a ring. They were living as a family. They were married in every way except a legal document. And how much did she need a legal document? She didn't need his name or his money.

On the other hand, the longer they went without a marriage license, the less he mentioned it. And the less he mentioned it, the more she questioned why. Was he having second thoughts? Did he think she was too old? Did he think she was too odd? Did he think she had forced him to propose? Did *she* think she had forced him to propose? Of course she had forced him to propose. She wasn't going to move to a generic suburb of a dystopian city for a fling. It wasn't joyficient.

But neither was feeling like she trapped him. Not that she trapped him. She had never trapped anyone in her life. Except for Jarrod. But it wasn't a trap. It was a pregnancy. He just called it a trap. And only when he was angry at her. Austin never got angry at her. And that concerned her. If he loved her, he would fight with her. Or fight *for* her. But Austin didn't fight. He got quiet. She didn't trust quiet. Quiet was where dark thoughts took root. Quiet was where doubts percolated.

She feared Austin was having doubts about her. Which made her have doubts about him. Which made her do stupid things, like snoop through his e-mail. And his office appointment schedule. (Like she was the only person who ever logged into her fiancé's work server!)

She mostly came up empty-handed. Except now her doubts had a name.

Naomi Bloom.

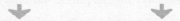

"When did your mom say she was coming back?" Dallas asked Mandy.

"She didn't." Mandy was where she had been for the last three months, sitting at Penelope's kitchen table, staring morosely into space and eating Häagen-Dazs out of the container.

"She had offered to babysit for Coal," Dallas said, perplexed that Penelope wasn't there and uncertain about interacting with Mandy, something she generally avoided.

"It's not a problem," Mandy said, taking another spoonful of ice cream. With her mouth full, she said, "The situation is under control."

Dallas had serious doubts about that, but she could hear Coal giggling happily in the next room as he played with Austin's old Hot Wheels set. Was it possible that Coal misbehaved only with her?

"I had wanted to ask her about something," Dallas said, and it wasn't about Coal. Dallas knew she shouldn't want to ask Penelope what she wanted to ask, and she also knew there was no way of stopping herself once something was gnawing at her.

"Is it about the wedding?"

"Kind of," Dallas said. She wondered if she should ask Mandy, which was an even worse idea than asking Penelope. "Do you have a cigarette?"

"You smoke?"

"No," Dallas said, "but sometimes I like to hold a cigarette in my hand. It calms me. Did you know in World War II the staging camps in Europe were named after cigarette companies?"

Mandy was staring at her blankly. "Has Austin said anything to you?" Dallas asked.

"About smoking?"

"About me."

"He doesn't talk about you that much with me," Mandy said.

"Well, has he said anything in particular lately?"

"Lately he's mostly been giving me grief about my current job status."

Mandy had no current job status. The closest she came to being productive was blogging about her lack of being productive. Dallas watched Mandy examine a lengthy strand of her unwashed hair as if it were a foreign specimen of dubious etiology. It wasn't the first time Dallas thought Mandy's obsession with her hair bordered on pathological.

"There's nothing wrong with dying your hair," Dallas suggested.

"Excuse me?" Mandy sounded taken aback.

"If you don't like the color of your hair, there are lots of options for doing something about it. Am I being too invasive?" It was a bad habit, and she was aware of it. She just didn't always have control over it. She shouldn't have said anything to Mandy about her hair—or about Austin. Now Mandy wasn't saying anything in return, which made Dallas more uncomfortable than she'd been to begin with. And when she was uncomfortable she babbled. "I lived with a guy who used to go through my underwear drawer when I left the house. Now, *that* was invasive. At first I thought it was my imagination. But I caught him on videotape, and there he was searching through my drawer. He said he was just counting my underwear. As a rule of thumb, one shouldn't date men who count your underwear."

"That would seem to be a good rule," Mandy said. Dallas wasn't sure if Mandy was being sincere or snarky. Dallas also wasn't sure why she had admitted to videotaping Jarrod. But she hadn't said it was Jarrod. And she wasn't the one who was barely functional.

"For the record, I don't want to dye my hair," Mandy said. "I just wish it was a different color. It's like wishing I was taller. Or Swedish."

"Swedish?"

"I don't expect it to make any sense." Mandy took another spoonful of ice cream.

"It's okay to feel sad," Dallas said. Mandy groaned. Dallas knew she was overstepping, but what was she supposed to say to a woman who probably hadn't showered in days, who was wearing a stained high-school sweatshirt and whose goal was to be Scandinavian? "You dropped out of school, and you're moping around your mother's house. Everyone knows you're sad. Are we supposed to tiptoe around and pretend we don't know? Are you going to keep pretending you don't know we're pretending? Mandy, there are red-light people and there are green-light people."

"Is that a chapter in your book?"

"If you had read it, you would know," Dallas said, less insulted that Mandy hadn't read the book than dismayed that she hadn't benefited from it. "My point is there's nothing wrong with being a red-light person. Just don't make things worse by feeling bad about who you are. If you're sad, feel sad. It can actually feel good to feel sad. As long as you don't beat yourself up about it. It's the beating yourself up that gets people stuck. And if you're feeling stuck, the trick is to just take a step away from yourself. It's easy to think you have to first know where you're going. But you don't. All you need to do is take a step. In any direction. Even if it's a step backward. Because once you're moving, a body in motion tends to stay in motion."

"Is that why you talk so much?"

Dallas didn't mind people being blunt. In fact, she preferred it. "Yes," she said, laughing. "I think so."

Mandy smiled. Well, that was something.

"This is your chance to start over," Dallas said. "There must be something you want to do. Something you dreamed of doing since you were a kid."

"I dreamed of being Dian Fossey."

"Who?"

"Dian Fossey. The woman who rescued gorillas in Africa."

"You're so fucking weird," Dallas said, laughing again.

"Coming from you, that's a compliment," Mandy shot back.

"It is," Dallas assured her, and for a moment she believed there was a connection between them. Or something close enough to a connection for her to decide that one blunt question deserved another. "Who's Naomi Bloom?" she asked.

Mandy seemed to hesitate before answering. "She's someone I went to school with in California."

"Did Austin go out with her?"

This time Mandy's hesitation was unmistakable. "No," she said.

"Are you sure?"

"Well, it's not like he tells me about every date he's ever gone on," Mandy said. "We don't have that kind of incestuous relationship."

"Don't even get me started on your relationship. I'm sorry. I'm being invasive again."

"No," Mandy said, "just offensive."

Dallas could see where she deserved that. "I think Austin's having an affair," she said.

"He's not." This time Mandy responded swiftly.

"How do you know? You just said he doesn't discuss these things with you."

"I know my brother, and I know he would never have an affair."

"You can't know someone," Dallas said, slumping into a chair. "You know things about someone. Things they choose to let you know or accidentally let you know while you're videotaping them going through your underwear drawer. But it's all peripheral. Who a person is deep inside and what they're capable of is something only they know, and sometimes they don't even know themselves." Sometimes her thoughts wandered so far afield, she needed GPS to locate them. It was foolish for her to have said anything to Mandy. Nothing good could come of it. When would she learn to keep her mouth shut?

"Austin isn't cheating on you," Mandy said with what seemed like genuine affection. "If you think something is wrong, then ask him."

"You never ask a question you don't want to hear the answer to," Dallas said. "And I don't want to lose him." As she said the words, she realized how true they were. She didn't want to lose Austin.

"I think he'll surprise you."

"Guys often surprise me, but they're rarely happy surprises."

"Just talk to him," Mandy said, suddenly the voice of reason on human interaction. "He's a guy. If you make things simple and direct, he can do that."

CHAPTER TWENTY

"You're going to have to get set up on EMR. And have you done a SWOT analysis?" Austin had no idea what Hope Cassidy was talking about.

"What is an EMR?" he asked.

"Am I losing you?"

He was lost before she arrived. Len had made it sound like Optimum Health was going to buy their practice as is. That turned out to be wildly optimistic.

"An EMR is an electronic medical record," Hope said. She was an attractive woman with chestnut hair in her late thirties. She talked fast, but that was probably a New York thing. She was warm in person. Warmer than on the phone. She was one of those people who seemed to be always juggling a dozen plates while also trying to drink a cup of hot coffee. She was actually always drinking coffee. She was already on her third cup since she'd arrived. Maybe that was why she talked fast. "All records at Optimum are electronic. Paper is very twentieth century," she said glancing at the framed antique eye chart on his wall.

"I don't use that chart with patients," Austin felt obligated to point out.

"That's a relief," she said. It wasn't until she smiled that he was sure she was joking.

"There are several different EMR systems on the market with different price points and different features. Unfortunately, they're not all compatible with Optimum's system, so you'll have to consult with tech support. Once you pick an EMR, make sure to include that in your SWOT analysis."

"Is that another newfangled electronic thing?" Austin asked. "I'm suddenly feeling very old."

"No," Hope said with a smile. "SWOT stands for strengths, weaknesses, opportunities and threats. It's a strategy tool. Something you use, well, *we* use to evaluate if you're a good business fit."

"If?" Austin was confused. "But you're here." Though it had taken so many months to coordinate the meeting, which he now realized he should have probably taken as a bad sign. "I thought Optimum was already committed."

"I'm here because we're committed to pursuing this opportunity. But the final decision is going to be made after a lot of number crunching about things like ROI and long-term growth rates. Of course, your market position will also be taken into consideration."

"You don't sound like a doctor," Austin said, his brain swimming.

"I didn't used to sound like this," she said with a rueful expression. She took a gulp of coffee. "I spent a decade as an ER physician at St. Vincent's in New York. But St. Vincent's went belly-up, and in the end the quality work taking place there meant a lot less than the value of the real estate, which is why a hundred-and-fifty-year-old hospital is soon to be the site of luxury condos. Medicine is a business these days, like any other. It's a brave new world."

As Austin recalled, things didn't end well in that book.

"You have to stop thinking of yourself as just a doctor. You're a service provider. You're an entrepreneur."

"But if I join Optimum, won't I just be an employee?"

"In this economy, being employed is no small thing," Hope said, gathering her short black trench coat and briefcase. "Well, I don't have to tell you that. Look what city you live in. Austin, once you get used to the new vernacular and protocols, you may end up liking them. Hell, I started using SWOT analysis on potential dates."

"How's that working for you?" he asked.

She paused on her way out the door, and her green eyes softened. "It's teaching me to be more aware of potential opportunities."

Austin spent his theoretical lunch hour trying to do a SWOT analysis of the practice. He divided a paper into four rectangles, as was done in the literature Hope left him. He labeled one square "Strengths," the next "Weaknesses," then "Opportunities" and "Threats." And that's about as far as he could get. The only rectangle he didn't have a problem filling was "Threats."

When Dallas knocked on his open door, he was going bleary-eyed trying to come up with reasons why anyone would invest in Farmington Eyes. He looked up, surprised and worried. She rarely came by the office.

"Is something wrong with Coal?" he asked.

"No," she assured him. "He's fine. He wants a dragon as a pet, like the boy in the movie he saw last week. I explained that dragons weren't real. So then he asked for a dinosaur. And when I told him that also wasn't possible, he asked if dinosaurs were real. And I thought maybe I should just tell him they're not, since that's what half the people in the Tea Party think, and it would be a lot easier than explaining evolution."

Dallas was babbling, which he knew from experience meant that she was upset about something. If she was upset with him, he was hoping it was for something like forgetting to put the toilet seat down as opposed to forgetting her birthday. He was pretty sure he hadn't forgotten her birthday. But all of a sudden his mind was a blank, and he couldn't remember her birthday.

"I just had something I wanted to talk to you about," she said, "and I thought it would be better to do it in person."

September. Her birthday was in September. He sighed with relief. "Is it possible we can discuss whatever it is tonight?" he asked. "I spent most of my morning with the Optimum rep, and I've got back-to-back patients all afternoon."

"We can't discuss it tonight because I won't be home tonight." That sounded odd. "I mean, I won't be at your home tonight. Our home. No, your home. I'm not doing this well."

"Doing what?" Now Austin was really worried. "What are you talking about?"

"I packed up my stuff. And Coal's stuff."

"What? When? Why?" Austin was sputtering.

"I'm moving out." She must have seen the befuddled expression on his face. "I started seeing someone."

Austin couldn't believe what he was hearing. It was only a few months back that she had been accusing *him* of having an affair. "Why would you do that?" It made no sense. "Why would you do that to me? Why would you do that to Coal?"

"It's Coal's dad."

"And that makes it better?"

"A little."

"No, Dallas, it doesn't. Not at all."

"Don't get upset."

"What the fuck am I supposed to do?"

"Don't yell at me!" She was crying. He should have been the one crying. "It's your fault!" she screamed at him.

"My fault!"

"You and Naomi."

"I told you nothing happened between us." They had been through all of this. He had told her everything. Or almost everything.

"Well, I didn't believe you."

"So it's my fault you didn't believe me?"

"I didn't believe you because it wasn't true."

"I swear to God—"

"I don't know what happened or what didn't happen. But I know what I felt. I know how you touched me. I know how you didn't touch me. I hooked up with Jarrod because I wanted to get back at you. Because I thought it would make us even. Because I thought since he was an ex, it was kind of a freebie. It wasn't like I hadn't been with him before."

She was talking. Words kept coming out of her mouth. But it was like they were in a foreign language. Austin couldn't comprehend them. He couldn't fathom their meaning. He was tumbling. He was falling down a flight of stairs. No, he had opened a door where he thought there was a flight of stairs and there was just a sheer drop. And darkness.

"I thought it would be just a one-night thing. I didn't plan this."

"Then why on earth are you doing it?"

"I know where I stand with Jarrod. I've always known where I stood. But with you, I feel like there's a big question mark about who I am to you and where the relationship is going."

"What's the question mark? We've been picking a date to get married."

"And we haven't found one."

"We haven't found the *right* one."

"Because there *isn't* a right one. When I'm with you, I feel like there's all this gray smoke in the air between us, making it hard to breathe. Making it hard to see you and see myself. It makes me want to smoke again, so I can be blowing smoke out rather than breathing it in."

"That's not what you told me in the past. You told me I made you feel safe. I made you feel protected. That's what you told me. And you tell me everything. For God's sake, Dallas, you vomit out every thought in your head, and you never told me any of this."

"Beware of people who tell you everything about themselves. They're the ones that hide the most."

Austin didn't know what to do with that. He didn't know how to process it. He wasn't even sure what it meant.

"What about Coal?" he asked. "I'm a father to him."

"Jarrod is his father," Dallas said, looking away from him. "Coal will be fine."

What about me? Austin wanted to ask. *Why aren't you concerned about me?* How could she just rip herself out of his life? And how could she take his son from him? Yes, after two years, Coal felt like his son. There were a half dozen pictures of Coal on his desk. Austin wanted to reach out and touch him. But he couldn't. And she was saying he would never be able to again. It was impossible. She was being impossible. No, she was just being scared. That's what Dallas did; she got scared about things. He understood getting scared. He understood the impulse to run like his mom did. Like Mandy did. But it wasn't something he did. It was his job to be strong. It always had been. If he could just get Dallas to calm down and see what a mistake she was making, they could work through it. They could somehow find a way to work through it. He reached for her hand, but she pulled away.

"Dallas, you don't have to do this. Or you don't have to do this today."

"You have no idea how hard this is for me. You have no idea."

"I do," he said. "I understand. Come back to the house."

"I can't."

"I'll get you a hotel room. At the Embassy Suites. You and Coal can stay there tonight. We'll talk tomorrow."

"There's nothing to talk about," she said. But she was wavering. He could tell.

"There's everything to talk about," he said. "You are everything to me. You and Coal."

"I'm everything to you?" she asked; she was crying again. He was getting through to her. Everything was going to be okay. "Do you love me more than anyone else in the world?"

If he hesitated, it was only for a millisecond. "Of course," he said to her. "Of course I do."

"Oh, Austin," she said. "You're such a fucking liar."

He didn't know what to say. There was nothing he could say. It was over. He had lost her.

"We don't fit together," she said, "and we never did. There are red-light people, and there are green-light people—"

"Don't you dare start in with your red-light, green-light crap." She had cheated on him. She was leaving him. He sure as hell didn't have to listen to her bullshit anymore.

"You can call it crap, but it's still true. There are people whose first impulse is no, and people whose first impulse is yes. Red light and green light."

"So I'm red and you're green." There was something superficial and simplistic about her and her advice. Mandy had been right all along. "Is that what you're saying?"

"No," she said sadly. "You're yellow."

CHAPTER TWENTY-ONE

"You look better in the blue," Lila said after Naomi changed outfits for the third time. "It brings out the color of your eyes."

"It's an interview, not a date."

"If it's a man, wear the blue," Lila said before returning her gaze to the copy of *Vogue* she was skimming.

Though it killed Naomi to admit it, her mother was right. She hated that she was primping for a meeting with a venture capitalist. She was nervous enough about the business plan she and Steffi had put together. But it didn't hurt to accentuate all her assets. The blue von Furstenberg wrap also had a lower neckline, and a little cleavage never hurt.

"I thought you were spending the day with Noah," Naomi said, hoping it didn't sound too obvious that she was trying to get rid of Lila. Now that Naomi and Noah both lived in New York, Lila's visits were becoming more frequent.

"He's got vendor meetings all day. I would never have guessed how much work goes into throwing parties." Lila would never have guessed how much work went into a lot of things was Naomi's thought, but she held her tongue. "I'm thinking of staying."

"At Noah's?" Naomi tried not to let her enthusiasm show. She was not enjoying having a roommate.

"In New York."

"For how long?" Naomi was now trying not to let her apprehension show.

"Don't worry. I'm thinking of getting a place." Why was that not a reason to worry?

"What does Daddy think about that?"

"I haven't told him. I'm running away from home. The way you used to do, when you would take off and we'd have to go searching the neighborhood for you."

"I was nine," Naomi pointed out. "And I didn't get very far."

"Well, if you had waited until your fifties, you would have had more resources." Lila clucked. "I want to live in New York. I want to go to parties with the titans of the cybereconomy. I want to tweet."

"You're sounding like a child."

"Good!" Lila exclaimed. "I want to be young before I'm old."

"You already were young."

"Not really," Lila said. "I want another life."

"Well, you can't have mine."

"Why not? I gave you yours. I gave you mine. Let me tell you, your twenties aren't as fun when you're nursing and toilet training."

"And what's Daddy going to do?"

"He can do whatever he likes. I raised his children. I entertained his business associates. I've braised enough chickens for a lifetime. I'm done. And it wouldn't hurt you to be more supportive."

"More supportive?" Naomi was about to lose it. "You show up unannounced, thinking I'm some kind of concierge hotel with free cable and Tab on tap. I have a meeting in an hour. A ludicrously important meeting that I've worked really hard to get. And instead of focusing on preparing I'm buying you magazines and dealing with your midlife crisis. What more do you want from me?"

"I want you to stop judging me."

"Judging you?"

"Ever since you were a child," Lila said, "you would scream if I didn't hold you just the right way."

"Are you talking about when I was an infant?"

"It never stopped. Nothing I did ever made you happy. The cupcakes were too dry. The macaroni and cheese was too watery. You were always watching me. With those thick eyeglasses. Watching my every move. Disapproving."

"Are you kidding me? All you do is disapprove. There hasn't been a day of my life when you haven't disapproved and criticized every single thing I say or do."

"You always exaggerate everything."

"AAAAGGGGHHH!"

"What? I'm not allowed to respond when you're attacking me?"

Naomi stormed into her bedroom to change clothes, slamming her door behind her.

Lila called out after her, "And you say I'm acting like a child."

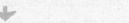

"I hate the name, love the concept," said Dov Levin, a twenty-seven-year-old wunderkind with spiky dark hair and penetrating eyes. "Who cares about 'Steffi's Stuff'? No one knows Steffi. Beyoncé's stuff. Yes. Steffi's stuff. Bleh."

"We're not married to the name," Steffi said. Naomi nodded.

"Good."

"Maybe we can use the word 'bazaar' to emphasize the international aspect," Naomi said, thinking that angle would appeal to Dov since he was Israeli.

"Bazaar makes people think of the Middle East. Makes them think of terrorists. Americans don't like international things. They like American things, like pizza, French fries and hummus."

He was funny in a fast-paced, did-you-get-that-too-bad-you-missed-it kind of way.

"I like the success you've had on eBay," he said. "But it's a big jump going from a store on eBay to launching a Web site."

"We have forty thousand followers on Twitter," Naomi reminded him.

"So does CeeLo Green's cat. When you have forty thousand repeat customers, then you're talking."

"CeeLo Green's cat doesn't have a twenty percent market share in a luxury brand sector," Naomi responded, more assertively than she had intended, but she couldn't help herself. Steffi shot her an uncharacteristicly nervous glance. But the blue dress was working. Naomi was feeling confident, energized and in the zone.

"I'm not knocking what you've accomplished," Dov said, "but the two of you are, well, inexperienced, to say the least, and I'm just not convinced this thing's got legs."

He was turning them down.

Naomi was stunned. It wasn't that she had any basis for expecting a better outcome, but her gut had told her they were acing the pitch meeting. And she had always trusted her gut. She was appalled she could have miscalculated so completely. She wasn't in the zone. She wasn't even in the stadium.

"Here's what I can do," Dov said. "I could throw a small amount of seed money your way. Like twenty thousand dollars. For a significant equity stake, of course."

"Of course," Steffi echoed, sounding relieved to be salvaging something from the meeting.

"It's a gamble," he continued. "But it's an interesting gamble. And I'm feeling charitable."

"Except you're not known for your philanthropy," Naomi said. He was bluffing. She was sure of it. Almost sure of it.

Dov spun his chair toward her, making a clicking sound with his tongue.

"What Naomi means," Steffi said, "is we wouldn't want you making an investment unless you have confidence in us and our product."

"And twenty thousand dollars doesn't seem very confident," Naomi added. He wanted in. And if he wanted in, he was going to have to up his ante.

He made the clicking sound again. "Where do you stand on current stakeholders?"

"Just a few family members," Steffi said. And one ex–family member, Naomi thought, noticing that Steffi had stopped wearing her wedding ring.

"Good. But remember, blood is thicker than water. Which is another way of saying that when you mess with family, they go for the jugular." He loosened his tie and started unbuttoning his shirt. What the hell was he doing?

"You see that?" he said, pointing to a scar on his neck. "My brother did that when I was five years old because I hid some of the quarters from our lemonade stand. There's no such thing as family when it comes to business. I'll put in two hundred and fifty thousand for a majority stake. I'll have my assistant follow up with the paperwork." Naomi hoped her face didn't give away how relieved and grateful she felt. "Any questions?" he asked.

"Just one," Naomi said, going on a hunch. "How did you really get that scar?"

"Playing Hacky Sack in my frat house at Cornell, I tripped and fell on a bong," he said. "It was a really nice bong."

He escorted them to the door, and as Naomi followed Steffi out, he asked her, "So, care to chat some more sometime about childhood scars? Perhaps over a drink?"

The blue dress was definitely working. "Not over a water pipe?"

"It could be arranged," he said, leaning against the doorframe. He was one of those men who had a permanent five o'clock shadow and deep olive skin.

"I have a rule about mixing business and pleasure," Naomi said. She had no such rule, but she thought she probably should.

"Does that mean you would find it pleasurable to have a drink with me?"

"I think I'm a little old for you," she said.

"What I lack in years I make up for in money." He smiled. And it was a fairly irresistible smile.

He took her hand in his. It was warm and a little rough. And larger than she expected, given that he stood only an inch or so taller than her. His shirt was still unbuttoned, and she could see thick dark hair sprouting from the opening.

"Let's stick to business," she said, "for now."

There were so many thoughts going through Naomi's head as she strode toward the marble elevator bank where Steffi was waiting. But the one that she resented was that she needed to thank her mother.

CHAPTER TWENTY-TWO

"Tell her she can't go," Penelope was beseeching Austin.

"Of course she can't go," Austin said.

They were talking about Mandy like she wasn't in the room. She wondered if anyone was going to comment on her new hair color. Her guess was no.

"First you complain about me not having a real job, and then you complain when I get one," Mandy said. "I kind of thought you'd be proud of me getting a job working for the UN."

"If you were working for the UN in New York," Penelope said. "Not the Congo."

"There's not a lot of gorilla rescue missions in New York," Mandy pointed out.

"Is this about a guy?" Austin asked.

Right. She was going halfway around the planet because she had a spat with a guy. Though she was kind of hoping there would be some strapping primatologist on the team. Preferably with a French accent. She really liked a French accent.

"Mandy, this is crazy," Penelope said. "Even if you weren't my daughter, I would tell you the same thing. I would tell you it's a dangerous place. It's a country at war."

"We're living in a country at war," Mandy said. "We've been at war almost ten years."

"It's not the same thing, and you know it."

"You're not going to do this," Austin said in the dad voice he'd been practicing since he was eleven. "You're not going. And that's final."

"What are you going to do? Lock me in my room?"

"If that's what it takes."

Mandy understood why her decision seemed odd to them, but it made complete sense to her. Everything shifted after her conversation with Dallas. She needed to take action. She needed to "take a step." As much as she hated to say it, she needed to stop being a red-light person and start being a green-light one. She almost had a desire to call and thank Dallas. Almost.

"This is what I've wanted to do my whole life," Mandy said. "Ever since seeing the movie *Gorillas in the Mist* with Sigourney Weaver, I wanted to be Dian Fossey. And Dian Fossey worked in the Congo."

"Dian Fossey was murdered," Penelope snapped.

"Not in the Congo," Mandy said, though she recognized this was not a major selling point.

"There are plenty of gorillas other places," Austin said. "Even places Dian Fossey worked."

"How about getting a job at the Detroit Zoo?" Penelope asked. "You used to love zoos."

"I'm not working in a zoo. I got hired to rescue gorillas in the Congo, and that's where I'm going."

Her answer further agitated her mother. "Do you think I don't know what it's like?" Penelope asked her. "To have your life turned upside down?"

Yes, her mother knew what it was like to be despondent. What her mother didn't know was what it was like to have watched her be despondent for almost a decade. She didn't know that Mandy had vowed never to be like that and that it scared her to realize how close she had come. "Then you should understand why I need to go," Mandy said.

"Well, I don't," Penelope responded. "I'm sorry, but I don't understand at all why there's not someplace in the world you can be of use without putting your life at risk. I don't understand why you have no middle speed. First you're moping around in a near catatonic state. Then you're running off to the Congo. Why isn't there something in between?"

"I don't know, Mom." She wished that she did. She could see that from the outside it could look like borderline clinical behavior. Over the borderline. Like Madonna, but without the sex, religion and bangle bracelets. But going to the Congo was far less risky than staying where she had been.

"If something happened to you, I wouldn't be able to survive. I couldn't go through that. Not again. How can you not know that?"

"Mom, nothing's going to happen to me."

Penelope stifled a sob as she rushed from the room. Austin looked at Mandy without saying anything. She hated when he did that. She could take it when he argued with her. But the stoic look of disappointment was his secret weapon, and she found it unbearable.

"I'm not doing this to hurt anyone," she said.

"Why are you doing it?"

"I told you. It's a way of jump-starting my life."

"So is going skydiving. Is that what you're going to do next?"

"Maybe," Mandy said defiantly. "If it's something I want to do. I'm not going to live my life being afraid."

"Then how about going snorkeling? How about scuba diving?" Now he was just being mean. "How about going sailing, Mandy? Or just going for a swim. You want to go for a swim? We can go over to my health club and—"

"Stop it! You've made your point."

"I don't think so. Not unless you're changing your plans."

"I'm not changing my plans," she said. "Don't you get it? If I stay, I will turn into *her*. And I won't even have two screwed-up kids to show for it."

"Hey!" he yelped. "Speak for yourself."

"Are you kidding me?" Sure, compared to herself, he was a paragon of psychological stability, but that wasn't setting the bar very high. "Last time I checked, you were still lamenting the woman who jilted you and working for a company you despised."

"I don't despise them," he said, his jaw tightening. "It's just a difficult adjustment working for a company when you're not used to it. And you're not going to turn into Mom. You didn't lose a husband."

"That's what makes it so much worse," Mandy said. Her mother at least had an excuse for losing it. What excuse did she have? "What if I hadn't come out of my funk? What if it had taken me as long as it took her? And don't say you hadn't thought about the possibility. Because I know you have."

"You don't know what I've thought or haven't thought."

She wasn't letting him off the hook that easy. "Are you saying that I'm wrong?"

"Jesus, Mandy." He squirmed in discomfort. "I was worried about you. You were ill. But this could just be part of the same illness."

"This isn't an illness. This is an opportunity. We're talking about the UN, Austin. I'll be working with extraordinary people. I'll be observing animals in person. Not on video. In landscapes I've dreamed about seeing. And I'll be doing something important. Not to mention getting a great credit on my résumé. There's only one reason not to go to the Congo. Only one. And that's fear. Fear that something *could* go wrong. But something could go wrong any day. I could get run down crossing the street. Or get shot at while at a movie theater. We have no control over these things. *You* have no control over these things. No matter how you try to believe otherwise. The things that happen to us are the things that happen to us. My hair is my hair."

"What the hell does that mean? And what did you do to your hair?"

"You mean you noticed?"

"Of course I noticed. It's nearly fluorescent. Whoever's manning the Space Station probably noticed."

"It's called Flaming Red, though it does seem more fluorescent than flaming. So much for truth in advertising."

"Mandy, what are you doing?"

"I'm living. Messily. Imperfectly. But I'm almost thirty-four years old, and the only thing I should be afraid of is dying without daring to be bold."

Mandy wasn't a hundred percent sure she believed that, but she was willing to give it a try.

CHAPTER TWENTY-THREE

"What are you doing here?" Steffi shouted, trying to be heard over the booming beat of the boffo drummer in the aptly named Boom Boom Room.

"What?" Austin responded, leaning in closer, which was hard to do given how close they were already standing in the crowded nightclub.

"What are you doing in New York?" she shouted in his ear.

"It turns out I'm not a very good employee," he said.

"What?"

"I'm looking for a job!" It wasn't really the kind of thing he wanted to scream out in public. Though it was doubtful anyone could hear him. It also wasn't the real reason he was there.

"Is Naomi around?" he asked.

"What?"

"Have you seen Naomi!"

Steffi grabbed him by the arm and led him down a dark, congested hallway, where the sound of the live band was replaced with hip-hop music thumping from overhead speakers. They continued up a flight of stairs and through a fire door, emerging on an Astroturf deck with circular Day-Glo–colored waterbeds. A red one made him think of Mandy's hair.

"How did you hear about the launch party?" Steffi asked. It was chilly outside in the spring night air, but it was a lot easier to be heard.

"Stu invited me," Austin said a little too quickly. He added, "When he heard I was going to be in the city."

"Of course," Steffi said. "My happiest investor. Is he here?"

"I haven't seen him," Austin said, looking out over the Hudson River from their nineteen-story perch. "I think he's in San Jose."

"Good," she said. Her glossy lips spread into a thin smile. "A continent between us works best."

"Have you seen Naomi?" he asked again.

"She's somewhere around. You know I got the idea for the name of Splurge.com from Stu."

"He didn't tell me."

"He doesn't know," she said, draining her pink drink. "Or maybe he does. Maybe he figured it out. He used to always complain about me 'splurging' on things. It was a constant 'thing' between us. He'd say, 'Don't you think that dress is a bit of a "splurge"?' 'Do you really need to "splurge" on another pair of shoes?' And that's how I came up with the name."

"I like the name." Austin looked around the dimly lit terrace to see if he spied Naomi. It was hard to see faces. A lot of shadowy figures intertwined. "And Stu likes the name. He's really proud of you, Steffi. He keeps saying how proud he is of what you've accomplished with this thing and how proud he is to be part of it."

"Well," she said, "he at least got something out of the marriage." There was a grimness in the way she said it. She had changed since the last time Austin had seen her. She was less bubbly. Less curvy too. She seemed to have been hitting the gym, given the flattering way her black cocktail dress clung to her. She looked good, but there was something hard about her and the way her upswept dark hair was shellacked in place.

"You were the only one who guessed right about Stu and me," she said. "Or the only one honest enough to say something."

"What do you mean?"

"You told Stu not to marry me."

"I didn't say that."

"You used nicer words. But he told me at the time what you said. That we weren't ready and that we were rushing into things. Now I wonder if that was his way of saying he thought you were right. Could have saved ourselves a lot of aggravation if we had listened to you."

"You loved each other."

"Did we?" she asked. She looked across the Hudson, but her gaze wasn't focused on the Jersey skyline. "Before I divorced Stu, I went to a therapist, and when I told him about our relationship, he said that he suspected Stu and I filled a void in each other's lives. But the truth was we created a void in each other's lives. I never went back to that therapist."

"You're sounding very cynical."

"Not cynical," she said, rotating the ice cubes in her glass. "Honest."

"I was there. I remember you guys being in love."

"Oh sure, at the start we thought we were destined for each other. Everything seemed so perfect. We knew each other since we were kids. Even our names fit together. When I saw him on Match.com, I thought I'd hit the jackpot. We both did. But I think deeper down I was a thirty-year-old woman afraid that almost all my friends were married and having children and I was being left behind. And I think he was afraid of the same thing. Maybe not the children part. Because, let's face it: Stu *is* a child. But maybe that was part of it too.

Maybe he wanted to prove that he wasn't a child. That he could be a man. Or at least wear a tuxedo for one night like one. It was a great wedding, though, wasn't it?"

Austin pictured Naomi lying in the Crystal Cove hotel bed with a breeze coming in off the bluff. "It was."

"Naomi told me that you hooked up that night," Steffi said, coming closer to him, and it wasn't so he could hear her. She was standing so close he could smell the rum on her breath. "She said you were very good."

"Thank you," he said, for lack of anything better. "I mean, that was nice of her to say."

"Was it?"

"Excuse me?"

She put a hand lightly on his arm. "Was it nice of her to say? Or was it simply the truth?"

The next thing Austin knew Steffi's mouth was on his, her lubricated lips open and thirsty.

"Steffi—," he gurgled.

He wasn't able to make much sound because her mouth was like a suction cup. It was as if she were trying to inhale his face. And her hands were moving toward his belt buckle.

He finally succeeded in pulling away. "Steffi, I think you're a little drunk.

"No, I'm not," she said. "I'm a lot drunk." Her mouth was coming in for another Austin-flavored big gulp. He leaned sideways, and her chin smashed into his shoulder.

"Ow!" she said, rubbing her jaw.

"I'm sorry," he said, wanting to extricate himself as quickly as possible. "So sorry. But I've gotta pee."

He ran back down the stairs. Once he reached the crowded

corridor below, he realized he really did need to pee. He headed down more dark, crowded corridors through a sweet-smelling mist coming from hidden fog machines, until he found the über-modern men's room, where a row of slick black-tile-and-chrome urinals lined a wall of floor-to-ceiling windows.

"It's a little like pissing on New York, isn't it?" said a guy standing at the neighboring urinal. Austin wasn't in the habit of starting conversations in lavatories, but he had to admit it was a unique sensation relieving himself while looking out a picture window high above Manhattan.

"What do you think of the party?" the guy asked when they stood alongside each other again at the sink. Austin noticed he spoke with an accent, something Mediterranean sounding.

"It's great," Austin said.

"Looks like you are enjoying yourself," the guy said, observing the large saliva stain on Austin's lapel as well as Austin's effort to remove Steffi's lipstick from the edges of his mouth.

"Are you involved with the Web site?" Austin asked.

"I own the Web site, or sixty percent of it," the guy said as he mussed with his thick black hair. "But I'm getting a lot more than that out of it."

"How so?" Austin asked, rubbing at his facial skin but still seeing a bloodred ring around his lips. Or maybe it was just that his skin was now red from the rubbing.

"Let's just say there are business mergers, and there are other kinds of mergers."

Austin wasn't sure he liked the sound of that.

"And when you find someone you want both with, you're a lucky man, am I right?"

"You are right," Austin said. "So you and Steffi are an item?" he asked, crossing his fingers the answer was yes.

"Steffi?" the guy laughed. "No, not Steffi. Naomi. You know her?"

"I do," Austin said, thinking his skin was now looking green.

"Then you know I am a very lucky man."

"I do."

Naomi was standing beside a sleek ebony bar, but her mind was elsewhere. Her mind was on a text she'd received from Austin more than an hour ago. It said he had a surprise for her. She had included him on the Evite list, half hoping, half fearing he'd respond.

"Naomi, the party is quite fabulous," said Godwin, with Noah at his side. "And you know how much I avoid using that word."

"Well, you know who gets the credit," Naomi said.

"And I love taking credit," Noah said.

"I thought you just loved spending on credit," Godwin said, wiping a stray crumb from Noah's fashionably plaid lapel.

"Only other people's credit," Noah said. "And speaking of taking other people's credit, where's Mom? Please tell me you didn't throw her from the roof deck. I get nervous seeing the two of you around sheer drops or sharp objects."

"She's perfectly safe," Naomi said. "Which of course means no one else is. Dov invited Barbara Corcoran from the show *Shark Tank*, and Mom is stalking her."

Godwin shook his head, a frown creasing his handsome dark features. "Has it occurred to either of you that your mother is actually a rather nice woman?"

"No," Naomi and Noah answered simultaneously, then looked at each other and cracked up.

"You're both incorrigible," Godwin said, walking toward a waiter carrying a tray of rumaki.

"Did Mom tell you that she's going back to California to visit Dad?" Noah asked.

"No," Naomi said, not interested in focusing at that moment on her mother's midlife crisis. She was more concerned that Austin might be at the party, and she was wondering if she should enlist Noah's help in finding him. But that would require explaining to Noah her relationship with Austin, which she wasn't sure she wanted to do. Nor was she sure that she could.

"Mom made a plane reservation for Labor Day weekend, and the only reason I know is she asked me if I had any gift suggestions. She wants to bring Dad something from New York."

Okay, Naomi had to admit that did sound like a step in the right direction.

"I think she's lonely," Noah said. "The problem with the whole second childhood thing is there's not a lot of other kids on the playground."

Naomi hadn't really thought about that. Perhaps she gave her mother too hard a time, but she found the notion doubtful.

She saw Dov approaching and had the same mixed feeling of attraction and dread that she always felt when she was near him. She had thought it was mostly due to having been burned in the past when she moved too fast, but after Austin's text she knew that wasn't the real reason.

"Noah, do you remember Austin Gittleman from when we were kids?"

"Austin Gittleman? Was he the one whose dad died in a surfing accident?"

"Yes." Naomi wasn't even sure what she was asking. How would Noah recognize Austin? She needed a different plan. "Have you seen Steffi?" Steffi was the only person who could help her.

"Is she with Austin Gittleman?" Noah sounded confused.

"No. Forget Austin. Have you seen Steffi?"

"Earlier."

"How's the most beautiful woman in the room?" Dov asked, sliding an arm around her waist.

She slipped out of his embrace. "Why do you keep telling people that we're a couple?"

"Because if you hear it from enough people, then you'll eventually believe it." He kissed her on the cheek.

"I don't get a kiss?" Noah said.

Dov clasped his hands around Noah's shoulders and kissed him on each cheek.

"Is that Acqua di Gio?" Noah asked, sniffing at Dov.

"Yeah."

"Very White Party 2008."

"I've been wearing this stuff since high school," Dov said.

"Exactly," Noah replied.

Naomi was barely following their conversation. She was keeping her eyes peeled for Steffi or Austin while trying not to look too distracted. It was kind of like playing Twister with only her head and shoulders.

"Would you like another drink?" Dov asked her.

"I'm fine."

"You seem tense."

"Aren't you?"

"Hell no," he said. "I'm having a ball."

It occurred to Naomi that if Austin really was there, she didn't want him meeting Dov. And vice versa. She tried to configure in her mind a way to avoid that happening.

"Noah." She turned to her brother, who was sipping a pomegranate martini and watching eye candy on the dance floor. "Let's go find Mom."

Noah looked at her like she had suffered a psychotic break. "Why?"

Naomi glared at him. "Dov, do you want to come with us?" she said, knowing full well he had a very low tolerance for her mother.

"Sorry, honey, I gotta check on the, um, thing with the club manager."

"No problem," Naomi said, smiling sweetly. Then she grabbed Noah and started moving quickly.

"You're going to make me spill my martini, and pomegranate stains," he said. "What's up?"

"Nothing. Why do you think something's up?" She jammed her way through the throng, with Noah in tow.

"I'm spilling!" he squawked. "It's a good thing your boyfriend is paying me a lot of money."

"He's not my boyfriend!"

They searched the dance floor and the hallway to the bathrooms. "Why are you so eager to see Mom?" Noah asked.

"Mom?" Naomi asked. "Right. Mom. Just want to make sure she's not getting into any trouble." Fortunately, there was no sign of Lila before they spotted Steffi as they headed toward the roof deck.

"Steffi!" Naomi called out. "Have you by any chance seen Austin Gittleman?" A blast of Lady Gaga surged from the sound speakers.

"Who?"

"Austin Gittleman!"

"No!" Steffi said sharply. "Why would you think I would have seen Austin Gittleman?"

"I think there's a chance he's here somewhere."

"There's a chance of lots of things, Naomi," Steffi said, wobbling on her heels, her voice thick and sour. "But the chances are usually slim."

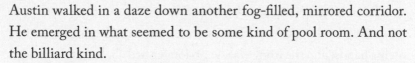

Austin walked in a daze down another fog-filled, mirrored corridor. He emerged in what seemed to be some kind of pool room. And not the billiard kind.

A giant disco ball hovered over a triangular-shaped whirlpool in a glass-walled lounge floating eighteen stories above the Hudson River. There was a 360-degree wraparound view mesmerizing enough to almost keep Austin from noticing two bare-breasted nymphettes frolicking in the pool with a fully dressed guy in leather. Above their heads was a sign made out of incandescent electric bulbs spelling out SPLURGE.

Despite the aquatic theme, Austin felt like a fish out of water. He didn't know anyone at the party. Other than Steffi and Naomi, and he had yet to lay eyes on Naomi. He should have guessed that she would have a boyfriend. Why wouldn't she? It was surprising she wasn't married. But if Austin couldn't be with her, he was at least glad she'd found someone who seemed good-natured and successful. Far more successful than Austin could ever hope to be. Though, shallow as it might be, Austin had noticed that the guy was shorter than him.

It had been a rash decision to come to New York. He didn't know what had come over him. It was really Mandy's doing. Not that she'd forced him to come. But she had gotten him thinking about the choices he'd made in his life. He tried so hard to make the right choices, but maybe he had defined "right" as safer rather than better.

Ever since Dallas had left him, he had been mourning not just for her and Coal, though he missed them terribly, but for the predictable life he'd had with them. He had known exactly how many minutes he could spend making Coal breakfast or having coffee with Dallas and still get to the office on time. He had looked forward each day to having two hours with Coal before reading him a bedtime story, and he could count on sex with Dallas twice a week (more if they didn't like the guests on the *Daily Show*).

He no longer had a reason to dawdle in the morning or to rush home after his last patient. He was acutely aware of having extra time on his hands, and the irony was he no longer had a job that demanded as much time. He was soon likely to have no job whatsoever, since he was constantly being reprimanded for spending too many minutes with each patient. With no need to stay late at work and nothing to come home for, he felt lost. The weekends were the worst. There was no reason to go to a park or a video arcade. Or to take a trip to the Belle Isle Aquarium. There were no mad dashes to the grocery store for more Cheerios. And no candlelit dinners after Coal was in bed. Sometimes he'd pretend Dallas and Coal were just out of town for a weekend custodial visit, as they had often been. Except it made Sunday nights even worse when they didn't return.

He felt like an amputee, suffering spasms from a phantom limb, but when he wasn't feeling overwhelmed by the vast emptiness of his days, he thought incessantly and obsessively about Naomi. As soon as Dallas left, his first instinct had been to pick up the phone and call Naomi. But it wasn't fair to do that to her. Or to himself. He needed time to grieve. He needed time to feel sorry for himself. And the truth was he didn't have the strength at the time to bear finding out that Naomi was with someone else. It turned out he still didn't.

He shouldn't have come to New York. No, the problem wasn't that he'd come. His mistake was that he'd come too late. He actually liked the city, much more than he expected. The crowds, the fast pace, the energy. He couldn't really see moving there. That was more Mandy's idea. He had scheduled a job interview while he was in town mostly to humor her. And it provided a good pretext for the trip. Still, Mandy was right about taking chances, though he continued to have reservations about her going to the Congo. But since she was scheduled to leave in the morning, she was unlikely to change her mind. He'd been hoping to hear from her when she finished packing, but she was probably still annoyed with him for the article he'd e-mailed her about a British tourist kidnapped in Kenya. He had sent the article to remind her how easy it was for people to take their safety for granted. It was only now that he realized that applied to emotional safety as well as physical.

All his effort to be careful about the things in life he could control had somehow led him to be careless with the things he couldn't. There was a lesson to be learned. A lesson he could contemplate on the flight back to Michigan. He wanted to find Naomi and congratulate her—on the Web site and the boyfriend. And then he wanted to leave. The mass of bodies surrounding him felt oppressive. He had never seen so many people at a party. Surprisingly, many of them looked vaguely familiar. Austin saw a teenage starlet whom he recognized from gossip stories posted on Facebook, and he spotted Barbara Corcoran, the real estate mogul. He and Dallas used to sometimes enjoy watching *Shark Tank* after Coal was in bed. Austin also recognized the woman standing next to Barbara Corcoran, but he couldn't place her face. Maybe she was also on a reality show. Then it hit him. She wasn't a celebrity; she was Naomi's mother. She was much older than when he had last seen her, but it was impossible not to recognize her; she looked like Naomi.

He could ask Naomi's mother where Naomi was holding court. Or, maybe better, he could just ask her to give Naomi a message. Nothing too complicated. In fact, just congratulations would do the trick. That's all that was necessary. Just let her know he was there and that he offered his good wishes.

No, man up, he told himself. No wimping out. No messages. He had come all this way, made up that cock-and-bull story with Steffi about Stu inviting him, and he wasn't going to leave with his tail between his legs. He was going to ask Naomi's mother where he could find Naomi. And he was going to see her one last time. He could do this. He wanted to do this. And he was about to do it when his phone buzzed. He pulled it out of his pocket, but it was a number he didn't recognize.

When he looked up, Naomi's mother was gone. Or she was no longer standing next to Barbara Corcoran. Austin swiveled his head from side to side. She couldn't have gone far. He navigated through the crowd in the direction he had last seen her. He shoved and shimmied between fashionistas and Silicon Alley swashbucklers, turning his head left and right, and he almost walked right into her.

"Mrs. Bloom?" he said.

"Yes?" Lila looked at him expectantly.

"I'm a friend of your daughter." Austin was relieved that they could hear each other talk. Though he still had to shout.

"I'm meeting so many wonderful friends of my daughter's tonight," she shouted back. "I can't tell you how happy it makes me."

"I'm actually a friend of hers from back in—"

"Godwin!" Lila called out.

An attractive dark-skinned man embraced her. "Are you having a good time?"

"I'm having the best time! This is a friend of Naomi's." Lila turned to Austin. "I'm sorry I didn't get your name—"

A waiter came between them with a tray of shrimp and some kind of green dipping sauce. There was a commotion around Austin as guests flocked to the shrimp, clearly a popular item, and he found himself cut off from Lila. His phone buzzed again. This time it was Mandy. Her timing was impeccable.

He answered, cupping a hand around his opposite ear. "Hello?" he shouted, hoping she could hear him.

"Mr. Gittleman?" It wasn't Mandy.

Austin pressed his hand tighter against his ear. "Who is this?"

"My name is Dr. Chun Kwan—"

"What?"

"My name is Dr. Chun Kwan. I'm a doctor in the emergency room of Beaumont Hospital, and I'm calling about your sister."

CHAPTER TWENTY-FOUR

Austin didn't know why Mr. Douglas had called him out of his fourth-grade math class. He didn't think he had been doing anything wrong. Or not terribly wrong. He was doodling in his notebook, making pictures of Superman fighting extraterrestrials, when he should have been doing his math problem set. But wasn't it his choice whether or not he wanted to do the math problems? If he didn't do well on the next quiz, then that would be his punishment. But if he could do well on his quizzes without doing all of the boring problem sets, he didn't see why that shouldn't be his choice. Patrick Henry said, "Give me liberty or give me death." Hadn't they just studied that in social studies class? Austin thought his social studies teacher and his math teacher needed to have a conversation.

Mr. Douglas opened the classroom door and followed Austin into the hallway.

"How are you doing, Austin?"

"I'm okay." Was he supposed to confess to his crime? Wasn't there a law that said you didn't have to? Your Amanda rights. That's what he heard them call it on TV. He remembered thinking it was the same name as his sister. But his sister didn't like the name Amanda. So everyone called her Mandy. Sometimes Austin called her Amanda just to get her upset. Mandy was pretty funny when she got upset. Her face would get all red until it almost matched her hair. Then she would try to hit him. But she was too small to hit him very hard. And she was a girl, so it's not like she really knew how to hit. Sometimes she scratched him pretty good, though. She was a good scratcher. He had to watch out for that.

"Austin," Mr. Douglas said, "I'm going to take you to the principal's office."

"I'm sorry about the doodling," Austin confessed. "I promise if you let me go back to the class I'll do all the math problems. I'll even do extra ones." Austin was not at all happy to make that offer. But he thought it was a good idea to sweeten the deal. He *really* didn't want to go to the principal's office. He had been sent to the principal's office only one other time, and his father gave him a spanking afterward. Of course, that time he had done something a little worse. He had called Charlie Flugelheimer a bad name. Austin thought Charlie Flugelheimer deserved it because he had spit at Austin. But the principal didn't agree. And neither did Austin's dad.

"Austin, don't worry about the math problems," Mr. Douglas said.

"I don't want to be in trouble," Austin said.

Mr. Douglas seemed very upset when he looked at Austin. But he didn't sound upset when he spoke. "You're not in trouble, Austin."

"I'm not?"

"No, you're not."

That made Austin feel a little better, but he still wasn't happy about having to go to the principal's office. And if he wasn't in trouble, he didn't know why he had to go.

When they arrived at the principal's office, Austin was surprised to see that Mandy was sitting in the waiting area. Had she also done something wrong? Daddy was going to be *really* angry this time. Austin sat next to her and asked her what she did.

"I ate a pink marshmallow," Mandy said.

That didn't sound all that terrible.

Principal Higgins came out of his office and Mr. Douglas left. Before he left, he clutched Austin's shoulder and squeezed it tight. He was acting kind of strange. Austin wondered if there was something wrong with Mr. Douglas. When Grandpa Joe had acted strange, he was taken to a hospital. And now he was living in a prison for old people. They had bars on the beds, and they weren't allowed to leave. Grandpa Joe rarely smiled anymore. Sometimes he didn't even say anything when they visited. But Daddy said he liked it when Austin visited, even if Grandpa Joe didn't tell him. But Austin didn't like visiting Grandpa Joe. He didn't like it at all.

Principal Higgins crouched down on one knee to talk to them. Austin didn't think he looked very comfortable. He told them that their mother was coming to pick them up from school.

"Are we being kicked out?" Austin asked.

Principal Higgins also looked upset. "No, Austin," he said.

Everyone seemed upset, and they were making Austin and Mandy leave school early. But no one was saying what Austin and Mandy had done wrong. That seemed very unfair to Austin. It was also unfair they had to wait in the principal's office. It seemed like they were waiting forever. Principal Higgins's secretary, Ms. Clark, kept asking if they wanted some water. Austin wasn't thirsty, but he asked Ms. Clark to give Mandy a cup of water.

When their mother finally arrived, she didn't look like herself. It wasn't that she didn't look like their mother; she just looked like a different version of herself. This version had puffy red skin, and her eyes were also red. Her shoulder-length dark hair looked like it hadn't been brushed and Austin's mother always spent a long time brushing her hair. A very long time. Sometimes Austin thought he was going to die waiting for his mother to finish brushing her hair. Then she would try to brush his, but he would shake his head until she left him alone. When it was Mandy's turn, there was always a lot of crying. Mandy didn't hate having her hair brushed the way Austin did, but she sure acted like it sitting on the bathroom counter and looking at her reflection in the mirror with her hair sticking out like a Chia Pet. Austin's mother would always tell Mandy afterward how nice her hair looked, but Mandy didn't seem to believe her. Austin thought it usually looked better before his mother brushed it.

But Austin's mother's hair didn't look better unbrushed and clumpy. She came running over and put one arm around each of them. And she held them tight like the time he got separated from her at Walmart, and he couldn't find her until a store manager helped him and called over the loudspeaker for her, saying, "Will the mother of Austin Gittleman come to the Sports Department." Austin was worried his mother would be upset with him because he wasn't supposed to give his name to strangers. But when she saw him, she came running up to him just like she did in Principal Higgins's office, and she held him just as close, so close not even air came between them. She rocked him back and forth and kissed his forehead, saying over and over how much she loved him and that everything was going to be okay.

CHAPTER TWENTY-FIVE

Penelope hadn't slept in three days.

She had lain down. She had closed her eyes. But she hadn't slept. Not really. Sometimes she thought she might never sleep again. She couldn't go through this. Not again. She barely got through it the first time. But she was thinking negatively. This was not the same thing. Mandy was going to make it.

Mandy was actually lucky. She could have discovered the aneurysm after she was in the Congo. Or she might not have discovered it at all. So she was lucky. Very lucky. Penelope kept repeating this to herself, in the hope she would start to believe it.

She needed to believe it. She needed to pull herself together. With Larry, she wasn't prepared. She was too young. She was only thirty-four. She was younger than Mandy. How was that possible? She was a different person then. A more foolish person. A person who still believed in free love and socialism. Yet a person who thought agreeing to live in a fancy beach town meant she was somehow protected from . . . from the things that happen to the people who don't have such options. It wasn't that she expected not to have problems. She just expected to have bourgeois problems. And compared to people in the Congo, she did.

Now she was older and less foolish. But she also had less stamina. Thank God for Austin. He had the stamina for both of them. The stamina to put up a brave front. He was there by Mandy's side, as he had been almost nonstop, while Penelope hung farther back, afraid Mandy would read the fear in her face. But Austin joked with Mandy. He teased her and rallied her. He helped her pretend everything was normal and fine, when neither could be further from the truth. Penelope didn't know what she would have done without him. He was still her little soldier. But he wasn't so little anymore.

She was worried about him. He seemed so sad, and not just now in the hospital. He'd been sad for some time. Even with Dallas and Coal. He just hid it better then. Both of her children were sad. Had she passed that on to them? It didn't seem possible, but she knew it was very much possible. She didn't spend six years getting two degrees in psychology and get nothing out of it. She had planned to do clinical work once the kids were grown. But she lost faith. Psychology was a religion in many ways, and Penelope had become agnostic.

But that was the easy out. The truth was there were many things she could have done with her degrees instead of remaining at a dead-end civil service job. There were few occupations more disheartening than being a human resources manager in the city of Detroit, where human resources sometimes seemed the only resources remaining. There were growing rumors about an emergency manager being brought in to run the city. There were also rumors of layoffs and pension reductions for all municipal employees. Penelope had no energy for rumors. And no illusions about happy endings. But she wasn't giving up on Detroit. If the city was a shadow of its former self, well, so was she, and she had somehow survived all the same.

Mandy was opening her eyes. She had been going in and out. Penelope knew it was mostly the drugs they had her on, making her sleepy. But every time Mandy closed her eyes, Penelope feared . . . No, what mattered was that Mandy opened her eyes.

"How you doing, champ?" Austin asked.

"I feel like crap," she said hoarsely.

"Well, you look like crap, if that's any consolation."

"Thanks a lot." She was speaking slowly, as if the words were coming from a great distance.

"Are you still feeling woozy?"

"A little."

"They have you on blood pressure medication."

"Is that a good thing?"

"Yes, it's a good thing."

Penelope didn't think it was a good thing. Nothing about this was a good thing. Mandy had survived the surgery. But the doctors kept saying things like "her age will work in her favor," which was very different from saying she was going to be okay.

Mandy had closed her eyes again.

"You still with us, champ?" Austin asked, wiping a wet cloth across her forehead. Penelope should be doing that. Why wasn't she doing that?

"I'm not going anywhere," Mandy said without opening her eyes.

"That's good." Austin smoothed her hair. Her crazy-colored hair. Even crazier now with half of it shaved off. What had she done to herself? She used to have such beautiful hair. Penelope used to brush it out when Mandy was a child, and it was like a red halo around her head.

"What are you thinking about?"

"Evolution."

"Evolution?"

She took a deep breath and made a soft guttural sound as she exhaled. "I was thinking that if evolution is random, what chance do we have on a day-to-day basis?"

"Ow," Austin said. "You're hurting my head. Don't you want to talk about something less taxing, like who George Clooney is dating?"

"What happened in New York? Did you see Naomi?"

Who was Naomi? Penelope's children had lives she knew nothing about. They lived so close to her, and they remained so far away. She had friends whose children couldn't get far enough away from them, who knew more about what their children were doing.

"I said something *less* taxing."

"Did you talk to her?"

"Why do you think I went to New York?"

Penelope thought he'd gone to New York for a job interview. That's what he'd told her. And to see his friend Stu. She thought he'd said Stu. But Stu lived in California. Or he used to. Or she was confused. She definitely was confused. Her brain was so tired she could almost hear the neurons firing in slow motion.

"That doesn't answer the question," Mandy said.

"Love is complicated."

"Don't plan a second career as a poet."

"I'll keep that in mind."

Mandy was silent a few seconds. Then she said, "You're getting old."

"Hey! No hitting in a hospital."

"I wasn't hitting; I was scratching."

They sounded like children again. Penelope wished they were children again. She wished they were all together in their Ford station wagon traveling to see Grandpa Joe in Phoenix. They used to torment her and Larry with their endless squabbling. She wished she could go back.

"But it's true, you know," Mandy said. "You're in your late thirties."

"Thirty-seven is not late thirties. And I think we should go back to discussing evolution."

"You're getting too old to be young and careless."

"That's okay," Austin said. "I was never good at being young and careless."

"No," she said, "you weren't."

This time it was Austin who was silent for a moment. "It's hard, Mandy."

"Being thirty-seven?"

"No. Yes. That's hard too. Love is hard."

"Love takes practice," she said, speaking even slower than before. "Like anything else. The idea of love is ludicrous. What could be less natural than love? What could be less natural than putting someone else's well-being before your own? It goes against every evolutionary instinct."

Penelope thought about that. Austin seemed to be thinking about it as well. She wanted to tell Mandy that she was right. Love *does* take practice. And you still get it wrong. And even when you get it right, sometimes it vanishes on a beautiful spring day. No, she didn't want to say that. But she realized it was too late. She had already said it too many times.

"So I guess we're back to talking about evolution," he said.

"I guess we are," Mandy agreed. Then she closed her eyes again.

"What did the doctor say?" Penelope asked. She was standing with Austin in the small waiting room, after purchasing the vending machine's last Junior Mints. She'd been popping them like, well, like candy.

"You heard him," Austin said.

"But I don't understand him."

"What don't you understand? He's talking in English, and you supposedly have two science degrees."

He was losing patience with her. It was like all the patience he had with Mandy used up his supply, and there was nothing left for her.

"It's not the same thing," she said, "and you know it. You're a doctor, and you know what these words mean."

"He said she's doing fine."

"And?"

Austin took a paper cup from the water cooler's dispenser. "And they're concerned about rebleeding."

Penelope knew what that meant. She had read enough about aneurysms in the last two days to know that rebleeding meant a stroke or death. "Well, what can we do?" she asked.

"There's nothing we can do but wait and see," he said, filling his cup.

"There must be something."

"Well, there isn't." Austin sounded so remote. He needed to stop being annoyed with her and think about his sister. He was a doctor. There was always some new drug or treatment they were testing. He should be able to find out about these things.

"There has to be something that we can do. Someplace we can contact. We can't just sit on our hands and hope for the best."

"Oh, now you want to do something?" he muttered.

"What's that supposed to mean?"

"It means you had your chance to do something."

"What are you talking about? I didn't know she had an aneurysm. How would I possibly know she had an aneurysm?"

"I'm not talking about the aneurysm." Austin threw his cup away. Water sloshed across the waste can as he headed for the door of the waiting room.

"Then what you are talking about?" Penelope called after him. "Come back here. Austin!"

He pivoted around. His face was red, and his eyes were squinched. She hadn't seen him look that way since he was a young child. Usually it was the expression on his face when it was time to leave the swimming pool on a day he hadn't taken a nap.

"You want to know what I'm talking about?" he said, his voice rising in pitch. "What do you think I'm talking about?"

"Austin," she said, wanting to soothe him. "I have no idea."

"I'm talking about Daddy."

"Daddy?" Now she was even more confused. "What does your father have to do with—"

"You had a chance to do something. And you did nothing."

Did nothing? Was he losing his mind? "I raced to the hospital like a madwoman. I pounded on desks and begged doctors to help him. I was beside myself. But there was nothing they could do. There was nothing I could do."

"And what about before that?"

"There was no before that. It was an accident."

"I don't think so."

The stress of dealing with Mandy must have gotten to Austin. Penelope couldn't believe he had forgotten what happened to his father. "It was a surfing accident, Austin."

"I don't see how it was an accident," Austin said with a cold voice. "He wasn't accidentally surfing."

"Austin—"

"He chose to go surfing."

"He didn't choose to be hit in the head with a—"

"He gambled and he lost. He gambled with his life. And he gambled with our lives. He was a man with two small children, and he chose surfing over us."

"You can't believe that." But she could tell by the look on Austin's face that he did. "Your father didn't even know how to surf."

"That part's pretty obvious."

"He didn't grow up by the beach, like you did. He worked in his father's appliance shop from the time he was twelve." Austin didn't understand. She needed to make him understand. "You were already ten years old—"

"I know exactly how old I was."

"Your friends were starting to take surfing lessons. And you were afraid to. He didn't want you to be afraid of . . . He didn't want you to be afraid of anything. He was taking lessons so he could teach you."

"Bullshit!"

"It's the truth." But how could she expect it to make sense to Austin, after all these years, when it barely made sense to her at the time?

"I didn't need to surf."

"That's what I told him—"

"I needed a father."

"But he was a stubborn man—"

"You should have stopped him."

"And he would have done anything for you."

"YOU COULD HAVE STOPPED HIM!"

"I couldn't even stop Mandy from going to the Congo! How do you think I could stop your father?"

That seemed to register. But only for a moment.

"It's your fault," he said. "Everything that's happened to Mandy and me our entire lives is *your* fault. And I wish it was you in that hospital bed instead of her!"

It was no longer her son's pained voice that Penelope heard, but the one that raged in the middle of the night, shredding her dreams.

"So do I."

CHAPTER TWENTY-SIX

Austin was uncomfortable sitting in a patient's chair.

It didn't help that the chair wasn't particularly comfortable. It was a big, heavily stuffed chair, but there was no give to it. When he sat back in it, he felt encased by it. But when he sat forward, he felt it made him seem nervous. He didn't want to seem nervous.

He had thought therapists still used couches, where patients lay down. Maybe some did. Actually, in his mind, he was picturing a tufted divan. He must have seen that in a film. Someone lying with one arm flung across his face, shielding his eyes from the glare of the doctor's truth. Or something like that. Lying down would definitely be more comfortable. But probably also more vulnerable.

Hope Cassidy had recommended the therapist, saying it was someone she had worked with at St. Vincent's. Austin and Hope had met for coffee a couple of times since he'd moved to New York. She said he reminded her of a good friend of hers. He took that as a bad sign for any romantic future. But he wasn't looking for romance at the moment, just a friend. A shoulder. Hope was actually pretty good in the shoulder department. But she had suggested he also try a professional. So he was trying. Or was about to start trying. He was still waiting for Dr. Obatola to arrive. The receptionist in the hospital waiting room said he was running a little late, and she deeply apologized. She had invited him into Dr. Obatola's office because she said it was more comfortable than the antiseptic waiting room. She didn't know Austin had been in far worse waiting rooms. And "comfort" was a subjective kind of thing.

What wasn't comforting were the well-intended sympathy cards and phone calls. It was exhausting having the conversations. And it was a weird circular logic that people felt obligated to call to make him feel better, and he felt obligated to talk to them to make them feel better. But the awkward and pause-ridden conversations didn't really make anyone feel better. And he felt the people who designed sympathy cards should be shot.

Why do they think that someone in mourning would enjoy looking at gloomy pictures of wilting flowers and barren trees? There was only one card he'd received that he liked. It was a picture of a footpath on a sandy dune, leading past a ramshackle wooden fence to a patch of shoreline. Austin liked the idea of Mandy being on a path to finally getting over her fear of the water. He kind of hoped that heaven was a tranquil sea in which Mandy was splashing lazily in serene circles. Austin didn't really believe in heaven as a place. But he did when he looked at that one card.

"I'm so sorry I'm late," Dr. Obatola said, coming in and shaking Austin's hand. He was a dark-skinned man in a white lab coat. He looked somewhat familiar, but Austin found everyone in New York looked more familiar than they should, given that he had just moved there. His brain had been so overloaded the last month, it was hard to know what was real and what was imaginary.

"I promise it won't happen again," Dr. Obatola said. He had a soft British accent that Austin hadn't picked up on at first. Austin didn't know what he felt about a therapist with a British accent. He kind of bought into the stereotype of Brits being stuffy. But Dr. Obatola seemed friendly, and he obviously wasn't tracing his lineage back to the Magna Carta. "I understand you know Dr. Cassidy," Dr. Obatola said.

"Yes," Austin replied.

"We worked together," Dr. Obatola said.

"She told me." Austin wondered if perhaps they had done more than work together. Dr. Obatola was a handsome guy, and Austin didn't see a wedding ring on his hand. Even though Austin wasn't dating Hope, he wasn't sure he felt comfortable seeing a therapist who had. Or maybe still was. Maybe Austin still wasn't comfortable with this whole therapy thing.

"You are also a doctor?" Dr. Obatola asked.

"Ophthalmologist."

"Then you know just how crazy things are getting. I've only been at St. Luke's a year. I worked at two hospitals that went bankrupt." Austin was under the impression that therapy was supposed to be about him. He wondered if he was going to be charged for this part of the conversation. "I don't know if Obamacare will make it better or worse. But a lot of doctors in New York are no longer taking insurance. Concierge service, they call it. Like a private club."

"A private *health* club," Austin said.

"Yes." Dr. Obatola smiled in a way that suggested they were having a "bonding" moment. But Austin didn't feel "bonded." He felt completely adrift. "In your message, you spoke about your sister. Do you want to talk about her?"

Austin realized that he didn't. He didn't want to tell this stranger about Mandy's life. About her death. This man couldn't understand who Mandy was. It made a mockery of what had happened to her. And what had happened to him.

"I'm not sure about this," Penelope said.

Austin and Penelope were standing along the narrow stretch of beach on Belle Isle. There were children near them running back and forth into the gently lapping water.

"Do you want to wait in the car?" Austin asked.

Penelope shook her head. "I made it this far," she said, burrowing a foot in the sand. "Did you ever bring Mandy here?"

There was a squeal of laughter as the children started splashing one another. "Are you seriously asking me that?"

She shook her head again and softly laughed. "No." She took a Kleenex out of her purse and dabbed at her eye.

Austin gazed out across the Detroit River at the downtown skyline. Towering Oz-like over the city were the gleaming cylindrical skyscrapers of the General Motors headquarters. Well, the new headquarters, since the old landmarked building now housed government offices, which was vaguely appropriate given the city's history.

He unzipped his backpack and took out the tin container. Penelope looked away. Inside the tin were the fluorescent red strands of hair.

"Mandy hated her hair," Austin said to Dr. Obatola, surprising himself by the disclosure.

"Why did she hate her hair?"

"I don't know," Austin said. "Yes, I guess I do. It wasn't the color she wanted. It wasn't as straight as she wanted. On rainy days, she looked like a redheaded Roseanne Roseannadanna, the Gilda Radner character on *Saturday Night Live*. She had this idea of who she wanted to be, of what she wanted to be, and she fell short of it. And she couldn't get past it. Except that's not true. I think she was getting past it. I think she was finally letting go of having this preconceived idea of what her life was supposed to be like. Because it never was going to be a picture-book life. I mean, it never was for us. There were no picture-book parents watching out for us. There was barely a mother. And mostly we watched out for her. I don't know what my mother would have done without my dad's life insurance policy. If she had to earn enough money to fully support us. Or maybe that's not true. Maybe if she had to earn more money, she would have gotten a better job and she would have been happier. Maybe Mandy would have been happier. She wanted to be happier. But at some point, I think she gave up trying."

"Until recently," Dr. Obatola said.

"Until recently," Austin confirmed.

"You seem to have been very close with your sister," Dr. Obatola said. Austin wondered if there was some mp3 file or DVD with pre-recorded comments for therapists to make.

"Well, yeah," he said. "It was pretty much her and me against the world."

"Against your mother?"

"No."

"You said against the world."

"The outside world."

"So your mother was on the inside?"

"Yes. No." Now Austin was getting confused. He thought he was a step ahead of the therapist until a question or two back. Now he was trying to catch up.

"So was the outside world where bad things happened?"

"I'm not sure if that's exactly how Mandy viewed it."

"How did you view it?" Dr. Obatola asked. He had gone from

being nearly silent to asking way too many questions. Austin was tripping over himself, and he was losing his train of thought.

"I'm not agoraphobic or something. I don't view the outside world as a bad place, if that's what you're asking. And that's not really what I'm here for."

"You're here for your sister."

"Yes," Austin said. "No. I'm here for me. To help me deal with my sister." That was implicit. Wasn't it? "You know, you're making this seem like I'm doing something bizarre."

"Am I?" Dr. Obatola sounded coy.

"Yes." Austin thought the whole point of therapy was to be supported. To have someone wrap you in the psychological equivalent of a warm towel and tell you everything you were feeling was normal. Unless what you were feeling wasn't normal. "You're making it seem like no one's ever sought therapy to deal with the loss of a loved one. As if I've landed from some spaceship from another planet where people get messed up when a family member dies." Austin was getting pissed off and was planning on telling Hope what a complete jerk this guy was. And he didn't really care if she was dating him.

"I'm so sorry," Dr. Obatola said. But something about having a British accent made his apology sound insincere.

"Are you sorry about making me feel bad or sorry that you can't help me?"

"You don't think that I can help you?"

"No." Austin felt he should leave. He was wasting time and money. And now that he was working at a public clinic, he didn't really have much of either. Not that he was complaining. He enjoyed working at the clinic. He was once again an employee, but he wasn't paid well enough for anyone to gripe about how much time he spent with patients. And Stu kept threatening to move in with him to help them both cut costs, but Austin wasn't clear how having a roommate was going to help if the roommate didn't have a job. Stu had been living off his savings for almost four years, hoping to come up with the next great app, which never quite happened. The savings were pretty much gone, and he needed a job. It seemed that there was one obvious dot-com CEO to ask for help. But Stu refused. Some people insisted on making things difficult for themselves.

"Maybe I'm not the right therapist for you," Dr. Obatola said. Austin was surprised he didn't put up more of a fight. "But maybe I can help you find the right person. Can you tell me what you're looking for?"

Austin was looking for someone with empathy for a start. He was looking for someone who understood what he was going through. "I'd like someone who had a close family member die."

"Someone who lost a sibling?"

"Or a parent. Or both parents."

"So I should recommend orphan therapists?"

Austin knew he sounded ridiculous. But better to sound ridiculous by his own doing than to sound ridiculous because of someone else twisting his words. "You asked what I want."

"I did."

"And that's what I want. I know it's irrational. But isn't everyone allowed to be irrational occasionally?"

"You think it's irrational?"

"Of course it's irrational. I'm a doctor. I know you don't need to have a patient's symptoms to treat them. But I also know what I feel."

"What do you feel?"

It was such a simple question, but the answer felt tangled like old fishing wires with the hooks still attached waiting to prick him if he wasn't careful. "When Mandy was born, my parents didn't say they had a daughter; they told people I had a sister. They said she was my responsibility. And she was. Pretty much from that day forward. I took care of her. Or I always tried to take care of her. But now I can't take care of her anymore. She was this sweet kid with freckles and weird hair and big brown eyes and a great laugh. And she's gone." His eyes were watering.

"And you want me to help you get her back?" Dr. Obatola asked gently.

Austin sniffed as he shook his head. Maybe this guy wasn't so bad at his job after all.

Austin pulled several strands of hair out of the open tin box, then held the box toward his mother so she could do the same.

"I'm not sure if Jews are supposed to do this kind of thing," Penelope said.

"It's not her ashes, Mom."

"I know," she said, but she seemed doubtful.

Austin wasn't doubtful. It was only a gesture, and one of which he was sure Mandy would have approved. He watched two kayakers paddling along the shoreline as they made slow and steady headway toward Lake St. Clair. It wasn't the Pacific, but it would do. Austin released the strands from his fingers, letting the bright red filaments twirl and tumble in the breeze as they sailed over the river below. Penelope let go of her strands as well, and somewhere off in the distance, beyond where Austin's eyes could see, they touched water.

"I'm sorry," he said to Penelope.

They were both still looking out toward the liquid horizon. "If I didn't think it was a good idea to do this, I wouldn't have gone along with it," she said.

That wasn't what he was apologizing for. "I'm sorry about what I said to you at the hospital." It had been weighing on him ever since, but with the funeral and the shiva, there never seemed to be the right moment to say something.

Penelope blotted the corners of her eyes with her Kleenex. "If we start apologizing to each other for things like that, I'll be apologizing to you till the day I die."

"So you forgive me?" He could feel his throat tightening.

"Oh, Austin . . ." She opened her arms, and he stumbled into them, allowing her to hold him to her the way she did when he was six or seven. She seemed so much smaller than he remembered, and it made him sad. He wanted to go back to when he was six. He wanted to go back and start everything over. But all he could do was cry, sobbing onto his mother's shoulder as she rocked him back and forth and told him everything was going to be okay.

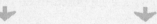

"People keep saying 'I'm sorry for your loss,'" Austin said, wiping at his eyes. "But I didn't lose my sister. I didn't misplace her at the mall. She was taken from me. So much has been taken from me."

"What do you feel has been taken from you?" Dr. Obatola asked in a kind voice.

"Everything," Austin said, knowing it sounded grandiose and not caring. "My father. My sister. My career."

He was about to say "my love." But Dallas wasn't really his love, much as he cared for her and much as he adored Coal. It was Naomi he ached for. And Naomi wouldn't even answer his texts anymore. Not that he could blame her. Love hadn't been taken from him.

It had been lost.

CHAPTER TWENTY-SEVEN

Naomi had lost her GPS signal.

She was looking for Sherlock Court. And she thought she had found it, but it turned out she was on Sherlock Road, not Sherlock Court, and since every road around seemed to be a one-way street, the next thing she knew she was on Moody Road. For the third time. And she was definitely getting "moody."

For some reason the GPS on her Prius had ceased functioning. Assuming she was pressing the right buttons, which was doubtful. Driving a Prius was like driving a computer, and she had never been very good with electronic equipment, which was ironic for someone who now owned a tech company. But the digital display said she was getting seventy-five miles to the gallon, so she was emitting minimal greenhouse gases while driving in circles. She otherwise liked the Prius. Well, she liked what it looked like and that she was saving the planet. But she hadn't driven regularly since she'd lived in Miami, and she had come to prefer letting a public transit worker navigate where she was going. Or a taxi driver when she was running late and felt like a "splurge."

Thanks to Splurge.com, she was able to splurge a lot these days. It had been less than six months since the official launch, and Amazon had already offered to buy them out. On the one hand, it seemed silly for Amazon to buy a company that in many ways did the same thing Amazon did but on a much smaller scale. On the other hand, Naomi felt that what Splurge really offered, more than the ease of its software interface, was the strength of its human interface. Human beings went to each of the locations and hand-selected local quality products. It was an online company that was very much about the offline experience, and Naomi was rather proud of that.

Yes, proud—and happy to accept Amazon's offer. Steffi, however, wanted to hold out for an even bigger payday, and it was her baby. But Naomi thought there was more than enough money on the table. How many times over does someone need to be a multimillionaire? Stupid question to ask while driving around Los Altos Hills, where you could easily spend a million dollars on a generic colonial house that would go for a few hundred thousand in Miami (and less in the Midwest).

But Dov wasn't going for a generic colonial. He wanted to stand out among the Silicon Valley arrivistes in a way that reflected what he had accomplished at a young age and, more important, what his plans were for the future. She didn't technically remember agreeing to move in with Dov, let alone buy a house together in Northern California, but it had all happened very fast. And her life in New York had sort of collapsed in on itself.

What should have been one of the best nights of her life had turned out to be one of the worst. She had spent the launch party searching for Austin, whom she'd never found. She'd come to the conclusion that the text she received from him was most likely intended for someone else. Because he never texted again. Or at least not before midnight, because that was the last time Naomi could remember seeing her phone. They tell you all the great things about backing up in the cloud. But what they leave out is that what can be put in the cloud can be taken out of the cloud. Whoever stole her phone deleted all the data from the cloud. So in a very interconnected world, Naomi was no longer connected to anyone. No e-mail addresses or snail mail addresses. No birthdays or business contacts. She didn't even have her brother's phone number memorized. She wondered if five-year-old children today still memorized their home phone numbers or if they all carried cell phones. Because Naomi was a lot more than five, and she had just taken for granted that she would always have all her contact information available at the push of a button. But now everything was lost. And she had no idea where to find it.

And that was aside from the not so minor detail that the thief had also opened up several credit card accounts in her name, thanks to all that useful data on the phone. So, yes, when Dov said he wanted to move to Silicon Valley to be closer to some of his clients, it was tempting to use his invitation to join him as an excuse to run away from the mess of credit reports and police reports that her life had become. And winter in Northern California beat winter in New York by a long shot.

On her fourth try, she found the turnoff for Sherlock Court. The address Dov had given her naturally had a private gate. She buzzed, and the gate opened, revealing a private road that seemed to wind around the hilly landscape for a mile before depositing her in front of a gargantuan three-story chateau on a promontory overlooking acres of forest. Dov was waiting for her by the six-car garage. Standing beside him was a busty twentysomething with spectacular legs and unnaturally blond hair. Her looks and attire seemed to scream out "real estate agent" or "porn star." Naturally, she was drooling over Dov. That was what Naomi couldn't figure out. Dov could have pretty much any woman he wanted, and he wanted her. With Carlos, she felt like she was always trying to prove that she was good enough. But Dov was the one constantly trying to prove he was good enough for her.

"What do you think?" he said after kissing her. She chastised herself for taking pleasure in the real estate agent's envious stare. "It's like living in fucking Sherlock Forest, right?"

"It's Sherwood Forest, Dov, and the house is French." She hated raining on his parade. But to her, it was just an admittedly pretty and very large McMansion, a rococo Disneyfied version that did sort of look like it belonged in a Robin Hood movie, despite the clearly Gallic-style turrets.

"It has seventy-five hundred square feet, five bedrooms, and eight baths," said Heidi, who introduced herself via business card before taking them on a tour.

"Wow," Dov said.

"Dov, what do we need five bedrooms for?" Naomi asked as they climbed the sweeping staircase.

"You never know," he said with a wink.

"There's also a fitness room, twenty-seat screening room, wine cellar, and safe room," Heidi said while showing them a colossal dressing room with a bay window. Naomi liked the sound of a safe room. Though she wasn't sure if "safe" meant it was a secure location or a receptacle for storing cash between merger negotiations. In Silicon Valley, anything was possible.

"How much are they asking?" Dov asked once they reached the terra-cotta brick deck and cerulean pool.

"Seven million," Heidi said, "and I think they'd accept seven point five."

Welcome to the upside-down rules of Silicon Valley real estate, where the asking price is the bottom of the bidding. "Dov, that's a lot of money," Naomi said.

"Not for this kind of house on this kind of lot. It's actually a bit of a steal." Naomi wasn't sure she wanted to live in a world where seven and a half million dollars for a house was a steal. But she supposed the bigger issue was that she wasn't sure she wanted to live in a house with Dov.

"You don't like it," he said, sensing her discomfort. For a self-confident Israeli, he was incredibly intuitive and sensitive.

"It's beautiful," she said.

"What are you really thinking?"

"I'm thinking you're incredibly intuitive."

"And sexy," he said, kissing her again. This time slower and gentler. This was nice, standing in front of a glittering pool on a sunny hilltop with a man who was, indeed, sexy and devoted to making her happy.

Her phone rang. Which was odd. Because almost no one had her new number. It was Noah.

"Mom has gone off the deep end," Noah said without saying hello.

"What has she done?" Naomi said, walking back and forth to find a spot with better reception.

"She served Dad with divorce papers."

"What? Why? I thought she was spending more time in California."

"She was. That's how she found out he was sleeping with one of her friends."

"Well, wasn't the point for them both to be 'free'?"

"Not that free," Noah said. "Turns out Mom thinks what's good for the goose is most definitely not good for the gander. Especially when the goose's dating life is dead in the water."

"What do you expect me to do about it?"

"I expect you to talk her out of it."

"When have I ever been able to talk her out of anything?"

"Well, I have a wedding to plan," Noah huffed. As if she could forget. Noah and Godwin had set their date as soon as New York legalized same-sex marriage. "I'm not sitting them separately and having an odd number of seats at two tables. I'm not doing it."

He also wasn't inviting cousins (too many). Inviting children (tacky). Having a cake (who eats carbs?). There was actually quite a long list of things Noah wasn't doing. And at the moment he wasn't helping.

"Did you ask Dad to talk to her?"

"He said that he spent thirty-five years giving her what she wants, and if she wants a divorce she can have that too."

Naomi's head was spinning. "When did you find out about this?"

"Just now. Aunt Leah served Dad with the summons. I've always suspected she didn't like him."

"What did you say to her?"

"To Aunt Leah?"

"To Mom!"

"I told her she was ruining my wedding. What do you think I said to her?"

"Naomi, if we want the house, we're going to have to put a bid down," Dov said, walking over to her. Then, noticing the stressed look on her face, he asked, "Is something wrong?"

She didn't want to buy a house. She didn't want to drive a car. She didn't want to keep her business. But most of all, she didn't want to turn into her parents.

"I'm just thinking how lucky I am to have found you."

CHAPTER TWENTY-EIGHT

"You're a hard man to find," Tad said to Austin.

Austin still wasn't entirely sure why this hipster musician had wanted to find him. He had shown up at the clinic without an appointment. But the receptionist had snuck him in at the end of the day because she thought he was cute.

When Austin entered the examination room, he found him rolling in circles on Austin's stool. He had a musical instrument case strapped to his back over a vintage peacoat, and Austin noticed a couple of piercings in his ear and the hint of a tattoo over the collar of the coat. Austin tried not to judge. There were parts of the city where everyone seemed to be pierced or tattooed or both. Austin couldn't understand why so many people would purposely disfigure their bodies. Maybe it was a doctor thing. Or maybe it was a Jewish thing. (The former Hebrew school student in him remembered his rabbi preaching that Jews with tattoos couldn't be buried in a Jewish cemetery.)

"Do I know you?" Austin asked. Tad looked to be in his early thirties, pale skin, receding hairline. Austin didn't recognize Tad's name, and he couldn't think of where their paths could have crossed.

"I knew your sister, Mandy," Tad said.

Austin felt his heart clench. He had gotten a lot better in the last eight months. He had to admit that therapy had helped, though he had been thinking he was ready to graduate. Still, one mention of Mandy's name, and he needed to hold on to the door handle to steady himself.

"We went out for a while," Tad said.

Austin crossed to the examining chair and sat down. "I don't remember her mentioning you." He vaguely remembered there was a guy that his mother said was supposed to come for Thanksgiving several years back. Or was it Passover?

"We kind of had a rocky relationship," Tad said, looking embarrassed. "Very on and off. Mostly off."

"I see," Austin said. Though he wasn't sure that he did.

"But when it was on, it was *very* on."

Austin said a silent prayer that Tad wasn't about to share intimate details about Mandy. Austin didn't think he could take it.

"Mandy's an amazing person," Tad said. "Was. She was an amazing person." It was possible that Tad was tearing up, or there was something in his eye. He blinked a few times, and then he seemed fine. "I just found out about . . . about what happened to her. I've been traveling a lot." He banged on the music case for emphasis. Austin noticed there was an Occupy Wall Street bumper sticker down one side. "I just wanted to say I'm sorry. I'm very, very sorry."

"Thank you," Austin said, feeling his heart beating a little steadier. Tad didn't seem to have anything more to say, so Austin stood up. "I really appreciate you making the effort to find me. It means a lot." Part of Austin wanted to grill Tad on everything he knew about Mandy. To fill in holes in Austin's knowledge. To make her seem present in his life again. But that was precisely what he shouldn't be trying to do. And if Tad had been a significant person in Mandy's life, she would have told Austin about him.

"I have something of hers," Tad said, placing his case on the floor and opening it. There was a trumpet inside and sheet music. And a large manila envelope. Tad handed the envelope to Austin. It contained some kind of manuscript.

"It's her dissertation," Tad said. "The one she wasn't allowed to do. She kind of did most of it anyway."

"She told me she threw out the dissertation. Destroyed the file."

"She did," Tad said. "But we also kind of lived together for a while."

Austin tried not to look as surprised as he felt. "For how long?" he asked.

"Well, that was also pretty messy," Tad said. "But maybe a year or two. Like I said, it was on and off, and I was on the road a lot."

Austin sat down in the examining chair again. What he liked about an ophthalmic examining chair was that it felt a bit like a throne. You were a foot or so above the ground. And the high back and arms surrounded and supported you. Sometimes after a long day, Austin would sit in the examining chair and turn on the visual acuity chart. He would sit in the dark and stare at the letters, trying to make sense of them.

"I know one or two years probably doesn't seem like a huge amount of time," Tad said, "but I haven't actually been with anyone else that long. Which probably doesn't say much for me. But the point is, Mandy was using my computer part of the time. So she *did* destroy her files, but she didn't destroy the files on my computer. It means what I have wouldn't have been her last draft. But it's really amazing all the same."

Austin looked up at him.

"She used her studies of the chimpanzees as a departure point to riff on the entire nature of human social and sexual interaction. It's kind of brilliant. She gets into all kinds of sexual role play. Kinky stuff too." Austin shifted uncomfortably on his throne. "Anyway, the point is she comes up with this whole theory of sexual aggression, and

I think her problem was she was in the wrong department. Instead of doing this as an anthropology dissertation, it should have been a psychology dissertation."

Austin was impressed. He flipped through the hundreds of pages in his hands. He didn't know what he was going to do with it, but he was glad to have it. "Thanks, Tad. I really appreciate you making the effort to get this to me."

"Well, she talked about you a lot, and I just kind of thought it was something you would want to have," Tad said. Then he looked down at the ground. "And I also have a bit of an ulterior motive for bringing it to you."

Austin was curious what it was. Maybe Tad needed an eye exam. He looked like he could easily be lacking health insurance.

"This music thing isn't going quite where I thought it would," he said.

Austin had guessed right. The guy needed health care. Or a job. Austin was happy to offer him either. They could always use an extra pair of hands in the clinic. Pay wasn't good, but it was exciting to be working at the forefront of what was being called a "revolution" in health care, with an emphasis on treating people rather than treating disease. And the truth was Austin wouldn't mind getting to know Tad a little better.

"I've been on the road a long time. I've been all kinds of places. Played in Europe. Played in Kazakhstan. That was pretty wild. But after so many years, I started to feel like I'm always moving, but I'm not getting anywhere. So I applied to grad school, and I'm going to be starting winter term at CUNY." Austin was a little confused where this was heading. "I'll be getting my PhD in psychology, and I'd like permission to use Mandy's dissertation as a basis for my own."

The conversation kept getting odder and odder. Austin wasn't sure what he thought about this new twist. He also wasn't sure what

Mandy would think. And he wasn't nearly familiar enough with the academic world to know how to protect her interests.

"I would give her full credit," Tad said. "It would sort of be like we were coauthors. I've already talked to an adviser at CUNY. I explained what happened to Mandy, and I showed him some of her work. I hope you don't mind." Austin shook his head. "And he's totally on board with me doing this. But I first wanted to get your blessing."

It was the word "blessing" that made Austin feel like he was going to lose it. It was like Tad was asking for Mandy's hand in marriage, and Austin was once again thrust into playing his father's role. Part of him resisted being pulled back in that direction. It was a role he had never wanted and never should have had. Yet he missed it. He missed taking care of her, and he was grateful to have one last opportunity.

"You have my blessing," he told Tad.

"Awesome!" Tad pumped his fist.

"On one condition," Austin added.

"I can't afford to pay for rights."

"That's not the condition," Austin said with growing fondness. "The condition is that we meet for coffee once a month, and you tell me how the work is going."

"Oh, cool," Tad said. "I was afraid you wanted sex or something." Austin had a moment of seller's remorse, but he chose to let it pass. "By the way," Tad said, "I have a working title I've been playing with. I'm thinking of calling it 'The Evolution of Love.' Do you think Mandy would like that?"

Austin tried to keep his voice from cracking. "I think she'd like it very much."

CHAPTER TWENTY-NINE

Steffi didn't like what she was hearing.

"It's not as if it's a surprise," Naomi said. "We've been talking about this for months."

"No," Steffi said. "We've never talked about you selling your shares of Splurge."

Naomi was throwing this at her out of the blue, and though she claimed she wanted a mutually beneficial solution, it felt more like she was asking Steffi to sign her own death warrant.

"We've been talking about selling the entire company," Naomi said as she stuffed Jacques Torres chocolate bars in glossy black swag bags for Noah's wedding. Steffi had already eaten three of the bars, which were definitely not on her diet.

"But we decided not to," Steffi reminded her.

"You and Dov decided. My vote didn't count, and the more I think about it, the more I'd like to be doing something with food."

"You're doing something with food. You're in charge of all the gourmet food vendors."

"I want to get back to doing something hands-on. Splurge was always more your dream than mine."

"And you're taking it away from me!" Steffi was trying not to sound as desperate as she felt. She wasn't succeeding.

"I'm not taking anything from you. If anything, I'm giving it back to you."

"You're not *giving* me anything," Steffi seethed. Like Naomi was offering her charity or something. "You're asking me to buy you out. Just where am I going to get that kind of money?"

Naomi didn't have a response to that. Obviously, she hadn't thought that part through. Typical.

"I bet you could get a loan," Naomi finally said.

"With what collateral? Am I going to give away my company in order to save it?"

"I'm sure Dov would be willing to—"

"Then it becomes *his* company. He already owns sixty percent. I worked too hard to let him take what I created."

"What we *both* created."

Steffi didn't respond. She wasn't going to say Naomi didn't contribute to Splurge. But it was Steffi's concept that had gotten it started and Steffi's drive that had made it happen. Though it might have been Naomi's tits that had helped reel in Dov. Steffi sometimes wondered if their roles would be reversed if she'd been the one rocking the low-cut DVF wrap dress at their pitch meeting.

"This is what you always do," Steffi said, unable to disguise her resentment.

"What are you talking about?" Naomi asked. "I've never started or sold a company before."

"You get bored," Steffi said. "You get frustrated."

"That's not what I'm doing."

Of course it was what she was doing. She'd been doing it since they were children. "We used to make beaded bracelets when we were kids. And if the beads in your pattern got out of order, rather than go back and fix it, you'd toss the beads back in the box and start over with something else."

"I don't remember doing that."

"Ask my mom if you don't believe me. Everyone always carries on about what a free spirit you are, flying off on a moment's notice to live in Rome or Paris. But usually it's the moment someone asks you to make a commitment." Naomi's jaw dropped open. "You have walked away from every job and every boyfriend since I've known you. And now you're doing it to me."

"I'm not 'walking away' from you."

"No, you're running away. But this time you're keeping the tycoon boyfriend. And your castle in Sherwood Forest."

"I don't live in a castle," Naomi bristled.

"No, you live in fucking Fantasyland!"

Steffi raced out of Naomi's apartment, fearing she was about to burst into tears. But the tears didn't come. Just waves of anger. She was angry at Naomi. She was angry at herself for trusting Naomi. And she was angry about becoming an angry person. She gulped water from the bottle of Evian she had gotten in the habit of carrying everywhere. But even after finishing it off, she was still thirsty. She was always thirsty lately. Overcome, really, with an intense parched sensation. It was like she was dehydrated on a spiritual level. No wonder she couldn't cry. She was becoming a brittle person. Who would ever want to be with a brittle person with a dehydrated soul?

She must have looked particularly forlorn, because a taxi pulled over right away. Or maybe that's the way karma worked. When something major is going wrong in your life, something small and inconsequential goes right. She knew she should be grateful for even small amounts of good karma, but she would have preferred ruining her heels walking all the way across town to worrying about Naomi going AWOL.

When the taxi pulled up at her apartment, there was someone sitting on the stoop of her Upper East Side brownstone. As soon as she saw who it was, she knew she had been premature in thinking there was any good karma coming her way.

"What the hell are you doing here?" she asked Stu as she pushed past him to the front door of the building.

"Nice to see you too," Stu said.

She was thirsty again. Maybe she had some kind of kidney disease. Her father had his first kidney stone at thirty-five. He said it was like giving birth to a stone pea. When Steffi said that didn't sound all that bad, he had laughed and said, "Wait until you try it." She wanted to call her parents. They would know what she should do about Naomi, but it was still too early on the West Coast.

"I'm not in the mood for games, Stu," she said, shoving the key into the hole.

"Neither am I. I need a job."

"Do I look like Monster.com?"

She tried to close the door behind her, but he had already jimmied his way into the open doorway. She headed upstairs. She wasn't going to fight with him. She just wanted to get home and get some fluid into her system. She would have killed for a bottle of Gatorade. Fuck the diet.

"I'm good at what I do," Stu said, "and no one knows that better than you."

It seemed that everyone drinking from her gravy trough had un-fettered belief in their own abilities and little in hers. "If you're so good at what you do, why am I the one with a potential job to offer?"

"Because I was the one who invested in you when your only talent was spending money."

They had reached the door to her apartment and the end of her patience. "If this is your idea of flirting, it's not working."

"Why would I be flirting?" he asked.

"Because you obviously want to get back together."

"Are you smoking crack?"

She was so close to socking him. "You want me to believe that you came and sat outside my building, waiting for me like a twelve-year-old, solely to get me to hire you."

"Yes," he said. "That tells you how desperate I am."

"*No one* is that desperate."

He banged his fist against the door. "You know what? You're right. This was stupid. Stupidest thing I ever did." He was leaning over her, his face flushed with anger. "No, the stupidest thing I ever did was propose to you."

"The stupidest thing I ever did was say yes."

"Then there's something we agree on."

"The one and only thing."

"Do you want to fuck?"

"God yes."

She couldn't get the door open fast enough. Their clothes were half off before they made it to the kitchen, where she guzzled half a bottle of cranberry juice, but it didn't even begin to quench her thirst.

CHAPTER THIRTY

Naomi dreamed she was drowning in her swimming pool, and each time she came up for air, Dov told her how much he loved her. She didn't know what it meant, but it couldn't be good.

Her natural impulse was to conclude that she needed to get away from Dov and from Splurge. But she didn't want to hurt him. And she didn't want to hurt Steffi. And she didn't want to "run away."

She was deeply troubled by what Steffi had said to her and had tossed and turned most of the night, which was probably why she was having bad dreams. Well, that and Noah's wedding, which was in T minus five hours. He had made her his combination "best woman" and "maid of honor." But really, she was just his all-purpose slave.

Noah had made it clear her primary job was keeping their parents from doing bodily harm to each other (until after the reception), but he had also assigned her a myriad of other tasks, including taking his and Godwin's Cole Haan shoes for polishing and their matching Dolce & Gabbana suits for one last pressing. Then there were Noah's custom-dyed shirt and socks, which required schlepping to a dye shop in Queens, before hightailing it back to Manhattan and making her umpteenth trip to the nineteenth-century West Village town house that Noah had chosen for the wedding.

There was no elevator, so she had to climb up to the "bridal" room, on the third floor of the four-story building, which was designed around a square-shaped central atrium, with a grand stairway wrapping around the atrium on each floor. The first time she climbed it, she felt like a character in a Henry James novel. By the twelfth time, it was *Les Misérables* that came to mind.

"Where have you been?" Noah asked, practically ripping the package out of her hands.

"You do know that Queens lies across a body of water, right?"

"Never mind. Happy thoughts. Only happy thoughts." He shooed her away, and she was halfway out of the room when he emitted an unearthly screech.

"What is *this*?" He was holding up a purple shirt that he had taken out of the box from the dye shop.

"A shirt?" she asked, wondering if it was a trick question.

"And what color is it!?"

She strongly suspected purple was the wrong answer.

"It's supposed to be lavender," he said. "Does it look lavender to you?" She couldn't say that it did. "I can't get married in a purple shirt. Who gets married in a purple shirt?"

Naomi couldn't think of anyone, but she wasn't aware of anyone who wore a lavender shirt either.

"Didn't you look inside the box?" Noah demanded.

"You asked me to pick it up, and I picked it up."

"The color scheme is lavender, black and white," Noah said. "Purple is not part of the equation."

"But purple's what you have," she said, trying to calm him.

"Not everyone spends their life going with whatever happens to be in front of them! Some people invest time and effort in their choices."

Where the hell did that come from? She invested time and effort in everything she did. Almost everything. Seventy-five percent of everything. "You think I just go with what's in front of me?"

"If the purple sock fits . . . Never mind. Happy thoughts. Only happy thoughts." She was tempted to tell him where he could put his happy thoughts. Instead, she trudged back downstairs, where her mother was rearranging floral arrangements that Naomi was fairly certain Noah had calibrated down to the last petal.

"Is that what you're wearing to the wedding?" Lila asked.

Naomi was in a halter top, shorts and flip-flops. "Obviously not," she said, trying to recall precisely when she had signed up to be everyone's punching bag.

"I don't take anything for granted anymore in this family," Lila said, in the aggrieved voice Naomi was getting weary of hearing. "Is *he* here?"

"Do you mean your husband?"

"I believe he gave up the right to be called that, and now it's only a matter of making the legal documents match the disgraceful reality." She had been making pronouncements like that for the past six months. This was the first time they were under the same roof. Fortunately, there were lots of rooms in the town house, and Naomi hoped for her father's sake that he was taking cover in one of the more distant ones.

"You know he's here, Mom," Naomi said, and then using her most patient voice, she added, "And it would mean a great deal to Noah and Godwin if you could be civil to him."

"I'm always civil." Lila fussed with a gargantuan lavender flower arrangement in the front hall. "Is your father's concubine with him?"

The notion that Naomi could mitigate her mother's behavior was preposterous. She had tried for thirty-five years without success.

"I know you think I'm acting ridiculous," Lila said. "But he didn't just cheat on me. He humiliated me. He could have had sex with some tramp at a hotel bar, and I wouldn't have thought twice about it, once he got a clean bill of health from Dr. Rosenberg. But he did it in our house. In our bed. And with someone from the neighborhood. So that everyone knows. *Everyone* knows. If I *don't* divorce him, I become a laughingstock."

"So you're better off being alone?"

"Oh, Naomi, I've been alone for a long time."

Naomi was putting that statement high on the list of things she wished her mother had never said to her. Naomi wanted to comfort her mother. But she also wanted to chastise her. Why would her mother say something like that on the day of her son's wedding? Why would she say something like that ever? There was such a thing as oversharing. Naomi feared her mother's chronic disappointment was contagious, or, worse, something she had inherited.

She found her father hiding out in a room on the top level of the building, near the French doors leading to a roof garden, and, more relevantly, next to an unmanned bar.

"How many of those have you had?" she asked, pointing to his tumbler of bourbon.

"Not nearly enough," he said.

Standing over him, she noticed how the silver hairs had vanquished the last of his dark ones, and how his cheeks were hanging lower on his strong-boned face. She sat down beside him on a purple antique sofa. "It's very nice of you to be walking Godwin down the aisle."

"Well, his parents are dead, and he doesn't have much family," her father said, swirling his drink. "So what am I going to do? He's like the *shvartze* son I never had."

"Daddy!"

"I'm kidding."

"You just lost all the PC points you got for being here."

"Aw, kiddo, I never had any. I'm here because your mother asked me to come." Naomi gasped. "Or should I say commanded me to come."

"She told me that—"

"Your mother says a lot of things. One of them was that she would never forgive me if I didn't show up. Okay, she also said that Noah would never forgive me."

Sometimes Naomi wished she came from a family of repressed WASPs. If no one talked about their personal problems, her life would be much less confusing.

"What the hell is going on with you two?"

"She wants to get divorced."

"And just because she wants it, you're going to do it?"

"That's pretty much how it worked when we got married."

"That's not the version of events I've heard for the last thirty-five years," Naomi said, crossing to the window. It looked like rain. Noah was not going to be so "happy" about that.

"*You* are not the reason we got married," her father said, waving his hand in front of his face like he was swatting at a persistent fly. "I was going to marry your mother either way. Just not at that moment."

"Really?" Naomi asked.

"Well, probably." He took a gulp of his drink.

"What about this woman?"

"Shirley?"

"I thought her name was Concubine." Her dad laughed. "Do you love her?"

"Love," he said, like he was encountering the word for the first time. "Do you love Dov?"

She hadn't anticipated his turning the tables on her. It was a question she'd been asking herself a lot. Since Dov had started hinting about proposing. More than hinting. She could easily come up with a hundred things she loved about him. But the pressure he was applying wasn't one of them. "I think so."

"Well, I think I love Shirley. But I also think that when it's really love you don't think. You know. But a lot of times by the time you know, it's too late. Or it's not enough. Or you're just not willing to fight anymore. Naomi, honey, your mother's a fighter. I know it comes from what happened to her family in Europe. I get it. But I don't like it. I'm tired of it. I'm entitled to some peace and quiet before I die."

"I'm sorry, Dad, but I think peace and quiet is what you get after you die."

He smiled and took another gulp of his drink. She watched him swallow. Then she took the glass from him and took a gulp herself.

"Hey!" he objected.

She grimaced as she swallowed the medicinal amber liquid. "Were you disappointed I wasn't a boy?" she asked, giving him back his drink.

"Where'd you get such a crazy idea?"

"It's how I felt when I was a kid. That you wanted a boy."

"I have a boy."

"Before Noah was around. I always felt that you didn't know what to do with me. That you wanted a boy to take to hockey games."

"I stopped going to hockey games."

"That's kind of my point."

"Naomi, you're being ridiculous."

"I'm not being ridiculous. I'm telling you how I felt."

"Well, your feelings are ridiculous."

"You can't tell someone their feelings are ridiculous."

"Of course I can. If you're saying things that are baloney, I'm gonna call it baloney. I didn't want a son. I didn't want anything. Jesus, Naomi. I didn't want kids. *We* were still kids."

Naomi's parents weren't going for warm and fuzzy wedding memories. Maybe the question wasn't why they were getting a divorce, but why it had taken so long.

A caterwaul erupted from the third floor. Either someone had died, or there was purple soap in the bathrooms.

Naomi ran to the bridal room, hoping she wasn't to blame for the latest calamity, but this time Noah's wrath was being directed at Godwin.

"All I said was I don't remember signing off on a purple shirt," Godwin said.

"Well, I don't remember signing off on plus ones," Noah barked.

"Just plus *one*," Godwin said. "One close friend asked as a special favor to bring a date, and I said she could."

"We had agreed we didn't want strangers coming to our wedding."

"He's actually a patient of mine."

"That just makes it all the more inappropriate," Noah huffed.

"So there will be five less shrimp to go around."

"That's not the way it works. There's seating arrangements. There's gift bags. There's—"

"Happy thoughts, Noah," Naomi said, trying to be helpful.

"Fuck happy thoughts," he replied before turning back to Godwin. "If you'd been paying any attention, you'd know what an ordeal it is to add someone at the last minute. But I guess throwing a wedding is too trivial a pursuit for a serious-minded mental health professional."

"If it's such a huge ordeal for you, then let's just forget the whole thing."

Noah staggered backward. "That's all it takes?" he exclaimed. "Just one little disagreement and you're ready to call everything off? Let me tell you something. I never planned to get married. I never wanted to get married. If the government hadn't gone all PC and decided to give us our forty acres and a mule, I would never have considered it."

"Noah," Naomi ventured, "you're sounding a little hysterical."

"Of course! I'm the hysterical one. And he's the calm, sensitive one. That's what happens in marriages. Each person gets assigned their role. And I'm stuck being the hyper, flamboyant one. Which is not who I am. No one even knew I was gay until I came out, and even then they weren't sure until I became a party planner." Naomi wasn't sure in what alternative universe this was true. "But here I am signing on for a lifetime of being the flighty gay sidekick to his straight-acting, centered monolith. And he's going to get all pissy just because I'm a little stressed-out?" He turned back to Godwin, practically shaking with anger. "You want to forget about it? Fine! Let's forget about the wedding. Let's forget about everything!"

"What I meant," Godwin said slowly and carefully, "was we can forget about the plus one. I'll call and say I made a mistake."

"Oh," Noah said, the color in his cheeks coming close to matching the shirt.

"Did you really mean what you said about assigned roles?" Godwin asked, sounding deeply (and perhaps professionally) concerned. "Do you believe that if I'm calm, you have to be crazed?"

"Not crazed," Noah said. "But not calm either. It's like you're occupying that space. We're yin and yang. That's the way partnerships work. But what if there are days I don't want to be 'wacky Noah'? What if there are days I want to be yin?"

"Then just be yin," Naomi suggested, putting in her vote for a less wacky brother.

"You can't have two yins," Noah snapped. "You mess up your Chakra Khan."

Godwin picked up the purple shirt that had been strewn across the tufted sofa, and he headed for the bathroom.

"What are you doing?" Noah asked him.

"What it looks like," he said. "I'm going to be yang today."

Noah's jaw fell open. He was speechless. Or the closest to speechless that Naomi had ever seen him. "Really?" he asked.

"Really."

Noah looked like he was about to cry. "There's matching socks," he said.

Godwin walked over to the box from the dye shop and retrieved the socks.

"I think we can squeeze in one extra person," Noah offered. "Just don't tell my cousin Janice."

"I won't," Godwin said, kissing Noah on the forehead.

Noah was blushing as he turned to Naomi. "Can you write up an extra place card for Table Five?" he asked her.

"Sure." She turned to leave, eager to give them some privacy, but then she realized she didn't know whom she was making the place card for. "What's the name?"

"Austin," Godwin said. "Austin Gittleman."

In Austin's experience, it was always the last patient of the day who would need emergency surgery. He had hoped to be changing clothes and on his way to Hope's apartment. Instead, he was calling her while prepping for a pneumatic retinopexy. "I'm sorry, but I've got a sixty-eight-year-old Ukrainian woman with a torn retina."

There was silence on the other end.

"Hope?"

"I thought you said you were getting off early today."

"I was," Austin said. "I just got waylaid."

Austin understood why Hope was annoyed. But it wasn't like this kind of emergency was unusual. She used to be an ER physician, so she should know better than anyone. He thought she had maybe spent too long as a desk jockey and was beginning to forget how things worked in the clinical world.

"Listen, if you don't want to go, it's okay," she said. "My friend Gavin can go with me. His wife's working tonight, and he's home alone anyway."

"I'm not saying I don't want to go. I'm just saying I'm going to be a little delayed."

There was another pause. He could hear Hope calibrating her response inside her head. She worked so hard at . . . well, at life. "How late?" she finally asked.

"An hour I think. Hour and a half tops."

"You're going to miss the ceremony," she said.

"These things never start on time. And maybe I'll be lucky and they'll have cocktails beforehand. Or maybe the bridegroom will have temporary cold feet."

"They're both bridegrooms."

"Right." Austin had forgotten. He had assumed for so long that Hope and Godwin had dated that he was having a hard time adjusting to the idea of Godwin being gay. "So double the chance."

Hope seemed doubtful, but she agreed to meet him at 632 on Hudson, the downtown event space where the wedding was taking place.

Austin focused on the procedure of injecting a gas bubble into the damaged eye of Ludmilla Marchenko and then cauterizing the insertion cut he had made with a laser. Everything was going relatively swiftly, until he tried to explain to Mrs. Marchenko her postoperative treatment.

"Okay, Mrs. Marchenko," he said as he finished up, "you're going to have to remember that you have an air bubble inside your eye helping to hold the back of your retina in place. And that air bubble can move around, the same way an air bubble moves if you turn a bottle of hand soap upside down. You ever done that?"

Mrs. Marchenko, who was only under local anesthetic, shook her head. "No need to move your head, Mrs. Marchenko. You've never turned a bottle of hand soap upside down?"

"Who use bottle of hand soap?" she said. "Hand soap go in hand. Not in bottle."

"How about dish soap?" Austin asked, looking at the time. "Do you use liquid dish soap?"

"Yes. Liquid dish soap is good. But I no use for my hands."

"That's okay. You don't need to use it for your hands. But have you ever turned a bottle upside down? Maybe while putting it in a grocery cart? Or taking it out of a bag of groceries?"

"Sure. Sure. Sometimes is upside down."

"Did you see any air bubbles?"

"No," said Mrs. Marchenko.

"You didn't see *any* air bubbles in the bottle?"

"How can I see air bubbles through bottle? Is white plastic bottle."

"Have you ever seen air bubbles in anything whatsoever?" Austin wanted Mrs. Marchenko to clearly understand how the bubble could travel through her eye if she wasn't careful. But he was running out of examples of viscous liquids and he was running out of time.

"Sure. Sure," Mrs. Marchenko said. "Air bubbles. In bath. My grand-children play with bubbles."

Austin rubbed his forehead. He was getting a headache. "That's not quite the same thing," he said.

"Is not air bubbles."

"It's a different kind of air bubbles. Here's the thing: For the next three weeks, you can't sleep on your back. Do you understand?"

"No sleep on back."

"No sleep on back whatsoever. No lying down on your back. Because the air bubble will move from the back of your eye to the front of your eye."

"Move," she repeated. "Like soap bubble."

"Kind of." It was as good as he was going to get, and he was exhausted.

He changed into his suit as quickly as he could and ran out of his Washington Heights clinic. But it had started raining, and available taxis or livery cabs were nowhere to be seen. The late spring heat wave was accentuated by the thick humidity, but he decided to chance it on the subway. Bad choice. The platform was mobbed. Which was odd for a Saturday, and it was usually a sign of a problem. But he had few options.

A train didn't arrive for twenty minutes, by which point there were so many people on the platform, Austin didn't walk toward the subway doors so much as levitate toward them. But the train was mostly full, and very few people got off. Austin was still two people away from the doors when they closed on a full car. Fortunately, the next train came only three minutes later, but it was also jam-packed. Austin succeeded in getting on board; however, the air-conditioning on the train didn't seem to be working, and he spent the next twenty-five minutes getting a free sauna experience, compliments of the Metropolitan Transit Authority. When he got off the train, he felt like he had swum to the wedding. But he had five blocks still to go. And the rain was heavier now. He had as good a chance of catching a taxi as of catching a zeppelin. And needless to say, he had no umbrella with him.

He arrived at 632 Hudson two hours late and drenched from head to toe. But he was there. And all he had to do was find Hope. And hope she didn't want to kill him.

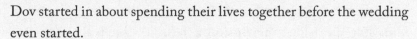

Dov started in about spending their lives together before the wedding even started.

"You know I was thinking as long as there's a rabbi here, we could make it a two-for-one special," he said. Naomi pretended not to hear him. "Instead of 'Three Weddings and a Funeral' we could make it 'Three Bridegrooms and a Bride.'"

It was a bad pun. A bad idea. And in bad taste. But Naomi knew it was her fault in a way, because he was trying, as usual, to flatter and amuse her. And, of course, he was trying to get her to marry him.

What he didn't know was that she had become a nervous wreck from the moment she'd heard Austin's name. She didn't know if it was the same Austin Gittleman. But Godwin had said that Austin was also originally from Huntington Beach, which ruled out just about any other possibility. Naomi had expected Noah to tell Godwin how uncomfortable it would be for Naomi if Austin was at the wedding. But then she remembered that Noah didn't know how uncomfortable it would be, because no one knew anything about her relationship with Austin. And that was because, well, it wasn't a relationship. It was . . . Oh, she had no idea what it was. But she knew it was going to feel awful to see him with another woman, and she wanted to circumvent it if at all possible.

She hid in corners and slunk along walls as the guests arrived, in order to prevent accidentally spotting him, but the more she did so, the more curious she became to see him. No, more than that. The more she yearned to see him, until it was a palpable part of her being. Like a tumor making her head feel thick and her skin feel prickly. She would have gone up to the roof garden to get some air, but it had started raining.

Dov, of course, knew none of this. And she intended to keep it that way. She had known for weeks that Noah's wedding was bringing out the romantic in him. Or the competitive achiever in him. But she hadn't anticipated a full-on assault about getting engaged from the moment he arrived. She tried to convince him she had her hands full as best woman, though by that point her responsibilities were pretty much limited to keeping her parents from launching into open warfare. But they would have had to talk to each other to harm each other, and so far they were still actively avoiding being within ten feet of each other. Dov, on the other hand, was like her shadow, as if he was afraid that if he let her out of his sight, she would disappear in a puff of smoke. And maybe she would. She was feeling so anxious, she almost felt capable of self-combusting.

Noah and Godwin had barely finished exchanging their vows in the Spanish-tiled atrium when Dov was at it again.

"This could be a good time for us to make an announcement," Dov said.

"Shhh," Naomi shot back, since Noah and Godwin were addressing their gathered guests.

She pulled Dov against a wall, which he took as a romantic gesture, but she was doing it mostly out of concern that Austin was possibly watching her from above. There were guests gathered all along the antique balustrades of the three-story staircase, applauding the couple whom the rabbi had just pronounced legally wed.

"I want to thank my husband," Noah said while holding Godwin's hand, "for marrying me despite planning a wedding with me."

"And I want to thank *my* husband," Godwin said, rather impressively carrying off the purple shirt, Naomi thought, "for making my life as beautiful as this wedding."

Everyone applauded again. Well, most everyone. Naomi noticed her father heading straight to one of the bars. But he had not only walked Godwin down the aisle; he had kissed both Godwin and Noah on the cheeks while lifting a prayer shawl over their heads. And Mom, to her credit, had held Dad's hand during the ceremony as they stood beside Noah and Godwin.

Dov was nuzzling Naomi's neck, something that usually turned her on but right now was irritating her. She glanced around the room, looking for Austin. But her vantage point was limited. Every vantage point was limited. There were too many nooks and crannies, corners and hallways, in the elegant but sprawling house. Why couldn't Noah have gotten married in a banquet hall like a normal person?

Now she was really losing it. And it was Austin's fault. For the second time, she was spending an important evening of her life thinking about him, instead of focusing on the things that were real in her life. Like Noah and Godwin. And Dov.

Why wouldn't Dov stop touching her? He was like a hormonal teenager. And one with no sense of propriety. She shifted her body out and away from his and slipped into a crowded lounge with tasseled lamps and another bar, which was a good thing. She needed a drink.

"How about we just tell your family?"

"Tell them what?"

"That you've come to your senses." She looked at him like he had lost his. "That I'm making an honest woman of you."

For some reason, that both insulted her and made her feel paranoid. "I've never lied to you!" she said hotly.

"That's not what I meant."

"Well, then maybe you need to think a bit more before you speak." She was being horrible. She felt horrible. But the bourbon burning her throat seemed to balance the effect. No wonder Dad liked it so much.

"Maybe you shouldn't take me for granted," he said chugging a vodka shot.

Now he was just being completely out of line. "What's that supposed to mean?"

"Let's just say there are a lot of other women who'd be very happy to be in your shoes."

He had finally said it. She almost felt relieved. "A lot of women?" she said. "How many women, Dov?"

"That's not what I meant."

"Then you're saying a lot of things you don't mean." They were both saying a lot of things they might not mean.

"I'm just saying that other people wouldn't be so damn ungracious about me proposing marriage."

"Then maybe you should ask one of those people to marry you." She didn't mean that. Maybe she did.

"Maybe I will," he said.

Naomi scanned the room, both hoping and fearing she'd spot Austin. Her attention was pulled back to Dov when he banged his glass down on the bar.

"Are you going to marry me or not?"

"Oh, that's romantic."

"It's a straightforward question. Are we in business or aren't we?"

And there it was. The reason he had continued to pursue her. The reason he had ignored all those other potential mates, who would always be there waiting for the right moment to pounce. She was something he wanted. And Dov always got what he wanted. Or at least tried. He wouldn't have been so successful if he wasn't so tunnel-visioned. But Naomi saw so clearly what would happen once she said yes. The thrill of the chase would be over. And she'd be moping around a seventy-five-hundred-square-foot home wondering what surgically enhanced blonde was making the moves on her husband.

"I'm selling my shares of Splurge," Naomi said, finally sure of her decision.

"What's that supposed to mean?"

"It means I don't think we should be in business anymore."

She ran out of the room. She ran into the dining room, where guests were feasting on coriander-crusted tuna and grass-fed hanger steak. She twisted and turned, not seeing Austin, not seeing which way she should go. She ran up and down the stairs, in and out of crowded vestibules. The rain was crashing against the windows in waves of agitation.

Naomi found Noah on the second-floor landing, speaking to a male couple in snug-fitting Thom Browne suits. She stood waiting for a break in the conversation, looking left and right, feeling the heat from the bourbon in her chest.

"Are you okay?" Noah asked her.

"No," she said. "I'm sorry. I need to make an early exit."

"Why?"

"Oh, Noah, please don't make me explain."

"You look like you've just seen a ghost."

"The problem is I haven't seen a ghost."

"Maybe you should lie down."

"I can't. I mean I can't stay. I'm so happy for you and Godwin. I'm so sorry."

She ran down the stairs like Cinderella leaving the ball, leaving her prince, leaving her sanity. She just knew she needed to run. She got down to the front hall before remembering she didn't have her purse. She had left it in the bridal room when she changed into her dress. She ran back up the stairs, nearly crashing into her parents. Talking. To each other. Like civilized people.

"Naomi." Her mother grabbed hold of her arm. "You look a wreck." She always knew what to say.

"I know," Naomi said, trying to reclaim her appendage.

"Have you been outside? Your makeup is running. You look like a raccoon. Doesn't she look like a raccoon, Ben?"

"A very lovely raccoon," he said with an attempt at fatherly sensitivity that sounded a whole lot more like tipsiness.

She didn't know which one of them was more annoying. How had they managed to spawn her? But at least they were agreeing on something.

"I need to go."

"Go?" her mother said. "What do you mean go? It's the middle of a wedding." As if that fact had somehow escaped Naomi's notice.

"Mother, please—"

"Please what? I'm worried about you. Now, I try not to say that. But this seems a good time to tell you that I'm—"

Naomi fled. She raced up the remaining steps to the room where the bridal party had put their belongings. Found her purse under the settee, where she had stuffed it. Did an about-face and froze in her tracks.

There, staring at her with a transfixed look on his face, was Austin. A very wet Austin. Dripping from head to toe. They both stood there looking at each other. For eons.

"I was looking for someone," Austin finally said, a small pool forming beneath him.

"Did you find them?" Naomi said.

Austin stared at her again. "I think so."

He came toward her so suddenly and with such intense force, she thought he was angry with her. But instead of yelling something at her, he took her in his arms and kissed her, the way he did on a train platform many lifetimes ago.

Seconds later they were on the settee, pushing shoe boxes and garment bags aside as they lunged at each other. Who knows how far they would have gone if Noah hadn't appeared in the doorway.

"I'm sorry," he said, looking embarrassed. "I just needed to get a mint out of my bag. Can you believe I forgot to have mints? How do you have a wedding without mints?"

Austin and Naomi stood up and straightened out their clothing. There was a large wet spot across her periwinkle blue dress.

"Congratulations," Austin said, extending his hand. "I'm Austin Gittleman."

"Oh," Noah said. "Hope's date," he added meaningfully.

"I've been looking for her," Austin said.

"Under the settee?" Noah asked. Austin looked abashed. Noah stood there, taking them both in and seeming to deliberate how he wanted to respond.

"Well," he said. "I don't want to be the bearer of bad news, but Hope seems to be thoroughly enjoying the company of a young Israeli venture capitalist." Naomi felt a twinge of anger mixed with relief and gratitude.

Noah picked up a knapsack from the floor and started rummaging through it. "Now, this is just me conjecturing here. But I'm thinking that Hope might enjoy her conversation all the more if she got a text saying her date was . . . rain delayed. But that's just a guess on my part."

"Sounds like a good guess," Austin said quietly. "Thank you."

"Oh, just call me a fairy god-brother," Noah said. "And if I'm ever asked, this conversation never happened." Then he closed the door behind him.

"We should talk," Austin said. Naomi nodded. "Maybe somewhere else?" Naomi nodded again. "Is there a back exit?"

"I don't think so."

They stood like that for several moments, pondering their options.

"Shall we do a walk of shame?" Austin asked.

"You first."

Austin headed out of the room and down the stairs, keeping his head down and avoiding eye contact. Naomi followed a few feet behind, doing the same. She couldn't imagine what she looked like in her wet dress. *Please let me not pass by my mother,* she prayed. *Or Dov,* she added. When they reached the front hall, they ran for the entrance like two children being let out of school early.

They were laughing and panting when they got outside, even as the wind and rain whipped around them. They dashed across the street, her clingy, long silk dress and strappy shoes terribly suited for the inclement weather.

"Do you know where you're going?" she asked.

"No idea," he responded. They laughed as they tried to catch their breath. And then they were all over each other again.

"We should stop," he said.

"You're right," she agreed.

"We should talk. We should date."

"Absolutely."

"We should get out of the rain."

"Kiss me!" she told him. And he did. On her mouth. On her neck. As the rain came down from the heavens.

CHAPTER THIRTY-ONE

Naomi was a beautiful bride. Lila told her so over and over all morning. She wanted to make sure Naomi heard her say it. And didn't try to claim later that she hadn't.

The wedding was going to be everything that Lila wanted it to be, because it was pretty much *precisely* what Lila wanted it to be. While it had been fun for her to help plan Noah and Godwin's wedding, Noah had very strong opinions about what he wanted and how many orchids should be in each centerpiece. Lila loved her son, but there was such a thing as too many orchids. If there was an argument to be made against gay marriage, it was that men made terrible brides. Noah knew how to throw a wonderful, or how they say, fabulous party. But there was something about a wedding that required a more delicate and—politically correct or not—a more feminine hand. Fortunately, Naomi had been willing, or, more likely, resigned, to letting Lila have her way. There were times Lila almost believed Naomi didn't care about the details of the wedding. Partly because she kept saying "I don't care about the details."

The only concessions were place and time. Naomi and Austin wanted to get married at the Crystal Cove. And as far as Lila was concerned, they couldn't have made a better choice. The timing was another story. Not only did they want to get married on New Year's, a social faux pas, but they wanted to get married on New Year's Day. Lila had pointed out that an evening wedding was more elegant and sophisticated. She also pointed out that guests tended to give better gifts. But Naomi was insistent. "This isn't the end of something," she said. "It's the beginning."

It was hardly the beginning, since they had known each other for almost thirty years. However, Naomi was intransigent, and since she didn't object or even question any of Lila's other suggestions (and since Lila herself had to admit that a daytime wedding outdoors at the Crystal Cove would look spectacular), Lila had dropped the topic with unusual alacrity.

Her initial plan was for the ceremony to be on the beach, but she had trouble figuring out how to transport the guests up and down the bluff. There was a gently sloping path that snaked its way down the mountainside, making for a lovely but circuitous route and turning the one-hundred-foot distance into a mile-and-a-half trek. It would take an eternity to get the guests up and down. There was also a stairway, which was less attractive but more efficient. However, Lila couldn't see the groom's mother making it up the 140 stairs. Lila considered looking into an airlift but then thought better of it.

So the beach was out, and the ceremony instead took place under a Venetian-domed gazebo on an expansive grassy bluff. The wedding party walked down an aisle lined with treelike arrangements of white roses and pink peonies with the Pacific beckoning on the horizon. As Austin and Naomi exchanged their vows, Lila noticed the breeze blowing through the chiffon panels hanging from the side of the gazebo, and it made her heart race a bit.

"I fell in love with you the day I first saw you," Naomi said, holding both of Austin's hands in hers. "I don't believe in destiny. But I believe in you. And I believe in the path that brought us together, no matter how much it twisted and turned."

"Naomi," Austin said, "I try to imagine my life without you, and it's impossible, because when I found you I found myself. My sister once told me that 'love takes practice.' I want to practice with you for the rest of my life."

Lila teared up. She had promised herself she wouldn't cry. Her makeup wasn't waterproof. She hoped Austin and Naomi would be happy together. Happy like her and Ben. She took her husband's hand, and he smiled at her. The same goofy smile he'd had at their own wedding. In the cramped social hall of her parents' Los Angeles synagogue. It seemed impossible that Lila had once been a young bride with so many plans for the future. Plans to live in New York and be a clothing designer. She had been applying for a job as an assistant buyer at Macy's when she found out she was pregnant. She remembered how much she'd resented Ben at the time. She had felt it was his fault, and technically it was, though that didn't stop his mother from accusing her of trying to entrap him. Lila could have chosen to have an abortion, but it would have destroyed her mother. "They kill enough Jews," she had spat at her; "you don't have to help them."

She had blamed Ben for having to give up the Macy's job. But the truth was the thought of moving to New York by herself had terrified her. She lacked Naomi's confidence and had feared failing in the cutthroat fashion industry and humiliating herself in the process. For all the women's lib rhetoric she spouted to Ben at the time, she'd been relieved when he proposed.

It was easy for her to forget that. So easy to forget how happy she had been to marry the man she loved. She wanted Naomi and Austin to be even happier than she and Ben. She supposed that's what every parent wanted for her children. To be happier. To be richer. To be wiser. Though if it truly worked that way, the world would be an increasingly bountiful place. And Lila didn't see that as a realistic possibility.

But maybe Naomi did. She had never been a very realistic person. Something she seemed to go out of her way to prove. A year ago she was in the *New York Times* business section, and now she was baking cookies again, in a "shop" that made an ATM lobby seem spacious. Lila couldn't even pretend to understand her daughter's choices. But Naomi was indeed a beautiful bride. And she would have been even more beautiful if she would just stand a little straighter.

Austin and Naomi were saying good-bye already. How was that possible? There was a too-hurried kiss. And a heartfelt hug. Lila was crying again. The day had gone by so quickly. Too quickly. Stu and Steffi were taking pictures. And so was Penelope. Was it Lila's imagination or did Naomi's hug of Penelope last longer than their own? Noah and Godwin helped the newlyweds get into a convertible red Miata, festooned with those silly ribbons and soda cans. They were going on an African safari for their honeymoon. Lila didn't see anything romantic about sleeping under mosquito netting, but far be it from her to criticize.

They inched the car forward with the family trailing alongside them, cheering and throwing rice. Lila had never thrown rice before. Or thrown anything else for that matter. She would never be accused of being a tomboy, but throwing rice at weddings had always seemed a particularly strange custom to her. She didn't understand the reason for it and didn't see the benefit of rice raining on a bride's hairdo and down her décolletage. But as she reached over and over into the box of Uncle Ben's Noah had handed her, she discovered there was something surprisingly liberating about flinging handfuls of grain into the air. Tossing them with abandon and watching them scatter in every direction.

As Austin and Naomi reached the end of the Crystal Cove

driveway, they veered to the right at the exit. But the highway was to the left. "They're going the wrong way," she said to Ben. He nodded.

"You're going the wrong way!" she shouted, but they didn't seem to hear her.

Then Lila did something she hadn't done in years. Not since school days. She ran. In three-inch heels. On a dirt road. She ran. She sprinted the few yards to the Miata, then was running alongside them. Her heart was pounding in a way she didn't remember it doing since possibly her wedding night. No, since the night she gave birth for the first time.

"You're going the wrong direction!" she called out. "You're taking the long way around."

Naomi turned to her with an amused expression on her face. Then she looked at her husband and smiled. "We know."

ACKNOWLEDGMENTS

Books are like children. It takes a village to make them strong. I'm fortunate to have many people to thank for keeping this book—and its author—out of harm's way. They are: Danielle Perez, Deborah Schneider, Stacey Luftig, Anne Newgarden, Badria Jazairi, Frank Basloe, Stephen Gaydos, Idra Novey, Robert Woletz, Tina Fineberg, Nicola Wheir, Heidi Giovine, Daniel Jussim, Shifra Diamond, Scott Sher, Eileen Finc, Darol Sipher, Sandy Sipher, Angelo Pacella, Jami Bernard, Jeff Nishball, Megan Gillin-Schwartz, Ami Angelowicz, Tasha Gordon-Solmon, Mort Milder, Rhonda Goldstein, Cathy Gleason, Victoria Marini, Loren Jaggers, Joseph Cortes, Sandra Engelson and Bruce Yaffe. And I'd like to thank Lisa Krieger for inspiring me with her strength and courage.

THE SCENIC ROUTE

Devan Sipher

QUESTIONS FOR DISCUSSION

1. Early in the book, Naomi tells Austin that there's no such thing as a wrong turn. Do you agree or disagree and why?

2. How would you describe a "manstrosity"? Do you know any?

3. Mandy theorized that the flawed choices humans make in their romantic pursuits are a genetic trait rather than a personal failure. Do you think that's likely true or wishful thinking? Were Mandy's flawed choices an implicit part of who she was?

4. Have you ever seen the Lumière film *Sortie d'Usine*? One version (of three) is viewable at the Institut Lumière Web site: http://www.institut-lumiere.org/english/frames.html. (Go to the "Lumiere Museum" section and click on "Films.") What stands out for you in the film? Do you think the film depicts something literal, metaphoric or both? Why do you think Naomi watched it over and over?

5. When Naomi told Austin she loved him, what should he have done? Was he morally obligated to be faithful to Dallas? Or was he being unnecessarily self-sacrificing?

6. Is Lila on to something with her plan to run away from home in her fifties? What are the advantages to waiting to sow your wild oats until your middle-age years? What are the disadvantages?

7. Do you believe there are "red-light people" and "green-light people"? What do you think are the characteristics of each? Do you believe a person can change from one to the other? And what did Dallas mean when she said Austin was yellow?

8. Why did Austin lash out at his mother while Mandy was in the hospital? Do you think Austin truly believes his father had a choice in his death? Why would Austin believe that?

9. Is Noah right about romantic partners each playing yin to the other's yang? Have you ever felt like you were locked in an unintended role in a relationship?

10. Austin starts the book wanting to follow a safe and cautious path in life. Was his problem that he chose an impossible goal or that he didn't do a good enough job of pursuing it? And in a world where we can't count on hospitals—or even cities—remaining solvent, what remains a safe bet?

11. Tad's title for Mandy's dissertation is "The Evolution of Love." Would that have been a good title for the novel as well? Why or why not?

12. If Austin had told Naomi he was falling for her when they first met, the trajectory of their lives for the remainder of the book would be significantly different. Is it a good thing or a bad thing that they ended up taking "the scenic route"?

Photo © Tina Fineberg

Devan Sipher is a writer of the *New York Times*'s "Vows" wedding column and the author of *The Wedding Beat*. He graduated from the University of Michigan, where he also attended medical school, and he received a master of fine arts from the Tisch School of the Arts at New York University. He was born in Los Angeles, grew up in Southfield, Michigan, and lives in Manhattan.

CONNECT ONLINE

devansipher.com
facebook.com/DevanSipher
twitter.com/DevanSipher